DANGEROUS DROP-IN

When I got to my office the next morning, I should have known right away that something was amiss. While my intuition was nagging me, my mind was racing with the minutiae of the case and I wasn't listening. By the time I was really aware of danger, I was inside, and the surprise was revealed.

I pulled my .38 and studied my trashed office. The roll-top desk had been plundered, all of its contents dumped onto the floor. Three of the desk drawers had been thrown down on the cement and the dovetail joints of at least one of them looked busted. All of the cubbyholes were empty and a carpet of paper littered the polished concrete. The desk chair and wastebasket were overturned in the middle of it all.

Two of the filing drawers had been similarly violated, and empty file folders were tossed upside down on the floor, their contents now in a pile with the rest of the papers. That alone sent my blood pressure skyrocketing, since I knew it would take hours of work just to sort through the papers and get everything back in place.

This case was not only dangerous, but now was hitting too close to home. . . .

THE LAST SONG DOGS

a Trade Ellis mystery novel by

SINCLAIR BROWNING

BANTAM BOOKS

NEW YORK TORONTO LONDON SYDNEY AUCKLAND

THE LAST SONG DOGS
A Bantam Crime Line Book / April 1999

Crime Line and the portrayal of a boxed "cl"
are trademarks of Bantam Books, a division of
Bantam Doubleday Dell
Publishing Group, Inc.

ISBN 0-553-57940-1

Published simultaneously in the United States and Canada

Bantam Books are published by Bantam Books, a division of Random
House, Inc. Its trademark, consisting of the words "Bantam Books" and
the portrayal of a rooster, is Registered in U.S. Patent and Trademark
Office and in other countries. Marca Registrada. Bantam Books, 1540
Broadway, New York, New York 10036.

PRINTED IN THE UNITED STATES OF AMERICA

WCD   10   9   8   7   6   5   4   3   2   1

FOR MY SIDEKICK, BILLY,
who's put up with more horse manure, howling dogs, rat
guts at the front door, and shin bumps on the trailer hitch
than a man really ought to have to . . .

. . . and for cowgirls everywhere.

ACKNOWLEDGMENTS

The author wishes to thank the following people for contributing their expertise to the writing of this book: Ace Bushnell, Lieutenant Leo Duffner, Pima County Sheriff's Department; John Redmond, Caesar's Palace; Ron Penning, Michael Downing, Pima County Medical Examiner's Office; Leon Ben, Jr., Geronimo Hotshots; Mary Kim Titla; Mike Cannon, El Campo Tires; Linda Laney, Alpine and Luna; Bob Schultz; Allen and Ginger Harding, general managers, Tal-wi-wi Lodge; Diane Balanoff; Dr. James ("Big Jim") Griffith, University of Arizona Southwest Folklore Center; Rose Walsh, Tanque Verde Guest Ranch; Karl Lasky, 6DOF Investigations; Assistant Chief Dan Newburn, Tucson Fire Department; Rosemary Minter; Ethel Paquin; Amanda Clay Powers; and last but not least, Lisa Baget for her ongoing words of encouragement as she struggled through my early drafts.

THE LAST
SONG DOGS

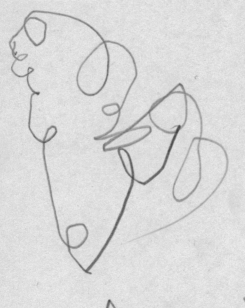

1

EVERYONE WAS TALKING ABOUT THE SEVERED ARMS, THEIR IMAGI-nations triggered by the gruesome page one story, complete with three-column black and whites of the trash bin where they had been found.

I skimmed the article with something less than enthusiasm. I knew better. Every time I pick up the papers I always want them to be filled with happy stories. They never are. But, instead of skipping all the gory stuff, I always find my eyes drifting back to the stories I promised myself I wouldn't read. They suck me in, and then I spend a few minutes off and on throughout the day grieving for the family killed in the fire, the child lost in the mountains, the raped coed—the list is endless, and always haunting.

So, last week it was the arms story. A street person hunting aluminum cans had found them. They were women's arms, too, which made the whole thing even more disgusting. No rings or fancy manicure, though. Just plain women's arms.

I had coffee with my cousin Beatrice the morning the story first ran. The police were searching for a body and I remember Bea, a television anchorperson with a morbid curiosity, wondering why they automatically assumed the woman was dead just because her arms had been cut off at the shoulder. At the time I'd thought her optimism misplaced until I remembered another horrible news story in which a California teenager's arms had been chopped off, and she had lived. But now a week had gone by and no body had been found, so maybe Bea was right.

It was hard to get the arms out of my thoughts, though. Just about every day a new story ran about them, adding to the information my saturated brain had already stored and didn't want.

My name is Trade Ellis. Weird name. My life is odd, too. I'm a rancher and also a private investigator. I always describe my investigative work the way the old-time cavalry troopers described theirs: weeks of sheer boredom punctuated by moments of total terror. If the PI work were anything at all like those television programs, I would have given it up long ago. My heart couldn't take it.

All in all, though, it's not a bad way to make a living. I set my own hours, write my own paycheck, and, thanks to the income from my ranch, can be fairly selective about my clients. It's also a great conversation grabber when people ask, "And what do you do?" That is, on the days I don't lie.

Today they found the owner of the arms. No body, just the identification. I got a funny pasty lump in my stomach when I read the name, Valerie Higgins. I knew her. She was a Song Dog.

She and I had gone to high school together, a long time ago in Tucson. Javelina High. The *j* was pronounced like *h* and we had all scribbled *Javelina Jigh* on our notebooks, thinking we were pretty cool.

Our mascot back then had been the javelina, or peccary. A funny-looking little wild pig-type animal with lousy eyesight. Indigenous to our state, Arizona. Terrific mascot. A blind piggy.

Anyway, Valerie had been one of the blind piggies and so had I. Of course, we traveled in different circles. She'd been one of the popular ones: blond, with straight hair I always envied. Not only envied, but tried to emulate as I laid my own curly black mane out on the ironing board and tried to straighten it with a hot iron. Why I still have any hair at all is a mystery to me. Must have something to do with my Apache ancestry, which had nothing to do with my curls.

It wasn't that I was wildly unpopular. I had plenty of friends. But I was never a cheerleader, a pom-pom girl, or Queen of Anything. Then, as now, I was pretty wrapped up in my horses and cattle, which set me apart from most of the student body.

Valerie Higgins was one of those girls who had Capezio shoes in every color and boys only in white. She'd been a cheerleader. One of the Javelina High Song Dogs, a cutesy name coined for the pep squad. Song Dogs was a slang term for coyotes and the student body pinned it on the cheerleaders, since they also howled. Some school.

Valerie and I had gone to Mrs. Wright's together, too. A waste of Saturday mornings, where we learned about important things like receiving lines, proper introductions, ballroom dancing and that if you sweat enough, it *will* seep through thin white cotton gloves and the boy you're dancing with *will* feel the sticky mess and pretend not to notice and you'll both be relieved when Mrs. Wright's little palm clicker finally announces the end of the dance.

I chuckled, remembering how I'd looked back then. Tall, like a long-legged colt, all gangly limbs, knobby knees and oversized hands. I had a wild look about me, with my black hair hanging down below my waist. As my father had said I would, I had eventually grown into my coltish body. Thankfully, I'm still thin and blessed with a heavy head of hair. Now it tickles the middle of my back, though, not my belt. I'm also probably shrinking, since I'm not much over five-seven.

The other thing I'd hated about Mrs. Wright's was the lines of boys and girls staring at each other from opposite sides of the room. The boys were supposed to ask the girls to dance, and we lingered, like vultures waiting on a cold morning for our wings to warm so we could fly. Valerie was always one of the first to go, I was always one of the last. And they say there isn't a caste system in America.

My attendance at Mrs. Wright's was a concession to my mother. I saw it as penance for the hours I spent on horseback helping my father with the ranch. I also blamed Manda Ortiz for my matriculation. The prod came when Grandma Rose came visiting in fifth grade.

Grandma was both hard of hearing and poor of sight, and we were driving her through the desert showing her the wildflowers when we came across two burros going at it.

Grandma Rose squinted and craned her neck out the open car window.

"George," she addressed her firstborn, my father, "what are those creatures doing?"

"Fucking, Grandma," I replied helpfully.

I never thought of my mother as a particularly fast mover, but she surprised me that day as she spun her body around to the back seat.

"*Where* did you hear that word?" Her face, normally the color of a long summer's tan, paled several shades. My mother, who was half Apache, had been raised in a culture whose language did not include swear words.

"Well, that's what Manda Ortiz calls it," I sniffed, without a clue as to my transgression.

Manda's father, Juan, worked for us on the ranch. Dad thought it was wonderful when Juan's daughter and I became fast friends. Mother, who considered Manda a bit wild, was not so sure. In spite of her doubts, she promised to make a valiant effort to overcome the historical enmity harbored by the Apaches against the Mexicans.

"She'll teach Trade Spanish," my father had assured her.

My mother was now seriously questioning the wisdom of the cultural exchange, and, thanks to Manda's tutoring, the foundation had been set for my years in hell. Two years later, the fall I hit seventh grade, I'd found myself enrolled at Mrs. Wright's. Along with the now dead Valerie Higgins.

Her photograph haunted me from the front page. I wasn't surprised to see an older Valerie. After I turned forty, I played a game with myself. As I saw or read about my old classmates, or anyone within a five-year range of my own age, the measurement now was always, "Does she look older than I?" I attribute this preoccupation to curiosity, of course, not to vanity.

Valerie passed the test. Most of the blond ones did. Must be something in the genes, because they all seemed to get wrinkled quicker than the rest of us. Maybe it was all that Noxzema they smeared on their faces in high school.

God knows I have had enough opportunity to spawn wrinkles. After spending my entire life outdoors, it's not that I don't have any lines, just not as many as a lot of my *comadres*.

I carefully read the article. So far the police didn't have any leads. Valerie had been at a happy hour with friends and had left early. Her locked car was found in the parking lot, but no one had seen her leave.

She had been a popular middle school teacher. No enemies. Happy home life. She'd been a real estate agent at one time and therefore fingerprinted by the state. The prints had been matched to the lost arms.

Valerie taught school on the far east side of Tucson. Her arms had been found down near the University district, in a trash bin on the trendy Fourth Avenue.

As the story jumped to page two, I saw a photograph. Apparently the brutality of the deed had captured the imagination of the University students, who had set up a makeshift shrine at the crime scene. Written on the ugly container, alongside gang graffiti and sexual suggestions, were odes to the late victim.

Someone, perhaps in deference to the English classes Valerie had taught, penned, "Death cancels everything but the truth." No attribution was given. Pots of artificial geraniums and small votive candles, coupled with discarded McDonald's containers, gave the trash bin the appearance of a bizarre pagan altar.

The news story included quotes from her principal and one of her friends. It was the usual: She was well liked and devoted to her family. She was survived by her husband Jerry, whom I couldn't place, and two kids in college.

Questioned about her jewelry, since none was found on the arms, the friend replied that Valerie always wore her wedding band and a watch.

I threw the paper down on the table and went out to feed the horses, disgusted with myself for reading all the grim details I had no reason to retain. After all, I hadn't seen Valerie Higgins in over twenty-five years.

2

THE COOL DESERT MORNING ON THE RANCH ALWAYS ENERGIZES me. Dudley Do Right attempted yet another cock-a-doodle-do when he saw me, probably his twentieth of the morning, as Dream and Gray, whose Arabian lineage is far fancier than their names indicate, nickered a greeting when I appeared with their buckets of pellets and vitamins. While most of my ranch horses are quarter horses, I prefer riding the more energetic Arabians. Their stamina never ceases to amaze me.

Mrs. Fierce, my neurotic cock-a-schnauz-passes-for-a-dog-but-thinks-she's-human, danced giddily around my feet in an effort at either love or suicide.

I love it here. La Cienega lies thirty miles north of Tucson, close enough to be convenient to the big city and its eight hundred thousand people. Tucson, a diverse mix of Indians, Mexicans, gringos, cowboys and retirees, is cradled in a valley surrounded by four mountain ranges. The largest of these, the towering Santa Catalinas, is the backdrop for La Cienega, so we're really right around the corner of the mountains from Tucson. But we're still far enough away to have all of the pluses of a small town. And a very small town it is. There probably aren't more than five thousand people in this neck of the county. Rednecks abound, with their trailers and hound dogs named Bones. Smith and

Wesson bumper stickers adorn their pickups and everyone knows everyone's name and everyone else's business. It's a place where you can still get chicken-fried steak with gravy as a breakfast special in the local cafe. Major dates are chronicled by the latest brush fire, and rain gauge measurements are argued with the vigor of a presidential debate. Water tables, roping times, and the weather are all favorite topics of conversation with the locals.

Unfortunately, La Cienega has also been discovered by the bicycle set, and now many a Saturday morning finds the local cafe littered with the fit, sweaty folks in their shiny latex pants mingling with the Levi's-and-cowboy-boots crowd. So far it's worked out, giving both sides additional conversational material when among their own set.

I've lived in La Cienega all of my life. My grandfather's inventions back East gave my father the luxury of becoming a gentleman rancher, and he did just that. Coming from Chicago to attend the University of Arizona, he had fallen in love with Tucson, found La Cienega, bought the Vaca Grande Ranch after graduation and never left.

The Vaca Grande had never been a big patented spread, but the state and Forest Service leases provided great forage for our herd of Brahma cattle. While there are only twelve hundred deeded acres, the grazing leases embrace 15,000. Which means that we actually have 16,200 acres on which we can turn our cows loose.

The ranch wasn't the only thing that Dad fell in love with on his trip west. While at the University he'd also found Mother, a fine arts major, and of the two I think she had the more interesting history.

Mother's mother, my *shiwóyé*, was a full-blooded Apache Indian and a powerful medicine woman. Shiwóyé met my grandfather, Duncan MacGregor, when he was teaching school on the reservation. Something clicked between the Scottish schoolteacher and the young Apache woman with a ravenous reading appetite. They married and that union produced my mother and her sister, Josie.

Duncan, whom I called Boppa but who was known to everyone else as Mac, was one of those special people who are born to teach. He taught all over Arizona, in all of the little mining towns, border places, rat holes and reservation hamlets scattered across the state. Boppa and Shiwóyé hit them all as he spread education and inspiration everywhere he went.

When my mother and her sister Josie came along, there was no question about their education. They attended the University and were two of only a handful of Native Americans who actually graduated. A double wedding followed, with my mother marrying Dad, and Josie hooking up with Charles Borden, an Anglo detective with the Pima County Sheriff's Department.

Then, one rainy July evening the summer after my eighth-grade year, Dad was returning from Douglas with Memo Ortiz, one of Juan's sons. Hauling a prized Brahma bull they had just bought, they were both killed when a drunk driver crossed the I-10 median and slammed head-on into the Ford pickup. In one of those queer twists of fate, the bull and the drunken driver both survived.

Somehow, with Juan's help, along with that of another of his sons, Martín, we were able to make it through the next six months. There was never any question of giving up the ranch; it was home to all of us.

The following March, Mother dropped dead from an aneurysm.

I was devastated. Barely into my teens and both of my parents were gone in less than a year. I was suddenly in the company of Tarzan (if abandonment counts), Oliver Twist and Little Annie. We were all orphans. A hard word. Orphan. For years afterward whenever someone in school mentioned her parents, I felt sick, afraid that someone would turn and ask about mine.

Boppa and Shiwóyé returned to La Cienega from the reservation where they'd retired. They took over my upbringing and stayed on the ranch with me until I finished college, and then Boppa died. Afterward, Shiwóyé returned to the San Carlos Reservation. Martín and Juan stayed on with me.

Taking into account my father's family, which was

predominantly Irish and Anglo-Saxon, and my mother's, Scottish and Apache, where do I fit in? I have a lot of fun with questionnaires. I insist on checking anything but Anglo. "Other" is one of my favorite choices. If I were in the dog pound, I'd have to be listed as a Heinz 57. A registered horse? Out of Texas by Trailer. Soda drink? A suicide, a blend of all the flavors.

I've always felt that being multiracial was a gift. Just like mongrel dogs are usually stronger and brighter than their pedigreed counterparts, my heritage has given me resilience and strength, two traits that have served me well through the years. I certainly can't discount my Scottish ancestors. There's something about being a descendant of Rob Roy that I find appealing. Those were tough folks—to claim the MacGregor name in the 1600s in Scotland meant instant execution in retaliation for clan acts against the British crown.

Through my years with them, Boppa and Shiwóyé also instilled in me a deep regard for my Apache ancestry. Not a bad thing at all, especially now that it's become so damned trendy to be a Native American.

Both cultures are known for their fierce fighting, making do with what they have, and putting great stock in the kinship of clan. These are good traits that will see me through tough times. My roots are strong.

As I came back into the adobe ranch house from feeding, I was greeted by a blinking light nagging me on the answering machine.

Brushing one of the cats from the kitchen counter, I pressed the play button. There was silence on the machine and I was hoping it was a hang-up, when a soft voice began speaking.

"Trade, this is Charlene." The voice was fading to a whisper. "Charlene Williamson. Uh, Carlton. I, uh, don't know if you remember me, but we need to talk to you. Call me back as soon as you can." She left her telephone number on the machine, and as I jotted it down on the back of a receipt from the feed store, I tried to remember who she was.

Charlene Carlton. I rolled the name around in my

memory bank and came up with the connection. Another blind piggy. From my era. Tall, redheaded girl with big boobs who got straight A's. That in itself had been even more memorable than her chest.

I dialed the number, talked to her machine. Another game of telephone tag had begun.

But there was something else about Charlene. She had been a cheerleader. Another Song Dog.

Suddenly the pasty lump was back in my stomach.

3

WHEN CHARLENE AND I FINALLY CONNECTED, I SET THE APPOINT-
ment for two o'clock the following day because I'd already
promised to help Juan in the garden. She hadn't been happy
with that. There was a real insistency in her voice that
turned to petulance when I insisted on an afternoon appointment. I knew that whatever her problem, a few hours
probably weren't going to make a difference.

Most people, by the time they get to me, think that
their problems are urgent. After eight years in this business,
I know better. Lose a kid in a shopping mall? Now, that's
critical—you want to get him back before one of the
weirdos grabs him. That's why people call the police.

But private investigators? We get the less than urgent
work: the skip trace, the cheating spouse, the lost heir, a little insurance fraud here and there, sometimes a missing person the police have either given up on or the client doesn't
believe the police are doing their best to find. But urgency?
Nah. Everything in this business can wait four hours.

And that four hours sometimes makes a big difference
in my mind-set. Like today.

I wanted to use the time instead to do a few things at
the ranch. Juan Ortiz, now into his seventies and deaf, and
his son Martín still live in the old bunkhouse. Martín, my
foreman, had just taken off for Mexico for a month on a

long-deserved vacation. So Juan and I began the morning by wrestling a cow into the squeeze chute and doctoring her for pinkeye. Pinkeye can be a big problem, as it tends to spread rapidly. So far the cow only had a diseased right eye. Most Brahmas are fairly opinionated and this one was no different. She squirmed and fussed and tossed her horned head while we sprayed her with furazone. We'd had some luck with the pinkeye patch, but we'd used our last one earlier in the week and now were forced to treat this cow with the spray until the new patches came in. She was slippery, but we managed.

When we finished, I helped Juan till some manure in the garden, getting it ready for spring planting. Then back inside I caught up on the never-ending stack of magazines I haven't had the guts to cancel. I even cleaned out a shelf in a bedroom closet. As for work, checking my messages revealed I had a couple of calls from clients, and then there was the appointment with a potential new one. Charlene Williamson.

I drove to my office before heading into La Cienega. I use the term *office* loosely, since it's really an old abandoned adobe stage stop that I've cleaned up. Located just a mile from the house, it only takes minutes to walk or ride there. I love looking out my office window at the Brahma cattle, all wearing the 9Z brand of the Vaca Grande. I wouldn't trade that view for anything.

The old stage stop isn't the best location for walk-in traffic, but this business never draws much of that crowd anyway. One advantage of my somewhat remote location is that it does afford the gun-shy client a degree of privacy.

Of course, I'm not wedded to the office. I've met clients in Tucson, in their own homes and even at Rainbow's Cafe in La Cienega. That one's tricky, since when I arrive there with a stranger, I usually get a grilling. That's just how it is in a small town.

By eleven o'clock I was settling in for what was left of the morning, switching the phone back to the office, brewing the coffee—that decaf stuff, otherwise I turn into a ten o'clock witch—and glancing through the weekend mail.

Part of my New Years' resolution was to deal with each piece of paper as it comes into the office. My tendency has always been to separate things into neat little piles, and the "to do later" one always grows until it threatens to engulf me.

Juan had collected the mail the day before and had thrown it on the desk. The first two pieces were bills, one each from the telephone and electric companies. Since I'd just picked up five heifers at the auction last week, I was a little short on cash and had no choice but to throw them into the bill drawer. I was already cheating on my resolution.

Next was a letter from Shiwóyé. That went to the top corner of the old rolltop, since I knew it would be a treasure, something to pore over when I wasn't pressed for time.

Then there was a letter from the Publishers Clearing House assuring me I was on the first list to win ten million dollars. I guess I'm either superstitious, or stupid, or both, but even though I know better, I always open those large brown envelopes, hunt for the appropriate stickers, and select the British racing green for my Jaguar. I don't want to even begin to think about how much time I've invested in filling out sweepstakes forms. And I wouldn't let Charlene come in early. . . .

At the bottom of the pile was a letter from someone named Daggett Early. It had one of those stick-on labels with a sailboat listing up in the left-hand corner. My name and address were handwritten, all scrunched up in the middle. The careful placement of the Elvis stamp obviously had higher priority than the sender's penmanship.

And then I remembered Daggett Early. Cheeze, another page out of high school. We'd had chemistry class together. He was a tall, goofy-looking kid with thick horn-rimmed glasses, who always wore ironed shirts and frequently forgot to zip his fly. He'd had the singular distinction of being the first one—actually more like the only one—in the class to totally memorize the Periodic Table of Elements. Pretty impressive guy.

I opened the envelope and was greeted by an invitation to a Javelina High reunion. I started to throw it in the trash and then I thought of Valerie Higgins and my pending appointment with Charlene. I read it closely instead.

In honor of our twenty-fifth reunion, the letter invited me for drinks on Friday night, March 14th, followed by dinner and dancing at the Tanque Verde Guest Ranch on Saturday night, and then a picnic on Sunday. It was hoped not only that I would be there, but that I would contact Daggett Early if I knew how to contact any of the below—a list of about thirty names. I skimmed them, but could only remember two distinctly; a few of the remaining names struck distant bells in my crowded brain. Once we get past forty, I maintain, there's so much stuff jammed in our heads that it's amazing we are able to retrieve any of it quickly, if at all. We've reached maximum capacity and it's no wonder that some of us short out.

Checking my calendar, I realized the reunion was three weeks away. I retrieved the envelope from the wastebasket and checked the postmark. Although it had been mailed two weeks ago from thirty-five miles away, by some quirk of the U.S. Postal Service it had only just arrived.

Anyway, I saved the notice. While I'd never been much on reunions, this one had all the makings of a doozy.

I updated a few files, both having to do with insurance claims, and took a call from Garrison Wright, a personal injury attorney in Tucson. I'd worked with Wright before, most recently tracking down a witness to a Nogales Highway automobile accident that had left a family of four dead. He was calling to tell me that locating Carlos Verduro had resulted in a four-million-dollar judgment. Not that it did me any good, since I charge hourly rates, not contingent fees. My next call was from Becky Greenough, who lived in La Cienega. She'd hired a local guy to paint the inside of her house, had advanced him a thousand dollars for materials, and hadn't seen him for two weeks. My explanation of my fees was met with a long silence before she said she'd have to get back to me.

As I hung up, my stomach started to complain. I glanced at the wall clock. Twelve o'clock straight up. Briefly I considered the stale Twinkie in my desk drawer, but, feeling virtuous because of the couple of hours I'd already put in, I decided to take myself to lunch at Rainbow's.

Downtown La Cienega—if a strip shopping center, Circle K, feed and video store (combined), hardware store, veterinarian and dentist's office (not combined) can be called downtown—is another world.

Rainbow's is one of a dying breed of restaurants, and the hangout of the Good Old Boys. Honest to God, some people drive all the way out from Tucson just to eat at Rainbow's. I think they're looking for something called Atmosphere— if Rainbow's were a classier place it might be considered Ambience.

The decor leaves a lot to be desired, even though small letters under Rainbow's sign proclaim, AND ART GALLERY. The art gallery part comes from a famous artist who used to live here and left a few of his prints in Rainbow's custody. While somewhat buckled from the humidity from the evaporative cooler used in the summertime, the prints do add a touch of class to the pockmarked walls.

Then there was the itinerant Indian guy who came through and painted the mural with Plains Indians on a buffalo hunt. It adds another touch of something to the place— although a Where's Waldo mural might have been more stimulating.

Decent food and conversations that are fun to eavesdrop on are the two main draws. As a regular, I've found myself a sometime eavesdropper and a sometime eavesdroppee. It all works out.

"Hey Trade," Rainbow greeted me as she ran through the restaurant with a parade of plates running up her right arm and a bowl of salsa in her left hand.

A person could sit in Rainbow's smoking section and have lung cancer before the order arrived. And the service is always fast with a capital *F*. I wasn't in a carcinogenic mood today, so I sat in the no-smoking room.

The Cienega Special includes turkey, bacon and jack

cheese melted on rye, thick-cut potato chips and a dill pickle. I am deeply committed to my cholesterol, so I ordered it. Working on an insurance file, I spilled catsup on only one corner of the papers, my measure of a successful working lunch. Sopping up the last chip, I paid my bill and returned to the office.

A little after two, Charlene Williamson arrived with another woman. They walked in, apologizing for being late; they'd had a little trouble finding the ranch turnoff. If Charlene hadn't made the appointment, I never would have guessed the fat woman with the puffy eyes and thinning red hair had been the tall, thin, peppy cheerleader and homecoming queen of Javelina High. Because of her height, she'd always been in the center of the cheerleaders' formations. I remember all the boys smirking about how stacked Charlene had been, but her stacks had melted into the rest of her bulk, and now were dwarfed by a new ledge below, all of which she attempted to camouflage with a long-sleeved gray caftan. As further defense, she clutched a large manila envelope to her body. Her large boneless feet mushroomed over the tongues of her matching gray tennis shoes.

Perhaps because her size limited her clothing options, she covered her body with jewelry. She sported only one hole in each ear, but each was filled with a huge diamond. Gold bangle bracelets sang on her right wrist, and as I glanced at them, I was struck by the fact that I couldn't see any bones beneath her skin.

"Hello Charlene." I extended my hand and watched it become engulfed in the Dough Girl's. I was suddenly sorry I'd eaten all of my potato chips. As she withdrew her hand, I spotted four rings squeezed onto her fat fingers, with pleats of skin radiating out from them. On her left hand she wore a simple wide gold wedding band that fit.

"You remember Buffy, don't you?"

I turned to the other woman. Buffy Patania, reputed to be the richest girl in high school, had been blond, tan, athletic and beautiful. Now she looked like the adult version of the All-American cheerleader—one of those tanned blond women with the shiny red lips and perfect teeth that stroll through Saks and Neiman Marcus. Whenever I'm in those stores, which is rare, I swear they have a little room in the back where they clone a model and then people their aisles with the Perfect Woman.

Buffy fit the mold. I searched her hair for gray, and thought maybe I saw a strand or two, but it was hard to tell—she was sporting one of those expensive dye jobs, the kind where your hair is yanked through a cap and dyed about four different shades.

Cradled in one of her arms, like a forgotten baby, was our high school yearbook.

"Trade." She extended her hand and gave me a soft shake. I noticed her French manicure, nails barely glossed. She had also been a cheerleader.

"You haven't changed a bit," Buffy said.

I muttered something about how great they both looked and hoped Charlene couldn't see the lie in my eyes.

"Do you still ride?" Buffy asked, walking into the middle of the room.

I nodded. "I've got a couple of horses."

"I've just started to," Buffy said cheerfully. "And I love it." Both women settled into the office chairs. "Maybe we could ride together sometime."

"Sure," I fibbed, leaning against my desk and facing them. I hadn't seen her in twenty-five years, so the chances of our riding together were fairly slim.

"You heard about Valerie?" Charlene asked, her voice catching.

"Uh-huh."

"God, isn't it awful?" What had been a cute button nose wrinkled, and I noticed for the first time that she had really big nostrils. Checking her out, I was ashamed to admit, even to myself, that I didn't mind cruel twists of fate. I always thought it would have been nice to be homecoming queen.

"Pretty gruesome," I agreed, not exactly referring to Valerie's death.

Buffy said nothing.

"She was a cheerleader."

"I remember."

"There were eight of us our senior year."

As if on cue, Buffy spread the yearbook out across her knees and began thumbing through it.

"And three of us are dead." Buffy didn't say much, but when she did, it was a zinger.

"Excuse me?" I caught the implication but was stalling for time to think, to try to remember. Had they died recently?

"Three of the squad have been killed in the past three months." Charlene nodded toward Buffy, who turned the yearbook so I could see the picture of the pep squad.

I'm blind as a bat and have worn contacts most of my life. Now the irony of aging is that even when wearing them, I also need reading glasses. I reached for them so the blurs could become faces.

Charlene's stubby finger pointed to a young face. "Valerie."

The finger moved on. "Debby."

It roamed before landing again. "And Elaine." It now stopped under Elaine Vargas, a pretty heart-shaped face with big brown eyes and dimples framing her smile.

"Elaine Vargas is dead?" I was stunned. For some reason, since I'd known her the best, it was harder imagining her dead.

Charlene fumbled with the envelope, withdrawing some stapled photocopies. "These are for you."

The one on top was a copy of a newspaper article from the *Albuquerque Journal* dated February 3rd. Elaine's face, older and somehow sadder, stared out at me from the Metro page, WOMAN FOUND DEAD IN MALL PARKING LOT, the headline read. I quickly skimmed the story. Elaine, taking advantage of a Midnight Madness sale, had gone alone to the shopping mall. She probably never made it inside: No shopping bags were found in her car and none of the clerks could remember waiting on her. Late that night, after the mall had closed, security guards had discovered Elaine's body slumped across her front seat. She had been shot twice, once in her right side and then in the back of the head. She'd been stripped of her purse and jewelry. The paper reported no one had yet been arrested in the case.

Elaine Vargas had left Tucson years ago, so I wasn't surprised that the *Arizona Daily Star* hadn't carried the story. If it had been in the *Citizen*, someone would have called me.

I turned the page. This one, a small obituary from the *Los Angeles Times*, was dated three months ago and chronicled the life of society matron Deborah Chamberlain. Cause of death was listed as salmonella poisoning.

The next few pages were photocopies out of the yearbook, a copy of the reunion notice, and the recent clippings on Valerie Higgins.

"We want to hire you, Trade." Buffy's voice cracked.

"We're scared." Charlene sounded breathless. "We think whoever has killed them is going to kill us."

"I admit that three out of eight is a strong coincidence," I offered. "But it sounds like Elaine was in the wrong place at the wrong time. And food poisoning isn't exactly murder."

"Connie O'Hara's missing," Charlene said. "She lives in Denver and was supposed to visit her mother in Tucson and never arrived. That was over a week ago. We've been checking on all the cheerleaders we could find."

"And the police?" I asked, distracted by Charlene, who was trying to move one of the rings around on her finger, but her flesh wouldn't yield.

"Nothing yet."

I mulled this over. We were now looking at a possible fifty percent fallout rate. I had to admit that seemed higher than coincidence warranted.

"Where are the other two?" I asked.

"Mina's living in Japan and no one knows where Bobette is." I loved these names. They sounded like the Mouseketeers. I could see the headline now: *Fluffy names with deadly futures.*

"You've gone to the police?" I asked again, hoping for more information.

"Yes. They're not sure about any connections. They say they're working on it, but they think we're just a couple of hysterical women," Charlene said. Something behind her sunken eyes reminded me that she was just fat, not stupid. "They won't give us protection."

"I'm sure." I knew about manpower shortages, budget crunches and lack of evidence. "But I'm not a bodyguard."

"Oh, we know." Buffy held up her perfectly manicured hands and I wondered who did the grunge work with her horse. "We don't expect you to protect us. We just want you to find him."

"What makes you so sure it's a him?" I asked.

"Well, women don't commit murder, do they?" Charlene's little eyes bored in on me.

"You know, if what you think is happening is really happening, this is a little out of my league," I said. While there was no denying that Elaine Vargas had been murdered, the others were gray blips on my screen. I wasn't yet convinced that someone was killing the Song Dogs. Still, Charlene and Buffy weren't budging. I had to confess. "I've never had a murder case before."

"We're just looking for a way to cover all of our bases," Charlene explained, a little too quickly. "And since you were in high school with all of us, and you have an investigator's license, you're the logical choice."

"We think it's someone we know," Buffy chimed in. "Someone we all went to school with."

"The reunion," I said. The connection they were making became clear.

"Exactly." Charlene picked at a Kleenex and began to tear it in tiny pieces and throw them at my trash can. "We'll be seeing a lot of people from high school, people we haven't seen in years. If someone is killing the cheerleaders, I don't think he'll be able to stay away from the reunion."

"That doesn't mean you'll catch him," I said, not buying into her liberal use of *we*.

"No, but it's the only shot we have." Buffy was really becoming talkative.

"Will you help us?" Charlene turned her piggy eyes on me. "Please."

I hesitated. What they had presented was flimsy at

best, and taking phantom murder cases was definitely not my style. Still, there were the unpaid bills in the desk drawer, and I wouldn't be shipping cattle until fall. How could just looking into it hurt?

I reached in the desk drawer for a contract. "I'll see what I can do, but I want you both to understand that I may not be able to accomplish anything. You may be wasting your money."

Buffy waved that aside. "It doesn't matter." Apparently she was still shot through with big bucks.

"May I borrow that?" I gestured toward the yearbook. I was sure I had one somewhere, but it would probably take me days to uncover it. "I'll need any lists you have of current addresses and names of our fellow alumni."

Charlene rummaged through her envelope and handed me a sheaf of papers. "I'm on the reunion committee," she said. "We're having a meeting Friday night. I'd like you to come with me."

"Sure," I said, figuring that would be as good a starting place as any. "I also want the two of you to make up a list of the people you and the other Song Dogs hung out with in high school. Your best friends, boyfriends, even boys you dated casually." As an afterthought I added, "And the teachers you had. Frankly, I think your murder hypothesis is pretty far-fetched. But if by some slim chance it does pan out, then there's got to be a common denominator."

Charlene scribbled on her envelope. Her handwriting matched her looks: large, round letters with small circles over the *i*'s.

"I'd also like current biographies on all of the cheerleaders: families, addresses, work information, hobbies, anything that might be useful or show a common thread. Basically, whatever you know."

We left it that way. The yearbook with me, the homework assignments for them. And I knew that the clue that would unravel the case—if there was a case—would probably lie in their work.

On her way out the door Charlene turned back. "Oh, I almost forgot," she said perkily. "Binky says hi."

"Binky?"

"I married him last year." Charlene turned her superstar smile on me. In it I could see a glimmer of her former persona.

"Remember me to him," I said as I closed the door.

Binky Williamson and Charlene Carlton. Go figure! Binky had been our star linebacker. Handsome hulk of a guy. He'd been the king of something, I thought, as I thumbed through the yearbook. I finally found him with the Rodeo Royalty. He was indeed the king. Built like a linebacker with dark curly hair and a little boy grin. The cleft in his chin didn't hurt his looks, either.

Now, Binky with the old Charlene would have made sense. Binky with the gone-to-hell one didn't and I was willing to bet, if the wedding ring was any indication, that she'd been this size last year, too. I still suffer from these stupid high school prejudices where I think that handsome matches pretty. Of course, I know better. But I was having trouble drawing the mental picture of the two of them together.

What the hell, I thought. He's probably gone to pot, too.

The picture in my brain was like one of those funny what's-wrong-with-this-picture cartoons where the guy has one plaid sleeve and one striped and is hitting a baseball with a golf club while a bird flies backward.

Something didn't fit. But what in the hell was it?

4

VALERIE HIGGINS MADE THE FRONT PAGE AGAIN THE NEXT MORN-
ing. Her missing body was found half buried in an abandoned irrigation ditch just outside the Tohono O'odham
Reservation west of Tucson. Cowboys out gathering cattle
had made the grisly discovery. The accompanying photograph showed a cadre of grim-faced policemen walking beside a shrouded body on a gurney. Detective Charles Borden,
my Uncle C, was one of the cops.

He's married to my mother's sister Josie and is the father of my cousins Beatrice and Top Dog. Top Dog disappointed him when he turned his back on police work and
went to live with Shiwóyé on the reservation. But Uncle C
likes the idea of Beatrice being a television anchor, and he
rarely misses her performance on the ten o'clock news.

In addition to being with the Criminal Investigation
Division of the Pima County Sheriff's Department, Uncle C
is an artist. He works in watercolors and India ink, painting
abstracts of some of his murder cases. I think his paintings
are grim, but there's an art gallery in Tucson that represents
him and he's even sold a few.

My uncle and I have a funny relationship. I'd had a
pretty checkered career after college. My degree in English
literature opened up few opportunities, most of them secre-
tarial. At that point in my life, I was eager to leave the ranch,

so, placing it in Juan's able custody, I took my first real job as-
sisting an interior designer who had been a good friend of my
mother's. A few months later, my head spinning, I quit. I
worked for a while with the telephone company, I peddled
real estate, and then I trained horses until one broke my arm
and ruined my best saddle. I traveled some, ending up back
in Arizona, and applied for a job with the Pima County Sheriff's Department. I made it through all the testing—the written and physical exams and the psychological review
board—and entered the Law Enforcement Academy. I lasted
two weeks. Couldn't stand the regimentation.

When I first applied, Uncle C grumbled. I think by the
time I entered the academy he was softening up, although
he had little use for policewomen. When I dropped out, I
was relieved . . . but he was shamed. And when I started
working with Tony Lorrenzo in private investigations, he
went berserk. If I wanted to play "goddamn girl detective" I
should have stayed in the academy and learned real police
work, he'd hollered.

After eight years he's mellowed a little. But not enough to
share any details about Valerie Higgins's murder. No, if I was
going to get any information, I'd have to find it elsewhere.

I read the rest of the paper, including the obituaries,
clipped Valerie's funeral notice out and tacked it on the bulletin board inside the pantry door. Her services were set for
the following Thursday afternoon.

Juan and I doctored the old cow with pinkeye again.
While I felt as though I should be working on the case, with
Martín gone I was worried about the pinkeye business. I
needed to check on the rest of my cattle, so I headed out to
the pasture and saddled a horse.

Dream, my bay Arabian, was eager to get out. We left
the thick mesquite bosques of the lower valley, crossed the
creek and began our climb up onto the flat mesas above.
Even in February the midday temperature was in the upper
seventies, ideal for riding. I spotted some of the Brahma
cows and headed toward them. Their mates, Hereford
bulls, had been doing their job, because each cow had a

baby by her side. We used to breed to Brahma bulls, but discovered that when we shipped them east they shivered off a lot of weight in the feedlots. The Hereford marriage gave the progeny a thicker coat and, for us, higher profit.

All of the cows I checked were clear-eyed.

I like cows. They're loyal to each other and they have a nice sense of community about them. Riding a little farther I found a gray mama baby-sitting six little calves. They take turns. One mother will baby-sit while the others go to water or just browse. The next day, a different cow will take her turn. And we think we're the only ones who appreciate good day care.

I headed up toward the Baby Jesus ridge. No one has ever figured out how it got its name. Some say if you look at the right angle you'll see baby Jesus in his cradle—all I see is a daunting rock pile. I stopped my horse near Green Rock and let him blow. I found myself wondering about the Song Dogs. If they were being knocked off, what—other than their long-ago cheerleading positions—did they have in common? There had to be a connection, but what was it? I shuddered, startling Dream.

We were halfway to the concrete water tank when I heard a familiar noise. A diamondback rattler, the first I'd seen this year and over three feet in length, rattled a warning. Although we were out of striking distance, he reared up, cobra style, and fixed his beady black eyes on me while his tail shook in anger. I hate it when they first wake up after their winter nap. They're hungry and usually cranky. We skirted him and headed for the tank.

I didn't see any cows up high. They had been there earlier in the week but now had drifted down below, lured by the six-week grass that had come up in the valley.

At the cottonwoods, I stopped for lunch. It was a spectacular picnic spot with the majestic Catalina Mountains looming to the east and a grove of ancient cottonwood trees, still naked from winter, acting as sentinels along the dry creek. The riverbed would begin running once the mountain snowmelt started. As I sat eating my potato and salsa sandwich I made a mental note to start my investigation by interviewing Valerie's family and the employees of the bar where her car had been found.

But it was too bizarre. Who would want to kill the cheerleaders? And why would he wait twenty-five years? None of it made sense, and I began feeling guilty about signing the contract.

They were wasting their money. There was nothing to it. I decided I would go with Charlene to the reunion committee meeting tomorrow night and then tell them they didn't have a case for me to investigate. No sense throwing good money after bad, I thought.

On the ride home I remembered something.

Elaine Vargas and Binky Williamson had been a hot number in high school. A real hot number. In fact, I remember Elaine telling me that the dean of women at Javelina High had called her in and lectured her about their "public display of affection" in the halls. Then something had happened their senior year and they broke up.

And now twenty-five years later, Elaine was dead and Binky was married to Charlene. Interesting, but still not a murder case.

I left the cottonwoods and cut cross-country to the north water tanks. There were no cattle milling about, but judging from the salt licks, which were almost gone, they had been there. I needed to bring some more salt in.

I reined Dream in just before dropping into the valley. From my vantage point I could see the cottonwood and mesquite grove that held the ranch headquarters below. With the coming of the spring grass, things were beginning to green up. As I dropped off the hill, a lone coyote scrambled out from under a mesquite tree. He stopped a short distance away from my horse, sat and scratched his ear. Cheeky things, these coyotes.

Binky and Elaine. I didn't stop thinking about them until I rode into my back pasture.

5

I HEARD GRAY WHINNYING FOR DREAM LONG BEFORE I RODE into the headquarters' pasture. Horses hear a lot better than we do, and I've discovered that those left in the ranch corrals always know when we're coming long before we're in sight.

My cousin Beatrice was waiting for me at the corral. Although she was a year younger than I, when she wore her hair long, we were sometimes mistaken for twins. Bea is the star in the family, and like her father, my Uncle C, I rarely miss her performance as anchor on the ten o'clock news.

"Good ride?"

"The snakes are out already." I didn't have to say *rattle-snakes*. When country people in Arizona say *snake*, they generally mean rattlesnake. The others don't count. "What brings you out?"

"Work. Stress. Same old stuff," she said. "I just needed an outdoor hit instead of just talking about it."

"You and two hundred million other people." I laughed.

"You're not going to suggest horseshit therapy again, are you?"

"Wouldn't hurt." I subscribe to the theory that if more people would just shovel horse manure, we could put psychiatrists out of business. There's nothing better for clearing out the cobwebs in the brain than good old-fashioned manual labor. After all, how many cowboys go to shrinks?

"Shiwóyé called to remind us about the tamales."

I groaned. With all of the Song Dog business that day, I'd forgotten about the Changing Woman ceremony. A big party had been planned for Alicia Cassadore to mark her passage into puberty. Since these shindigs are always expensive for the family, Shiwóyé had committed Beatrice and me to ten dozen beef tamales. We hadn't even started them yet.

I undid the horse's breast collar and flank cinch before pulling his saddle. Grunting, I dragged the saddle into the tack room.

When I stepped back outside, Bea handed me the brush. I'm always amazed at how you can think you have a clean horse but when you pull your saddle off after a ride, there are mud slicks outlining the edges of the saddle blanket. I began brushing at these and across the horse's back. "When is it?"

"The seventh."

"Well, that gives us some time."

"A couple of weeks. But you know about tamales."

Unfortunately I did. Tamale making is a celebration of sorts, a great excuse for a party and drinking a few margaritas, but it's also a hell of a lot of hard work. Like about two days' worth.

Gray nudged the gate, eager for his pal to join him.

I untied Dream and led him to the pasture. Once I turned him loose, he ignored Gray and trotted to the first sandy spot he could find. He circled for a minute and then, finally satisfied, dropped and rolled. He smashed his head into the dirt, rubbing his face where the bridle had been. Then, without warning, he rolled all the way over.

"Hundred bucks," Bea said.

"Right." She was referring to an old cowboy adage. They used to say that every time a horse rolled completely over he was worth a hundred dollars. If a horse rolled over three times, he was said to be worth three hundred dollars.

Of course, some of them were worthless—they couldn't roll over at all.

Gray fit this category. To scratch his back after a ride, he'd do one side, then stand and drop and roll on the other. Sometimes he'd get screwed up and forget which side he'd done and end up doing the same side twice. Funny creatures, these horses.

Like most old cowboy sayings, there was some truth to this one. You can tell a lot about a horse's back and hindquarters by how he rolls. A healthy horse will have little problem easily dropping to roll and will be able to roll over. A horse that can't drop easily, roll over and get up smoothly, usually has a problem somewhere in his back, hips, stifles or hocks. The one exception is the high-withered horse. They can be structurally sound and still have trouble rolling. Gray was such a beast.

"How's the new case going?" Bea asked as we crossed the yard. I paused long enough to fill the bird feeder. A stupid excess when one has cats around.

"I'm giving it up. There's nothing there." We walked through the screen porch and into the kitchen. I washed my hands and stepped into the pantry. "Twinkie?" I held up a cellophane-wrapped little darling.

"No thanks, I'm trying to quit." Bea and I are a lot alike, but nowhere more so than in our eating habits. She, too, loves chocolate and junk food and goes on spurts of healthful eating. We have a lot of fun with our food. Luckily we're both tall and thin or we'd be on the Overeaters Anonymous Top Ten Most Wanted list.

"So how'd Charlene and Buffy look?" Bea had been a year behind me at Javelina and knew the two cheerleaders.

"Fat. Gorgeous."

"Which one was fat—Charlene?"

I nodded.

"You're not really going to give up, are you?"

I carefully bit off the end of the Twinkie until just the beginning of the white stuff was starting to show.

"I just don't see it making sense." I started on the other end, saving the middle until last.

Beatrice shuddered. "My bones tell me you're wrong. I think something happened to those cheerleaders."

"We'll see," I said.

After she left I did chores, fed Mrs. Fierce and the horses and chickens, and sprinkled scratch around the pond for the ducks. Then I built a fire in the rock fireplace, closed the curtains on the big picture window, had another Twinkie for dinner and curled up and read the *Western Livestock Journal*. My idea of a perfect evening.

6

I MET CHARLENE IN THE PARKING LOT OF A DUNKIN' DONUTS IN Tucson the next evening.

I locked up Priscilla and left her there. She is the love of my life. A white Dodge turbo-charged three-quarter ton pickup truck, complete with bug guard and mud flaps. I could go on and on about her. Suffice to say that this is a Big Girl Truck. Gets some of the boys out on the highway thinking about things. After all, her guts are a smaller version of the Cummins engine, the one that powers over half of the semis out there. With a twinge of regret I left her in the lot.

"You look nice, Trade," Charlene volunteered as I slid into her silver Mercedes. "Those earrings are terrific."

I had on long turquoise hoops, a gift from Aunt Josie years ago. Charlene's clutch of bangle bracelets looked like a Slinky moving down her arm.

Ten minutes later, she turned her car onto a residential street.

"You know, I'm really looking forward to this," she said.

"The meeting?"

"No," she laughed. "The reunion."

"March seems like a strange time for a class reunion."

"Well, the committee talked it over, and we decided

that it would be a great incentive for anyone living where it's cold. Everyone wants to come to Tucson in winter."

"Spring," I corrected her. Everyone who lives here knows that March is spring. Even the Arizona-Sonora Desert Museum lists five seasons for the Sonoran Desert, and spring runs from February through April.

Daggett Early had a remodeled adobe in the El Encanto district, a ritzy neighborhood in the middle of town. Part of what made it so exclusive was its "rural" nature. Each house was situated on at least an acre.

If Daggett's home was any indication, memorizing the Periodic Table of Elements hadn't hurt him any.

Charlene smoothed her red plaid caftan with one of her pudgy hands and wiped the lipstick off her teeth before ringing the bell. I gave up on that stuff long ago. There's really only so much you can do. I'm always wrinkled. I'm just one of those people who will go through life with little creases in my clothes, shoes, and now even my face. I could pat all day long and it wouldn't do a bit of good. I have discovered, however, if you wear your Levi's tight enough, the wrinkles kind of smooth out. I've also, on really important occasions, resorted to squirting my blouses with water and letting my body heat kind of iron them.

We stood there, Charlene wanting to give me some of her weight, and me wanting to grace her with some of my wrinkles. Fat people are kind of like stuffed Levi's: They smooth out the wrinkles. Life is so perverse.

If I hadn't known where we were, I wouldn't have recognized Daggett Early, that's for sure. The guy who opened the door was a hunk, pure and simple. As he greeted us, I found myself wishing I'd washed my hair.

"Hi Charlene." She had all the luck—he hugged her.

"You remember Trade Ellis."

"Sure." Although he was polished about it, I knew Daggett had checked me out. He extended his hand and gave me a warm, firm grip.

"Daggett." My voice didn't sound like it was my own. Suddenly I felt like I was back in high school. Feelings of uncertainty and self-consciousness flooded me. It's been a long time since I felt that way, but this new Daggett Early was something else. Through some quirk of nature the nerd had been replaced with a stud. The horn-rimmed glasses were gone, exposing deep brown eyes with long thick lashes. Some men have a spark in their eyes. Maybe he'd always had one and the Coke-rim bottles had hidden it, but there was no denying it was there now. I've always had good luck with those sparkling-eyes guys.

Daggett's body had filled out, too. Very nicely. I noticed that he had learned to zip his fly. Damn! I hate it when everything changes.

"Come on in."

As he closed the door, I spotted a stainless steel panel sporting several buttons. Alarm systems always make me nervous, especially if I have to do anything with them—as in when they're screaming their heads off and I have to shut them down. Fortunately this one was content to just wink at me with one green eye. Security systems are getting more common, but I always wonder what people have that makes the inconvenience worth it.

Daggett led us past a plant-filled atrium that resembled a miniature jungle, other than its sprinkler system, white tiled floor and center drain.

"Trade's going to help us with the reunion," Charlene said.

"It looks like you've got everything under control," I said lamely.

"We can always use help," Daggett's hand slid down my arm to my elbow as he guided me into his living room. "Would either of you like a drink?"

I quickly scanned the room to see if anyone was really drinking. They were. "Red wine."

"Me, too," echoed Charlene.

As I was introduced around, there was only one person I didn't remember even when prompted: Jericho Jamison. With an alliterative effort like that you'd think it would have been easy. Memory overload again, I suppose.

Charlene was the only Song Dog on the reunion committee. There were a few girls from the pom-pom line; a guy who had made it to the regionals in diving; Mr. Jericho, of course; Calvin MacKenzie, the past editor of the *Javelina Journal*; the class twins Ron and Don; and Mr. Weston, our old dean of men.

As they settled in to their lists and planning, I dropped to the leather couch, sipped my wine and checked out the room.

It was done in the less-is-more style. Daggett Early, whatever he was doing now, was obviously very successful. From my short stint working for the decorator, I recognized the sleek leather Roche-Bobois furniture. Mirrored tables and thick Berber carpeting, the expensive kind, graced the room. The walnut floor-to-ceiling bookcases harbored leatherbound volumes and looked as though they were treated to a gentle dusting by the cleaning lady a couple of times a week. Inset lighting highlighted several original oil paintings on the walls, all contemporary. The one over the marble fireplace was an original Taber-Borcherdt. Big bucks.

Everything was so neat and structured I had trouble equating the room with someone who would send me an envelope with scrunched-up handwriting. It's been my experience that the neatniks' habits usually overflow into their penmanship. Maybe his secretary did it, or maybe they all sat around addressing envelopes in their earlier committee meetings.

I set my drink on a mirrored coffee table in front of the couch. A heavy crystal obelisk was the only other object on the table.

Opposite me, a walnut and glass lit cabinet held two more glass sculptures, a carved ivory head, some small brown blocks, an ugly wooden and steel box, and what looked like an antique gun. On the bottom shelf there was a small object inside a case—a redundancy, glass inside of glass. I couldn't make out its contents from the couch.

A fire blazed in the fireplace, but it was insulated by a glass screen. That, together with the spare decorating and the rest of the glass cases, gave the room a cold feeling. While it was all tastefully done, it gave me the creeps. It was too perfect, too sterile, too kept. The chairs were stiff and uninviting—it would be a challenge just to curl up in them and read for a couple of hours, even if there had been good reading light. Taking all of this into consideration, I judged Mr. Warm and Bubbly Hunk had a few hang-ups. Maybe major ones.

"So, Trade, what have you been up to?" Daggett pushed a couple of kilim-clad pillows out of the way to sink into the leather beside me.

"Just working and getting along."

"What do you do?"

There it was. That wonderful question that I sometimes can't wait for people to ask, and more frequently can't stand for them to ask. It's right up there with "What's for dinner?" in my book. I used to get that one a lot when I was married. Since then the "do" question has edged out dinner.

Briefly I thought about lying. I frequently do. But he looked so good, I couldn't bring myself to do it. Besides, I thought he might find me sexy since I have what, to most people, sounds like a sexy job.

"I'm in investigative work." I said, seeing no need to tell him I was also a rancher. There was no need to get that personal.

"Journalism?" If his eyes had been sharks they would have eaten me.

"Private investigation."

Something flickered in his sparkling eyes. Just enough to tell me that I didn't want to stay on the subject. Could he have something to hide?

"That must be very interesting," Daggett cupped his wineglass in his hands. "We were just talking about the cheerleader thing before you got here."

"Did you know any of them?" I asked. He'd handed me the perfect entrée. How well could he have known the cheerleaders in high school?

"Charlene and I had senior English together. I took Connie O'Hara out twice. The others never gave me the time of day." Although he was matter-of-fact about it, his voice sharpened a little. "Can't say as I blame them." He laughed and took a slug of his wine. The hail-fellow-well-met was now back, but I found it curious that he had not only dated the missing cheerleader, but twenty-five years later remembered exactly how many dates they had had. He had been such a dork, I was much more surprised that one of the Song Dogs would have gone out with him.

"I didn't date much so it's easy to remember the few I had."

It was eerie, as though he had read my mind. I didn't like the feeling.

"I didn't really know Valerie, but I was sorry to hear about her when I got back."

"Back?"

"I was in Denver on business last week."

Bingo. Although Daggett Early now had the singular distinction of being the first person on my suspect list, he'd just jeopardized his position with an alibi.

"You're not married?" He abruptly changed the subject.

"Not anymore."

He nodded and flashed me a Colgate smile. "Maybe we could have dinner together sometime."

"Sure." The words were out of my mouth before I could stop them. Although I like men with spark, I don't date ones who quiver my antennae. I was still wondering about the danger signals, but my mouth was already in gear. I relaxed when I realized that dinner would give me a chance to find out what he knew about the Song Dogs. Chalking up my quick acceptance to hard work made me feel a lot better.

"So then we'll have a cash bar, right?" Charlene's voice cut into our conversation. "Is that okay with you guys?"

"What?" Daggett asked.

Charlene waved a pudgy hand, exasperated that most of her report had been missed by her handsome host. Her motion set the bangle bracelets singing. "The ranch wants to charge us too much. We can't price the dinner at fifty dollars a plate. The nondrinkers and poor folk just won't come."

"I'll handle it," Early said easily. He was obviously used to picking up tabs.

"God, Daggett, we might have a couple of hundred people there," Charlene countered, clearly amazed at his offer.

"It's all right."

If he'd intended to impress us with his largesse, it had the opposite effect on me. His extravagant gesture was too grandiose for my taste. I'm not that keen on show-offs.

A few more committee reports were given, then plans to meet again were made, and we all started to drift out. I made a point of walking next to the fireplace, which led me past the lit cabinet. Daggett Early was on my heels when I paused in front of it.

"You have some lovely things," I said.

"Thank you."

Now that I was close I could see that the small brown blocks were actually dice.

"Those look old."

He opened the unlocked case and handed them to me.

"From 1888. They're loaded. That box"—he pointed to the ugly wooden thing—"is a dice shaver. I collect this stuff."

"Old things or dice?" I asked curiously.

"Old gambling things." He reached for the gun, which wasn't larger than the length of my hand. "This Remington derringer, for instance, was used by the old gamblers as a hideout gun. They stashed them so the other players wouldn't know they were armed." He rolled the derringer over in his hand and I could see two three-inch barrels, one on top of the other.

"Is it loaded?' I asked.

"With .41 rimfires," he said, snapping the gun apart and showing me the two bullets.

I thought it was pretty stupid to keep a loaded gun in an unlocked case in full sight, but maybe collectors did that sort of thing.

He put the gun and the pair of dice back in the case and pointed. "Two pretty shelves"—his hand passed by the top two shelves—"and my collection shelf."

Charlene walked up and hovered near the case, obviously eager to be included in our conversation.

"And that?" I pointed to the glass case inside the glass case. From this distance I could see that it was a carved head of some sort.

"Oh, that's my prize," he said. "This is my exotic shelf." He reached for the glass box. Once he got it out of the case, he removed the top. "A shrunken head." He said proudly, lifting it out.

In spite of myself, a shiver went up my spine. "A real one? I mean, this was really a person?"

"From Colombia. My grandfather brought it back years ago when he was working for Foster-Wheeler." He held the head by its long black hair and dangled it in front of my face as though I wanted to inspect the damned thing.

"That's creepy," Charlene said.

"Well, it kind of grows on you," Daggett laughed, dropping it back in its box.

We quickly said our "good nights," and walked out. As I let myself into Charlene's Mercedes, I wondered what in the hell Daggett Early was doing with a shrunken head.

7

By Monday morning I was ready to go back to work on the case. I had spent the weekend riding the ranch, checking on my cattle and putting out salt. Since the bulls run with the cows year-round, we get early calves. After riding all day Saturday and most of Sunday, I had several new arrivals logged in my tally book.

I spent a lot of my time in the saddle thinking about the Song Dogs, and I had decided to go for it. Charlene and Buffy's timing was good, since my case load was fairly clear and I had time to devote to their cause. I really didn't have much to lose. Worst-case scenario was that I would have to give back the retainer. In the plus column was the rush I felt whenever I thought about handling my first murder investigation.

It helped to have a suspect. Daggett Early. That shrunken head business really made me wonder. A guy that had dead people's heads on display in his home was very suspicious. My first step would be to find out how ironclad his alibi actually was.

One of my team penning partners, Emily Rose Kibble, lives in La Cienega and is my conduit into the Pima County Sheriff's Department. She's worked in the Medical Examiner's Office for thirteen years. All county suicides, traumas and homicides, along with any other death where a doctor isn't present, are brought into the examiner's office, so I knew they had Valerie Higgins.

As I pushed the glass doors open, Emily Rose looked up from the telephone. She waved as I approached the counter. The office also contracts with nine other counties, including some in the northern part of the state. While these autopsies should logically be done by Maricopa County, the Phoenix medical examiner is too overloaded with that massive population to do them. Since the office can be pretty hectic, I was glad it wasn't a busy morning.

"Hello Trade, here to see Em?" Sharon Roberts, one of the filing clerks, greeted me. I was always here to see Emily Rose on "personal business."

My friend hung up the telephone and came around to the counter. She had permed her short hair and now vaguely resembled a cute poodle.

"Curls again, and blond," I said. It was a running joke with us. I never knew if Emily Rose was going to show up curly or with a short wedge cut, blond or brunette. She was always saying we cut our hair to grow it, and grow our hair to cut it. That was true with Emily Rose anyway. She was like a chameleon with her crowning glory. Pretty and petite, she had a body like steel due to her fanatical hiking habits. At least three mornings a week Em hiked three miles up to the Romero Pools in Catalina State Park and back before coming in to work. Her one bad habit was chewing gum. It was always in her mouth and she loved to snap it.

"What are you doing here?"

"I've got a new case."

"You don't do murder," she said, clearly surprised.

"I do now."

"Let me guess." She walked over to her desk, rummaged through her out box and handed me a sheet of paper. It was a signed autopsy order for the missing Connie Eugenie O'Hara. "They're beginning to stack up."

"Shit." I said to no one in particular. Any concern I had

about the Song Dogs being a phantom case evaporated as I studied the order. With O'Hara's death the odds had increased that someone was killing the cheerleaders.

Emily Rose was clearly pleased she'd picked the right one.

"They brought her in early this morning. Bad news, she was also cut up pretty good. They're working on her now."

I knew that if they were doing the autopsy, her next-of-kin had probably been in and identified the body.

"Where'd she turn up?"

"Out near Picacho." Picacho Peak was about thirty miles north of Tucson, halfway to the Gila River. Its claim to fame was that it was the site of the only Civil War battle—if twenty-eight soldiers duking it out can be called a battle—ever to be fought in Arizona. Now another body had been added to its legacy.

Picacho Peak is in Pinal County. Valerie Higgins's arms were found within the city limits of Tucson, and her body was located just off an Indian reservation in Pima County. Jurisdictional problems could complicate things. It was also possible that if a multiforce task force was thrown together, my chances of getting information would be better than if only a few detectives were involved.

"The Higgins and O'Hara murders are definitely connected. Same knife was used on both women. The tea leaf guys have already been called in," Emily Rose said helpfully.

"Tea leaf?"

"The feds. They're doing a personality profile for us. Unfortunately they don't have much to work on."

Emily Rose returned to her desk and rummaged through some papers. She handed me a manila envelope folded in half. Without a word I tucked it inside my suede jacket. Sharon Roberts hunched over a file she was working on, happy to ignore our exchange.

"That's not very pretty." Though Emily Rose nodded at my jacket, I knew she was talking about the contents of the envelope. "And this one won't be, either." She snapped her gum. "He likes his blade."

My stomach rolled. Another mutilated Song Dog.

"And that"—she gestured again to the files at my chest—"isn't exactly good bedtime reading."

"Thanks, Em, I appreciate it," I waved my goodbye as I exited her office and headed for my next appointment.

Forty minutes later I was seated in Valerie Higgins's living room with her husband, Jerry. His kids had both come home from college to be with him. I felt like the interloper I was, asking him about his dead wife. He assured me that he would do anything to see her killer brought to justice, even talk to me.

We talked at length about all of the cheerleaders as I took notes, but he couldn't tell me anything I didn't already know. Higgins apparently attributed his wife's death to a robbery gone awry.

"She never took off her wedding ring, even when she had a bad hand rash from doing dishes," he said, his voice beginning to crack. "She kept it on since the day I put it there. He took it and killed her."

Feeling guilty for wasting his time, I left him and drove down to the University district. I parked Priscilla and walked to the trash bin and ersatz shrine.

While I had seen the newspaper pictures of the battered dumpster, but seeing it in person was even more chilling. Gang graffiti, big puffy letters that were the latest trend, sprawled across the beleaguered trash bin. A line of votive candles and one lonely fake geranium rested at the base of the metal box, along with something that looked suspiciously like a used condom.

The whole thing gave me the creeps. Rosary beads dangled from one hinge. It was like those white crosses draped with colorful plastic flowers that are put up alongside the highways where a pickup full of teenagers has overturned. *Pay attention,* these icons caution, *lives were lost here.*

I left the alley and walked down Fourth Avenue. Although trendy, this is one of our "areas in transition," as they say. Favored by street people, a food co-op and a few boutiques, it also has some good restaurants, a Salvation Army thrift shop and several watering holes.

It was not yet ten in the morning, but there were a few

diehards bellied up to the bar when I stepped into Justin's, the bar where Valerie had last been seen. Rheumy eyes checked me out only long enough to ensure that I wasn't one of them, before they went back to their pick-me-ups.

I perched on a stool and ordered a Virgin Mary.

The bartender, a big guy with a diamond in his left ear, plopped a stalk of celery in my drink and slid it across the polished mahogany. I stared at the diamond and wondered if he was gay. I can never remember which earringed ear is the clue.

"Any more excitement around here?" I asked, shamelessly trolling for information.

"Lady, what are you talking about?" He polished a glass with a dirty rag, slipped it beneath the counter and retrieved another wet one from the small sink.

"I meant that body the other day."

"Hell, that wasn't a body, that was just arms." His tone told me he thought he was talking to a moron.

I shuddered involuntarily. "I read she was in here before it happened," I said.

He gave me a funny look. I wasn't being very discreet about the whole thing, and this guy had probably seen a steady stream of curiosity-seekers come through his door asking questions about Valerie Higgins. So far, I wasn't doing too hot on interrogation technique for my first murder case. Nothing from Jerry Higgins, and this was looking like a no-go.

"You one of the looky-loos huh?" He lit a Camel and blew the smoke toward the side of my face, but far enough away so that I wasn't sure if he was deliberately trying to aggravate me.

"I knew her," I said, waving the smoke away from my face. He'd scored, if that was his intent.

"Uh-huh."

"We were in high school together." I slipped my card across the bar. He looked down at it like it was a squashed cockroach.

"So do you remember her?"

He gave me a wild look. "Lady, we get three hundred

people in here on a good night, and that one was a good night. You think I remember everyone who comes through that door?"

"I just thought you might. She was with a group of women."

"So that's unusual?"

The guy was clearly an asshole, but I continued my quest.

"But there were other people working that night?"

"Yeah, yeah. Leave me a couple of your cards and I'll have them call you." He picked up the single card and squinted. "Miss Private Ey-yi."

I left a few on the bar top, paid my bill and headed for the sunshine.

Just outside Justin's, three transients slumped against the building.

"Hey lady, got any spare change?"

I was walking fast, eager to leave them behind me, when I started thinking about routines. Everyone has routines, even street people. I turned back and fumbled in my jacket.

"Have you ever seen this woman?" I handed a dollar bill and a newspaper clipping with Valerie's picture on it to the one who was awake.

"I can't remember," he said sullenly. "You're kinda cheap, ain't ya?"

I scrounged in my jacket and came up with a couple of bucks, which I handed over. I felt like I was feeding a shark and didn't want to get close enough to actually touch him.

He pocketed the money and handed back the clipping.

"Nope, never seen her." He pulled his filthy brown cap down over his eyes and fell back against the building, returning to his morning nap.

So far, the trip to Fourth Avenue had produced nothing but celery strings in my teeth.

8

WE DIDN'T HAVE AN APPOINTMENT, SO I WAS SURPRISED TO FIND Charlene and Binky Williamson sitting on the brick tree well in front of the stage stop on the ranch lane. They were both sipping take-out cups of coffee from Rainbow's. I pulled in beside their tan Explorer.

"Hey Charlene."

Binky helped her to her feet.

"You remember Binky, don't you?" she said.

"I remember Binky, but I doubt he remembers me." I extended my hand.

"Blue Chevy pickup, primer on the hood." He cocked a finger at me.

"Right." These super memories were beginning to get to me. First Daggett Early remembered how many times he'd taken Connie out in high school and now Binky recalled a truck I drove twenty-five years ago. I can't even remember what I ate for lunch two days ago. "Come on in." I fumbled with the office key, opened the door and turned on the lights.

"I wanted to drop this off." Charlene handed me a check that was folded in half. Without looking at it, I threw it in the desk drawer.

"Also"—she rummaged around in her oversized handbag and extracted a piece of paper—"this came in yesterday's mail."

I looked at the paper she had handed me. "The lost has been found," I muttered sagely. It was a reunion reservation form from Bobette Jarcik.

"That's just it, Trade. We don't have an address for her. It's not in any of the reunion records, so we didn't send her an invitation." Charlene's already small eyes narrowed as she shared this piece of information with me.

I looked at the form. If it was to be believed, Bobette was now living in Luna, New Mexico, a small town near the Arizona border. A post office box was listed and no phone number was given.

"So no one knew how to reach her?"

Charlene shook her head.

"We thought this might be important," Binky added, reminding me that he had never been a mental giant. He, like Charlene, had also pudged out, only not as seriously. He now carried that bulky, potato-sack look that old jocks get when they don't continue to work out or watch their weight. Pockmarks that I didn't remember marched across his face. His neck was thick and corded. He sat with his legs far apart. The ability to cross them, one on top of the other, had disappeared long ago. When he walked, I knew he would look like a bulldog with his legs spread so his thighs wouldn't bang together.

What was left of his dark, curly, Rodeo King hair had settled on top of his ears. Still, he was attractive in a used sort of way. Especially when he turned on his megawatt smile. I wondered if he and Charlene had kids. With their combined grins I envisioned a whole pack of Williamson brats toddling around like those windup teeth, chattering and skittering across the floor.

"Did you save the envelope?"

Charlene rummaged around again and produced a wrinkled, torn envelope. I checked the postmark. Luna, New Mexico.

"Someone has her address," Charlene whispered dramatically.

"It could be anyone." Although I still jump to conclusions, my work as a private investigator is teaching me to cultivate a more cautious approach.

"It could be, but I think it's *him*." Although it was cool in the office, perspiration was starting to condense on Charlene's upper lip.

"If he's got her address, why doesn't he just go to Luna and kill her?" I was really asking myself, but the question came out loud.

"It's a post office box." Binky smirked. "He doesn't know where she lives." He crossed his arms over his heavy chest, as if to say, *Stupid*.

"Right," I said, trying to get the discussion back on track. "But then again, a classmate could have gotten the reunion notice, known how to contact her and sent it on. If that happened, then that person either Xeroxed her copy before sending the original or isn't coming."

"I thought of that," Charlene said. "I checked the registrations. They're all the original forms, no copies. And no one has sent in Bobette's address even though the missing names were on all the letters that went out."

"That's not too ominous," I said. "If the person knew where she was, the important thing would be that she got the notice, not that the reunion committee knew how to reach her."

The telephone rang and I ignored it. The machine would pick it up. But when Emily Rose's voice came floating through the air, I grabbed for the phone.

"Em."

"They just finished the O'Hara autopsy. We're looking at ventral wounds to the abdomen." She was in her clinical mode. "The cause of death was penetration to the left anterior chest wall, which avulsed the pulmonary artery, causing massive internal hemorrhaging."

"Okay. Anything else?" I wanted to ask, *Like missing arms?* but felt inhibited by the Williamsons' presence.

But Emily Rose caught my drift. "The dorsal sides of the arms were cut, also her right palm."

Not necessarily mutilation. Probably just self-defense on Connie's part.

"They vacuumed her thoroughly and got some skin from under her fingernails. Forensics is still working on it. The FBI's profiling a male suspect and the photos are in on the tire tracks from where the body was dropped."

"Can you get me copies?" I asked. I knew I was pushing it.

"They won't do you much good without the car. They're like fingerprints," she said. "But I'll see what I can do. Gotta go." The line went dead.

I replaced the phone and turned back to the Williamsons. I decided to share what I had learned with them. Maybe Charlene would think she was getting her money's worth. Besides, it would be all over the evening news. "Connie O'Hara's body was found this morning, out near Picacho Peak."

"Oh God," Charlene stuffed a fat fist into her mouth and bit on it. "Connie."

Binky shook his massive head and put a hamhock arm around his wife. "Another one."

I tapped the eraser end of a pencil against the rolltop desk and tried to carefully phrase what I was about to suggest. "You know"—I turned to Charlene—"you might want to think about some kind of protection. You and Buffy."

It was the wrong thing to say. Binky began huffing and puffing. "I'll protect Charlene," he said. "We don't need some goon to do that."

I had to agree with him. One goon was enough.

"Can you be with her twenty-four hours a day?" Charlene had told me that her husband was in the insurance business, and even insurance salesmen had to put in a few hours at the office.

Charlene's eyes darted around the room. She was obviously running scared. "Won't the police do something?"

"I doubt it. There are four of you left, and surveillance

details around the clock are expensive. They don't have the money or the manpower."

"You don't bodyguard?" Charlene's voice had gotten huskier. Binky snorted.

"I shook my head. "It's out of my realm." As was investigating murders, I thought. I fumbled in the cubbyholes of my desk and found a sheet of paper. "Here's a list of professionals in Tucson. Most of them start at about twenty-five an hour."

As Charlene reached for the paper, Binky grabbed it, wadded it up and shot for the wastebasket. "You don't need any damn protection with me around!"

The paper lay crumpled to the right of the trash can. I was glad he missed. I reached for another list and purposefully held it out of his reach. "Give this to Buffy," I said, handing it to Charlene. She really looked peculiar, and I couldn't tell if it was because she was afraid for her life or terrified by her husband.

"Okay," she said in a small voice. "Oh, I've got these for you." She handed me the biographical information I had asked for, including Buffy's.

Binky stood and pointed a threatening finger at me. "You just find this son-of-a-bitch. Before he gets to her." He pulled his wife to her feet. With her bulk, if she hadn't cooperated, he probably wouldn't have been able to budge her. "That's why they hired you."

As they left my office, I wondered why he had said *they* had hired me, and not *we*. I reached in the desk drawer and pulled out the check. It was for five hundred dollars.

They might have hired me, but the check was written on a trust account in the name of Buffy Patania.

9

I THREW THE BIOGRAPHICAL STUFF ON MY DESK, GRABBED VALERIE Higgins's autopsy reports and a map and headed for Rainbow's. It was as good a place as any to do my homework.

"Hello Frank," I greeted the chow dog sitting beside the front door.

I was disappointed when I saw that the Philosopher was in. He was holding court in the smoking room, and I knew that it would be hard to concentrate on my work as his voice filled the cafe. A nonstop talker, I think his mother must have been bitten by a parrot when she was carrying him. He was always eclectic in his choice of subject matter. It ranged from which was the most venomous species of rattlesnake to what the CIA was doing in El Salvador. The Philosopher had opinions on everything and was not the least bit hesitant to share them with the Good Old Boys or the rest of the cafe, even the bicycle crowd, who thankfully were absent.

It looked like the Philosopher had an audience of one today—German Jack, whose days were usually spent patiently searching for the "Mine with the Iron Door." Jack, his trusty blue mule Sarah and dog Frank spent days on end camped out in the Catalinas searching for the legendary lost gold mine. Coming back from his jaunts, he usually appeared at the cafe.

Rainbow waited on me herself. Her real name was Rebecca Liebowitz, but she'd changed it to Rainbow Dancer back in her flower child days. A left-wing New York transplant with a talent for pastry, she had settled into Arizona's most liberal county. Still, she fancies us not quite as intellectual as her fellow New Yorkers. On a really bad day, she holds court with the Philosopher.

"Great crêpes today, Trade," she offered. "Broccoli cheese with hollandaise."

Since I'd had a bagel with cream cheese and cocoa for breakfast hours ago, I worried my cholesterol count might be slipping, so I ordered the crêpes. "Is there lots of chocolate pie?"

She stuck her head around the corner and checked with Joe Bob, the cook. "Couple of pieces."

"Save one for me," I said. Nothing is worse than having two pieces of chocolate pie in a cafe when you come in, ordering lunch, and then finding them gone by the time you are ready to eat dessert. It's best to plan ahead.

I opened the manila folder. There were two autopsies inside—the first one had been done on the arms when they'd been found. It was nine pages long, not much shorter than the autopsy on the rest of the body. Since the arms had been unidentified when they were found, the autopsy on them contained reports from both the forensic pathologist and a forensic anthropologist. The dorsal sides of Valerie's arms had been cut, defensive wounds that indicated they'd been part of her body at the time of the assault, and that she had probably been conscious when they were cut off. The flesh bore jagged cuts and the bone examinations revealed that a serrated blade had been used. The other autopsy consisted of a lengthy narrative report outlining the condition of Valerie's body, followed by a toxicology report. While it was fairly dry reading, I found myself remembering Valerie and getting a bit queasy. I was glad I was looking at it before lunch arrived.

I skimmed the autopsy report until I found "cause of death." There it was: "Stab wound to the left anterior chest wall." If the guy had indeed started out somehow poisoning Deborah with salmonella three months ago and then moved on to shooting Elaine Vargas, he had now found his preferred method and was aiming for the heart. It was working.

Since Emily Rose had told me about the skin under Connie's fingernails, I knew that at least one of the women had put up a fight. Whoever the killer was, he should be sporting some battle scars.

On my legal pad I scribbled, "Rural locations." Picacho is no challenge for the average passenger car, and Valerie's body had been found along a rural boundary of the Tohono O'odham Reservation, parts of which were remote and would definitely require four-wheel drive. I needed to know exactly where Valerie's body had been found. I wrote down and circled, "Four-wheel drive or pickup?"

There had to be a common thread. Someone who had a bone to pick with eight women, or at least with three of them—Elaine Vargas, Valerie Higgins and Connie O'Hara. I wasn't ready yet to chalk up Debby Chamberlain's salmonella death as intentional. All of the women had been cute and popular in high school. What could they have done to warrant this? I wondered as I put the autopsy reports back into the envelope.

The crêpes were as good as advertised. Light and fluffy, with broccoli in a rich cheese sauce, covered with a creamy hollandaise. I had several bites, trying not to drip sauce over my notes. Then I paused long enough to unfold, then refold the map I brought with me into a nice compact square and continue eating.

Running my finger up the eastern margin of Arizona, I stopped on Luna, New Mexico. It was just across the line from Alpine. Although it was February, we hadn't had a lot of bad weather, and I figured I could get through the White Mountains and into Luna in about six hours. The drive would be worth it if I found Bobette Jarcik. And I had to find her before the killer did. The clock was ticking and I had a horrible feeling that the murderer wanted them all dead before the class reunion, less than three weeks away.

The chocolate pie finally arrived and was adequate.

There are few things I am an expert on, but one of them is chocolate pie. This one rated a six, considerably less than the French Silk produced by Village Inn. Still beats carrot cake, though.

I bundled up my stuff and drove to the Rail X, our local feed store, where I bought duck and chicken food and some pellets for the horses. I still had a couple of tons of hay in the barn and could limp along without buying any more until the second cutting this spring.

Feed stores are one of my addictions. They are simply the neatest places in the world. From the moment you walk in and are greeted with all those wonderful, fresh smells, you know it's special. There's no way that Neiman Marcus can hold a candle to a good old-fashioned feed store. Once I lived in the city for a couple of years. I remember driving to a feed store and walking in the front door just to get a hit of country. It's kind of like the horse manure thing: Some people go to therapists—I shovel and mainline feed stores.

After chatting with Curly, the owner, I checked the bulletin board for new additions. I love reading the notices people post—ads for tack and animals for sale, posters for ropings and barrel races, offers for horse-training services, or the rare benefit for the family who lost their home to fire or needs money to bury someone. As I headed outside to Priscilla, I ran into Sanders, one of my closest neighbors, and a good friend.

"Howdy Trade." Sanders is originally from the north country, South Dakota, and he is one heck of a cowboy. In fact, he also runs some of his own cattle, the Quarter Circle Running N brand, on the Vaca Grande in exchange for helping me out. Sanders is probably the best-looking man in this part of the county, a fact that is lost on him. Lean and well over six feet tall, he has a deep voice that rivals Sam Shepard's. He always wears a cowboy hat—straw in the summer, felt in winter—and, unlike a lot of cowboys, actually has a full head of hair underneath it when he takes it off. Those Marlboro men have nothing on him. He's single, too, since he lost his wife to a heart attack a few years ago, but never dates as far as I know.

Sanders is also something of a local celebrity. He's a cowboy poet and goes to the annual gatherings every year in Elko, Nevada. Too shy to read his own material, he's always surrounded by young cowboys eager to make a name for themselves reciting his poetry, a lot of which has been published in various cowboy poetry anthologies.

"Getting feed, huh?" Sometimes my feed store conversations run to the obvious.

"A little bit," he drawled. "Say, have you seen those Shorthorns lately?"

I shook my head. He had a handful of Shorthorn cattle running in with my Brahmas. Since La Cienega was growing, there were more frequent encounters between the two-legged creatures and the four-legged. So far this year we'd lost two head to vehicular calf slaughter, and one to some crazy with a gun. So we like to keep a close eye on them. "And I rode all weekend."

He nodded.

"You going out?" I asked.

"Yep, I guess in the morning. Wouldn't hurt to look around some."

"Well, I'd like to ride with you, but I'm taking a short trip tomorrow and won't be back until Wednesday. I'll try to get out later this week."

" 'Preciate it," he said with a grin as he climbed into his Ford and I got into Priscilla. He headed left into La Cienega, and I turned back to the right toward the Vaca Grande.

I stopped at the old stage stop on the way to the ranch and retrieved the biographies. Charlene and Buffy had attempted to fill out information for each of the dead and missing Song Dogs. I knew that I'd eventually have to fill in the blanks. After glancing through them briefly, I tossed everything in the manila envelope before heading out the door. Suddenly, I remembered something. I went back inside and grabbed Buffy's Javelina High yearbook.

Mrs. Fierce was waiting for me halfway up the drive. If I ever get burglarized, I'm going to blame the dog. She's a beacon. If I'm gone, she trots down the lane and waits for me. All the neighbors know where I am by the dog's location.

I'm sure any enterprising burglar could figure it out. "Stupid dog," I muttered with affection as I drove in.

I backed the truck into the tack room area and unloaded my feed. The duck and chicken sacks are easy. At eighty pounds a bag, the horse pellets take a little maneuvering. But if you wrap them in a big hug, and balance them on your thighs, and then sort of do a duck walk, you can usually get them into the feed bins. I always feel like Superwoman when I unload feed. Thank God the Rail X feed store stacks the hay. When Martín's around, he'll usually do it, but I don't like to ask him for the help. As it is, he does enough around here.

As I unloaded the feed I wondered how big a person would have to be to load up Valerie Higgins's body and dump it out on the Indian reservation. It would have been light, without her arms. Still, it would take someone strong to be able to handle all of that dead weight. Or more than one person, maybe.

Dream and Gray came running, their long Arabian tails flipped up over their backs. I thought they were thrilled to see me until they rolled back at the pipe fence and tore off down the pasture. Just another game of equine tag.

When I finally got the feed in, I fed the horses and chickens and collected eggs. As I came across the yard I scattered some scratch and duck feed for the quackers.

Once inside, I lit the fire and poured myself a glass of red wine before checking the answering machine. I was surprised to find a call from Daggett Early. When I returned it, he asked me out for dinner Thursday night. I eagerly accepted it. I wanted to get to know him better, but for all the wrong reasons.

10

A GOOD STIFF BREEZE, UNUSUAL FOR MORNINGS IN OUR VALLEY, plagued me as I packed Priscilla the next day. There were no clouds in the sky, but a wind like that could stir up a storm. Briefly, I thought about canceling my trip to Luna, but decided I should track down the missing Song Dog as quickly as I could. There was no telling if the killer already had Bobette in his sights, and the pressure was on me to locate her and alert her to the possible danger. I also needed to get a hold of Mina Arthur in Japan.

Mrs. Fierce did a funny little hopeful dance around the truck.

"No, Juan is going to take care of you," I explained patiently.

Destroyed, she lowered her tail, gave me that I-can't-believe-you're-doing-this-to-me look and sat under a mesquite tree, pouting as I drove out.

I headed north out of La Cienega up Highway 77, past the Biosphere, a controversial recycling experiment. I left the desert behind as the road climbed into the scrub-oak-covered hills of Oracle, then dropped down again at the San Manuel turnoff. The huge copper smelter there belched out a gray slab of smoke that hovered over the area. As I slowed to thirty-five driving through Mammoth, a notorious speed trap, I could see the lush San Pedro valley below. When

I crossed the bridge I noticed the river was a thin ribbon of water.

The two-lane road began a steady climb up through Winkelman to the Globe turnoff. The Gila River was to my right, spewing froth on the rocks at its curves. It's popular with the rafting crowd, but no one braves it in winter, not even in sunny Arizona.

By midmorning I arrived in Globe and turned east, continuing my climb before dropping into the spectacular Salt River Canyon, one of the last Apache bastions during the famed Indian Wars. Five miles wide at the top, the vertical walled gorge is two thousand feet deep, and with its sedimentary rock layers clearly visible from the road, it's easy to imagine how my renegade ancestors holed up in the high canyon caves watching the cavalry's pursuit as they navigated the treacherous ravine.

Three hours from the ranch I passed Show Low, one of our White Mountain communities, and maybe the only town in Arizona that owes its name to a poker game. Back in the 1800s two partners arguing over the town's ownership agreed to a game of cards. "If you show low, you win," one goaded the other. "Show low it is!" replied his disgruntled partner as he threw his low cards down. The name stuck, and the main street bears the name of his stroke of luck, Deuce of Clubs Avenue.

I found a diesel station combined with a mini-market there and loaded up with road food: Twinkies, a diet Pepsi and a box of Cheez-Its. The Cheez-Its are an integral part of any trip I take. They are absolutely a requirement for a successful journey. Part of the success formula is, of course, that the box come home empty. Cheez-Its are ecumenical in that they can serve as breakfast, lunch or dinner. They are also a fine foodstuff to have in the car on those occasions, which I confess are many, when I worry about not having enough to eat. This is, of course, just another one of the hang-ups of traveling for investigations.

As I headed up toward Springerville, I noticed a bank of dark clouds gathering on the eastern horizon. I'd had the radio tuned to country stations all morning long, and the weather reports had been growing more ominous as I drove.

The first snowflake hit as I drove down into Luna. Luna, New Mexico, is a tiny town. Actually there are two of them, on just about the same latitude—one east and one west of Socorro. And then there's Los Lunas north of Socorro, south of Albuquerque. The New Mexicans have a thing for the moon.

This particular Luna sits in a hollow, surrounded by mountains. It's a pretty little place with cottonwoods acting as sentinels for the San Francisco River, which runs along the south edge of town. Most of the trees were cleared out by early settlers to make room for the now fallow farm fields.

The Luna post office shares an ancient log building with one of those old-fashioned country stores. When I walked in, the four or five people gathered around the woodstove in the middle of the room stopped talking, checked me out and then went back to their conversations. It wasn't much different than Rainbow's.

The postmistress was eating a homemade chocolate chip cookie and she offered me one from a chipped blue plate. They were delicious and I told her so. That started a heady discussion on the merits of various cookie recipes and we agreed that the one on the back of the Nestle's package was best. We were divided on whether or not to refrigerate the dough before baking, but came back into agreement that eating the raw dough was even better than gobbling up the actual cookie.

At any rate I really thought I had her nailed, but when I got around to asking about Bobette Jarcik the friendly cookie maker's face became a Darth Vader mask of doom.

"She has a post office box here." I withdrew a copy of Bobette's reunion form. "See?"

The stone face nodded.

"It's really important that I talk to her. I think she might be in danger."

Nothing.

I fumbled for a card. Sometimes it works, especially in

small towns. That "private investigator" piques people's curiosity, and they often spill their guts.

But Cookie Postmistress took her job very seriously, and she was having none of it.

"I can't give out that information." She was clearly suspicious.

"Is there anyone here who might be able to help me out?" I looked over at the stove and noticed a few of the clan had dispersed.

She shrugged and began weighing mail. "Don't know."

Although I was pissed, I thanked her for the cookie. I stopped at the woodstove and warmed my hands. Only an elderly couple remained.

"Cold day," I said.

"Cold winter," the man replied.

"I'm looking for someone and I wonder if you can help me."

"Well, if they live in Luna, we probably know 'em," the man said.

His wife nodded.

"Bobette Jarcik."

A flicker in his tired gray eyes told me I'd hit my mark.

"Do you know her?"

"That's Jessie's granddaughter, ain't it?" The old lady nudged him. "The one who come back."

"Yep."

"Do you know where I can find her?" Their backs were to the postmistress, who was now giving me dirty looks.

"Up the valley, 'bout a mile or so. Blue house on the right, white railin' on the front porch."

"Thanks a lot." I smiled. As I left the store I wondered why I'd bothered with all the cookie shit. I should have gone straight to the stove.

11

As I climbed into Priscilla, I could see the postmistress through the front window. She was on the telephone, probably talking to Bobette.

It was a lot colder now, and I grabbed my down jacket off one of the rear jump seats and pulled it on.

Driving past the Mormon church, a staple in many of our small Arizona towns, I took the main road up the valley and started looking for the blue house. What the nice old man had not told me was that there were a lot of blue houses—all of them the same shade.

Someone had gotten a hell of a deal on paint, or maybe it was like naming your kid. Some years were good for Gordons and Jessicas and Seans and Ashleys, and others were good for blue paint. I dropped Priscilla to twenty-five as I crawled along the edge of the road looking for the right house with the white porch railing. It was the sixth blue house. I pulled into the snow slush in front of it, grabbed the yearbook and headed for the front door.

The bell was one of those obnoxious ones that sounds as though you have just electrocuted something. I had just removed my finger from the button when the door opened.

"Yes?" A tiny woman with a head full of permed blue hair stood in the doorway.

"Hello, my name is Trade Ellis. I went to high school with Bobette. Is she here?"

"Oh dear." The woman pulled her paisley wool shawl tight around her scrawny shoulders. "Just a minute." She started to close the door, then reopened it. "What was your name again?"

I repeated it and wondered if they already knew about the Song Dog murders. I also wondered if there was any chance that Bobette would remember me. The only memory I had of her was the yearbook photos. She had short dark hair worn in a pixie cut and one of those chunky gymnastic-type bodies. She had been the most athletic of the cheerleaders. She did the best cartwheels and was the only one who could handspring across the gymnasium floor. Of course, this was in the days before steroids; now they all can do it.

I waited on the porch as the snow began falling in earnest. I blew on my hands and rubbed them together. Checked my watch. Stomped my feet. And finally Bobette Jarcik opened the door.

"Come in," she said.

This one I never would have recognized. The shiny black hair had gone to a dull gray. She was wearing it longer now, a chin-length pageboy. The solid gymnast's body had withered to anorexic proportions. Her face was lined and worn and she was wearing way too much makeup. The black kohl rimmed her eyes and thick green eye shadow, caked in the crevices of her eyelids with the wrong shade of blush, gave her a clownish glow. The sadness in her eyes rivaled some bloodhounds I'd seen.

Bobette led me to a glassed-in sitting room at the rear of the house. It had probably been a screened porch, but with the wicked Luna winters it had been transformed into a room that was usable year-round.

"Have a seat." She pointed to an old wicker rocker with stained chintz cushions.

"I'm Trade Ellis. We went to high school together," I began.

"Did we?" Her eyes were a cloudy blue, but there was still a clarity about them. One I began to suspect had not always been there.

"I'm sorry, we didn't really know each other. We were just in the same place at the same time. But there's a problem I want to talk to you about."

"The murders," she said. "The police told me."

Of course, Charlene would have given Bobette's address to the Tucson homicide investigators.

"You saw them?" I asked.

"No. They called yesterday." She lit a cigarette. "I wasn't any help. I haven't seen any of those girls since high school. They didn't like me then. I was a Song Dog, but I really wasn't popular, you know what I mean?"

I nodded, totally mystified.

"How did you get the reunion stuff?"

"They asked me that, too. It just came in the mail. I didn't save the envelope, didn't know it was going to be a big deal."

"And you're still going?"

She laughed. "It's a way of confronting my past." She took a long drag on the cigarette and I saw that her hands were shaking. "Of exorcising demons."

"Demons?" I was beginning to think I had something here.

"Look, Trade, I'm going to be candid with you. High school was not a happy time for me. Hell, my whole life hasn't been a happy time for me. I think I'm finally getting it together. And maybe going back will help some of the pieces fall in place." The sorrow never lifted from her eyes.

"Would you mind looking at some pictures for me?" I opened the yearbook and found the Song Dog page. "What do you all have in common?"

"I don't know." She crossed her skinny legs, and one of them bobbed up and down. "I can't think of anything."

"Did you maybe date someone that one or more of the other cheerleaders dated?"

She laughed. "I didn't 'date' any of the boys that went out with those girls."

I turned to the football page and pointed to Binky Williamson. "Did you know this guy?"

She laughed again. "Yeah, I knew him."

"Ever go out with him?" She was acting weird.

"Not exactly." She took the book from me and studied the football team. "I just screwed him."

"You mean . . ."

"Yeah, I mean." Her finger ran across the football team. "And him and him and this one. Oh, there's Jerry and Warner." In all, she had screwed half the starting lineup and a lot of the second stringers.

I tried to pretend I wasn't fascinated. It wasn't even a winning team.

I didn't fool her, though. "I told you it was a really unhappy time for me."

"I can understand that."

"No, I don't really think you can." A hard edge had come into her voice. "It set me up for a lot of grief." She rolled up her sleeve, exposing the inside of her elbow. A herd of small red bumps paraded across her arm.

"Heroin?" I asked. It was the hard drug in the days before crack and PCP. And making a comeback, I heard.

"Yeah. And the groundwork that I got at Javelina helped me buy it." She laughed at her pun. "I went to St. Louis and started hooking." She pulled up her shirt and exposed a nasty scar across her stomach. "Until the black hookers got mad at me for horning in on their territory."

I shook my head. This was not the way cute cheerleaders were supposed to wind up.

"There were a few overdoses," she offered, pulling another cigarette out of her pack.

"And now?" It was a hard question, but I figured I had nothing to lose.

"These are my vice," she held up her cigarette. "I don't drink. Can't have kids."

"You went through a program?"

The cynical laugh was back. "Oh yeah, you could say that."

There was a long silence. I didn't know what to ask, but I felt if I was just quiet, more would come. I was right.

"There are a lot of programs in prison," Bobette said. "A lot of them."

"You were in prison?"

"Eight years. I got out in January and have been with Granny ever since."

She must have seen the surprise on my face. "It isn't any secret. The police know."

"They would."

"I'd appreciate it if you wouldn't tell the others."

"I won't." The way I figured it, Bobette had enough problems without my squealing on her. "What were you in for?"

The blue eyes grew cloudier. "Self-defense, but they called it murder. Someone tried to kill me and it didn't work out. It was unlucky; I don't want to talk about it."

Shit. *Self-defense, but they called it murder?* She looked scrawny, barely strong enough to carry her own weight, much less Connie O'Hara or the body of Valerie Higgins. But she may have had help. As painful as Bobette's life had been, I was afraid I was going to have to put her on my list.

I flipped through the yearbook and asked about a few more faces as we tried to figure out who sent her the invitation. We went over the reunion committee—the pom-pom girls, the diving guy, that Jericho fellow, the *Javelina Journal* editor and the twins, Ron and Don. She'd screwed both of them.

When we got to Daggett Early, she remembered him. "Smart guy," she said. "He was in my biology class."

She saw it in my eyes. Damn! Sometimes they tell too much. I'm still working on that impartial observer thing, even after eight years. I'd have to practice more in the mirror.

"Surely you're not suspecting him?" she asked.

"Everyone's a suspect right now."

"God, he couldn't even dissect his frog; he almost fainted. I had to help him with it. He was a brain, though, got the best grade in the class."

Interesting. If Daggett had trouble dissecting a frog, could he carve up a woman?

"I know, I had him in chemistry." I gave her a questioning look.

"God no," she said. "The guy was a geek. He probably hasn't been laid yet."

I said nothing, letting her keep her fantasy.

We talked awhile longer, and then I said my goodbyes.

On the way out to the truck I wondered why Daggett hadn't remembered that he'd had biology with Bobette Jarcik.

12

A COATING OF SNOW BLANKETED PRISCILLA, AND MY HANDS shook with the cold as I opened the truck door. In spite of the weather, she cranked right up and soon Luna, New Mexico, was in my rearview mirror.

It was dark now and a slow thirteen miles back to Alpine. I stopped there at the Sportsman to see about a room and dinner. I was starving, and when I found out that all of the restaurants, along with the market, were already closed, I decided to continue driving into Springerville.

The snow was really coming down. I'm not all that fond of the stuff. I guess it's okay if I'm inside by a fire admiring it through double-paned glass, but outside I find it slippery and mushy and, well, cold. As for driving in it, I'm ignorant. Like most desert rats, I'm discombobulated by snow. In spite of all admonitions to the contrary, I'm sure that if I got to sliding on a slick stretch of highway, I'd slam on the brakes and turn directly into a tailspin.

Snow flurries were whirling around the truck and, caught by the headlights, they appeared to be dancing ghosts. A car pulled out in front of me on the outskirts of Alpine, and I fell in behind it as it maintained a comfortable speed through the miserable night. I was going to school on its headlights, and when it turned off after a mile or two, I felt abandoned.

While my attention was fixed on the road ahead of

me, the rearview mirror reflected a high pair of headlights behind my truck. They were moving fast, faster than I thought prudent in the snow. I tapped my brakes to let the driver know I was there and going a lot slower. The gap between us was shrinking fast as his headlights grew larger in the mirror.

I could see a curve ahead and because there was no slacking in his speed, I knew the idiot behind me was going to attempt to pass. I slowed down so he would have enough room to get back into the right-hand lane in case there was a car coming from the opposite direction. Sure enough, he pulled out and began to pass.

My eyes were riveted on the road ahead. The passing vehicle, which loomed large and white, a snow-covered box; was beside me now. It paused there for a moment, long enough to catch my attention. I looked over but could not make out the driver, only that the vehicle was some kind of sport model.

Suddenly the driver swerved into my lane. Had I not been looking, the car would have clipped Priscilla. I turned sharply to the right, and the front wheels of the Dodge caught the snowy shoulder of the road. The truck slid off the highway into the slush and mud and spun out and around. I fought the steering wheel to gain control as I felt the rear end slide and fishtail around the verge.

It was over in seconds. Priscilla was still. Miraculously, we were on the edge of the road, and I could see the diminishing taillights of the passing car disappear into the snow-bound night.

"Son-of-a-bitch," I finally snarled when my heart stopped pounding, "ought to learn how to drive." I sat there for a few minutes, collecting myself, thankful that Priscilla's fine engineering had avoided a wreck. I could just as easily have been smeared in the ditch.

Back on the road after extracting my truck from the embankment, I saw a sign for the Tal-wi-wi Lodge, and it didn't take much encouragement for me to turn in. I was in luck—there was not only room at the inn, but wine and food.

It's funny how we take so many things for granted, and

my near miss that night had me savoring everything. The glass of merlot held new meaning, the chicken was the best I'd ever had, and even the apple cobbler vied, at least for that night, with the best chocolate pie I'd ever eaten.

After dinner I pulled out the manila folder and the background information on Charlene and Buffy. Charlene had sent hers through a computer, which meant no typos, but there was some red stuff smeared on the papers that looked suspiciously like strawberry jam. Buffy's material was written in a straight-up-and-down hand that was easy to read, although dispassionate.

A lot of the same names appeared on the sheets. They both, of course, listed all of the girls who had been cheerleaders, as well as those in the pom-pom line. They both remembered they had been in the same math class and Buffy remembered that she had had biology with Bobette Jarcik. Which, based on what Bobette had told me, meant that she'd also shared the class with Daggett Early. I found it interesting that the top two suspects on my list had not only shared a biology class, but had done so with one of the last living Song Dogs, who, in spite of her retainer, was also under suspicion. I had to consider all of the four remaining cheerleaders as suspects. After all, there was a connection somewhere, and I couldn't count any of them out. Not yet.

Charlene had gone steady with Tom Sorenson her junior and senior years. After high school he'd gone to Vietnam and didn't return.

For the first time since I'd known her, I learned Buffy's real name—Virginia Morgensen Patania. Her dating list read like a Who's Who of Javelina High, but she hadn't emphasized anyone in particular. Binky Williamson's name appeared on her list. I circled it and wondered if Charlene knew that her fellow Song Dog had dated her current husband. He was so disagreeable now, I had to think he must have been more charming in high school to have done as well as he did with women. He wasn't doing too badly with me, either. Unbearably macho, nasty and abusive, he was third on my list, right behind Daggett and Bobette. His history with so many of the Song Dogs was also beginning to make him look like a common denominator. Although I really didn't believe it, could Charlene be my killer? Reluctantly, I placed a red check beside her name.

Charlene had been married three times. The first two had no Javelina High connections. She had one son by her first husband, Oscar Ramirez. He was attending Pepperdine outside Los Angeles and living with his father in Malibu. Her second husband had been killed in a hit and run. Her parents were living in Tucson. She also listed a deceased sister, Laverne Carlton. Charlene's hobbies included cooking, needlepoint, crossword puzzles and reading. Not the kinds of things that are real calorie burners. She listed several women friends and three asterisks by Buffy Patania's name, indicating that this was her very best friend. Charlene didn't have a job.

Neither did Buffy. She had been married once. Briefly. Like six weeks. To Vance Packard, the quarterback of the football team. Vance hadn't escaped Bobette's identifying finger during our yearbook discussion, so he had been one of the notches in her belt. I circled his name to remind myself to check his whereabouts. Seeing Packard's name reinforced Bobette on my list. I couldn't afford to discount her—there were a lot of old coincidences, intertwining her life with those of the other Song Dogs.

Buffy definitely had a more active life than Charlene. She played tennis, gardened, rode horses, painted and worked as a silversmith. And those were just her main hobbies. Buffy, an only child herself, had no children. Both of her parents were dead: her mother to cancer, her dad a suicide. I placed a dollar sign in the margin and circled it. Buffy had probably inherited a fortune.

Under friends Buffy listed three names. One of them was Charlene's, but there were no asterisks next to it.

I compared Charlene's and Buffy's sheets. In addition to being Song Dogs, the one thing they had in common was that Bobette Jarcik had screwed both of their husbands in high school. I wondered if either of them knew that. The only noticeable distinction between them now was that Charlene's name had a red check, Buffy's didn't.

The red check system was probably stupid, but it made me feel as though I were doing something. It was kind of like grading papers. In reverse. The one with the most red marks under my system would get the A. Besides, when I looked at all the checks, they actually helped me focus on my suspects.

Tired from the long day, I gathered up my papers and headed back to my room. I quickly undressed and slipped between the crisp cotton sheets.

It was like counting sheep. Newspaper headlines of the dead cheerleaders taunted me as Buffy Patania, Charlene Williamson and Bobette Jarcik pranced through my head.

My last thought before drifting off to sleep was that I needed to contact Mina Arthur in Japan.

She was now the only missing Song Dog.

13

AFTER BREAKFAST THE NEXT MORNING, I PAID MY BILL AND WENT out to load Priscilla. I opened the passenger door, flipped the front seat forward and stowed my gear in the back.

When I walked around to the driver's side, I could see something dangling from the door handle.

I felt numb as I stepped closer.

There, swinging in the morning breeze, was a rag doll. It was naked.

And around its neck was a perfectly fashioned hangman's noose.

I checked the snow around the truck, but it had started to melt and was deteriorating into slushy mud. There was no way to make out any tracks.

I debated calling the police and then dismissed the thought. I was in Apache County, and not only would I lose most of the morning explaining things, but whoever left the hanging doll on my truck was definitely not from Apache County.

And the passing car last night was not just a bad driver.

For some stupid sexist reason, the hanging doll seemed like a woman's touch. Suddenly the prospect of a woman killer was gaining ground. But which one? Bobette was the logical choice. She was just down the road in Luna and following me to the Tal-wi-wi Lodge would have been easy for her. That sweet little grandmother of hers probably wouldn't have even known she'd been gone. Although I felt sorry for Bobette and admired her honesty, she now topped my list.

Retrieving a plastic bag from the truck box, I carefully slipped the doll into it—probably a useless gesture, with the difficulties of lifting fingerprints from cloth. Besides, I didn't really expect whoever had left it to be stupid enough to leave such a signature. I tried to shake off the numbing chill I was still feeling, and I climbed in the truck and headed home. I had less than three weeks to find the killer before the reunion. Maybe I was getting close to something, I thought, shivering again, although the heater was on full blast, But what?

I got back to the ranch about one in the afternoon and Emily Rose Kibble was waiting for me on Hank, her big palomino gelding.

"We going penning?" she hollered at me before I had even cleared the truck. "They're starting the buckle series tomorrow."

With all of the Song Dog business, I had completely forgotten about team penning. Sanders, Emily Rose and I always rode together as a team. While someone could fill in for me, or for them, it was never as good as when the three of us teamed up together.

I climbed out of Priscilla and was assaulted by Mrs. Fierce, who did a peculiar little two-legged hop as her front feet grabbed my Levi's. As she humped my leg, her tail wagged wildly in rhythm. The dog's got talent. That's one good thing about having a dog—they're always tickled to see you.

God, with all I had to do, I really had no business thinking about going team penning.

"Did you talk to Sanders?" I asked, half hoping he'd said no.

"He's ready."

Then I remembered the rag doll and how scared I'd been when I'd almost been run off the road. And the best glass of merlot I'd ever had and how truly grateful I was to be alive. Life was too short. Maybe shorter than I thought, so I did the only sensible thing.

"Okay. Let's do it," I said.

"I've got these for you." Emily Rose turned in her saddle and unzipped her cantle bag, pulling out some folded pieces of paper. "The photos on the tires."

"No molds?"

"Not anymore. New technology. These are taken with a scale in place ninety degrees with flash illumination. Direct overheads."

I looked at the photographs, but there was nothing distinguishing about them. While tire marks aren't quite as individual as fingerprints, they are identifiable. Each tire wears a little differently and if the suspect vehicle can be found before it's driven too far, it's possible to match a tire on it with the track it left. Tire prints are tattletales. *If* the vehicle can be found.

"Have they got anything yet?"

"They're running the tires now, and still trying to work up a suspect profile. But they're having trouble—they don't have enough evidence."

"Sounds familiar," I said. I felt the same way. A lot of suspects but no one coming out strongly on top.

"The serrated knife went in past the hilt," Emily Rose volunteered.

I shuddered.

And then I remembered what I wanted to share with her. Reaching back into the truck I retrieved the plastic bag. I filled her in on the rag doll I'd found hanging from Priscilla at the Tal-wi-wi Lodge.

"My God, Trade, what can I do?"

I thought for a moment. "Well, do you think you can have someone try to run prints?"

She took the bag and studied it.

"Am I missing something here? Cloth, right?"

"I know."

"Can you bring it to the penning tomorrow?" she asked.

Her generosity was overwhelming, because I knew she'd have to impose on a cop, who would eventually ask for a return favor.

"Gotta go." Em turned her palomino toward the front drive. "I'll see you tomorrow." She settled the horse into an easy singlefoot and disappeared from sight as I started unloading the truck.

Juan walked up to help me.

"Anything new here?" I asked him.

"Busted water pipe. We were at eighteen this morning."

There it was again. The weather. Those of us who live in the country are obsessed with it.

"I came through a big storm up north," I said, looking up at the dark sky. "Looks like we might get some here tonight."

"Red sky this morning. I turned the cow out."

"Her eye's better?"

He nodded. "Sanders came by. He found a dead calf down near the Sutherland tanks. Lion."

I hate it when we lose calves, but unfortunately it does happen.

"I'm going to town; you need anything?" he asked.

"No thanks." Now that Martín's my foreman, Juan spends a lot of time running to town. This could mean anything from the five-mile trip into La Cienega into a longer sojourn into Tucson. It's his way of filling his days. He'll most likely stop at the feed store, the cafe and maybe the Circle K. Later in the day he might drop in at the Riata and tip a few beers, shoot the bull with the boys and flirt a little with the barmaids. I think these are basically scouting expeditions, because he always comes back with some piece of local gossip. Besides Shiwóyé, Juan's been the one constant in my life. I hate it that, like my grandmother, he's getting old. I can't stand the thought of not having him in my life and I know that one day that will happen.

In the house I grabbed a Twinkie and perched on the kitchen stool as I listened to the messages on my answering machine. It was family day. The first message was from my cousin Bea, who wanted to make tamales the following Tuesday.

Some of the Twinkie goo had gotten stuck on the plastic wrap, so I licked it off as I listened to the next message. It was from Uncle C. He rarely called me and I jotted his name down on a scrap piece of paper next to the phone. There was also a call from Charlene Williamson.

I called her back first.

"Hi Charlene, this is Trade."

"Oh Trade." Her soft little-girl voice grated against my ear. Funny how someone that big could have such a tiny voice. "I just wanted to call and find out what was happening."

Briefly, I told her I had met with Bobette Jarcik.

"Did you know anything about her reputation in high school?" I asked.

"You mean like all those guys she slept with?"

"Right."

"Sure, everyone knew about that. Didn't you?"

I ignored the question.

"I didn't get much from her," I said, neglecting to mention Bobette's jail record or that she had slept with Binky in high school.

"Have you seen the paper this morning?"

I told her I hadn't, since I'd been traveling all day.

"Well there's a big story on the reunion and Val and Connie."

"Shit. Who did that?"

"I don't know. Maybe MacKenzie. He freelances."

MacKenzie had been the editor of the *Javelina Journal* and he was on the reunion committee. He probably couldn't resist selling the story.

"I've been getting calls all morning from strange people wanting to come to the reunion."

I groaned. "What did you tell them?"

"Well, I said they couldn't, of course. That this was just for alumnae. You know we can't have that. I mean, the facilities are limited."

"Right." My mind raced. If the killer showed up at the reunion, it would be difficult at best to ferret him out from among the known. If a cast of thousands arrived, it would be impossible. "Good decision."

"We're up to a hundred and three now."

"Including spouses?"

"Yes. But we've got a few more weeks." Charlene went on to tell me many more reunion details than I cared to know about. But it was her nickel, so I listened patiently as I attacked another Twinkie, trying to disguise the crinkling of the cellophane. She asked me a question while my mouth was stuffed and I squished it into one cheek in an effort to sound normal.

"What?" I stalled so I could swallow. Although I'm fond of them, I'd hate to choke to death on a Twinkie while talking on the phone to Charlene Williamson.

"You are coming, aren't you? I mean, you haven't sent in your form."

"Oh no, sure, yes, of course I'm coming."

"Trade." Charlene's voice dropped to a whisper. "Binky's bought a gun."

"A gun," I repeated.

"And he's got it in the house."

I didn't think that sounded like such a bad place for a gun. "Does he know anything about them?"

"I don't know. He says he does, but I don't know." Her voice was still low, leading me to believe Binky was somewhere close. "I think he's getting worried."

Bright boy, I thought. "Well, he probably just wants to protect you." I entertained thoughts of Binky shooting himself in the foot, or worse, shooting Charlene in the middle of the night, mistaking her for the Song Dog killer. "But Charlene, he really ought to know what he's doing, or he has no business with a gun."

"I *told* him that, but he says it's okay, that he knows what he's doing. I can't stand the idea of having a gun in our *home*."

I didn't know what to say. From what I'd seen of Binky

Williamson, I was pretty sure he was going to do what he wanted to do and the protests of a mere woman were not going to dissuade him.

"Do you have a dog?" I asked.

"Duke, our Labrador. He's wonderful."

"Good. If you're home alone, keep the dog with you. He'll be some protection."

"I've been doing that. But he's an outside dog, and he's piddled on everything. But we're working on it."

I smiled to myself. A little piddle was nothing compared to a lot of blood.

"And Charlene, try to keep Binky from accidentally shooting the dog," I said before I hung up the phone.

I called Bea back and left a message on her machine setting Tuesday as tamale day.

When I finally reached Uncle C he had just come in from the golf course. We exchanged pleasantries and family news for a few minutes, then he finally got down to business.

"Trade, Beatrice tells me you're messing around with this cheerleader thing."

"Well, I've taken on a couple of clients in conjunction with it, if that's what you mean." I replied, already defensive. Family can make you crazy.

"Clients." He cleared his throat.

I grimaced. We've had a lot of arguments over that one. He says clients are what lawyers have, and the people who hire me are customers. I guess the way he figures it, if you pay more, you get to be called a client.

"A couple of the cheerleaders. They're just covering their bases." I decided to downplay it, hoping to save myself some grief.

"Yeah, I know." When he cleared his throat again, I knew that something was bothering him. "Are you getting anywhere?"

"Chasing rabbits so far. How are you boys doing?"

"Using lots of time and men with damn little to show for it. We've got this goddamn task force now. Too many chiefs."

Fifteen silent seconds passed.

"Listen Trade, you've got to give it up."

"Pardon me?" I really did need him to repeat it. He'd never asked me to let a case go before.

"This one, Trade. I want you to turn it back."

Jesus, he really was asking me to do it. While I knew he loved me and was just concerned, I was also pretty pissed, but I tried to stay calm.

"I can't do that, Uncle C."

"Why the hell not?"

"My clients are counting on me." As long as I was standing my ground, I'd be damned if I'd use the word *customers*. "And I'm beginning to think I can help."

"I don't know what in the hell you think you can do that the police can't."

"I went to school with all of them."

"Yeah, yeah, I know."

"And I think the killer may be someone we know."

"We're following up on that angle."

"Well, another pair of eyes and ears can't hurt."

"That's not the point, goddammit." Even with the distance between us, I imagined his full face turning the shade of a midsummer tomato. "The point is that you could be hurt."

I smiled. Most of the time Uncle C teased me about my loser cases, chasing down errant husbands or deadbeats. This was almost a welcome change.

"I think I'm all right. I was one of the dorks, remember? Not a cheerleader." A shudder went through me as I thought of the car last night and the hanging doll this morning, but I said nothing. If I raised his anxiety level any higher, he'd really be insufferable.

"You weren't a dork, Trade. You were just smarter than the rest of them." It had always been a sore point with Uncle C that I had just missed being class valedictorian. "If this son-of-a-bitch thinks he's in danger, he's not going to stop with them. He'll do whatever it takes to protect himself. I've seen the shots of that last woman. The son-of-a-bitch is a butcher."

At least in Uncle C's mind the killer now had a name. Son-of-a-bitch. And a gender. Male.

"I know. Let's just hope we find him before he does it again. There are still four of them left."

"Honey, I'm just worried about you. Won't you leave it alone?"

"I'll think about it, Uncle C," I lied, feeling badly even as I did so.

"Do it for me," he said as he hung up the phone.

I went out and caught Gray. The overcast sky kept the afternoon warm, and as I brushed the horse, handfuls of gray hair came off, a sign that hot weather was not far away. As I saddled him, Mrs. Fierce hopped up and down with a stupid little dance that could have earned her a blue ribbon in cock-a-schnauz dance class. She doesn't always get to go with me, only on the shorter rides. I didn't think it would take me long to check on the dead calf, so I invited her along.

I headed down the valley. We rode in the Sutherland Creek most of the way. Our Arizona riverbeds, when they don't get too deep, make wonderful riding. Deep with sand, that is. In our country we have these strange riverbeds. As Mark Twain said, "You fall into a river in Arizona and then get up and brush yourself off." That's for most of the year. When the monsoon season hits, along about July and August, then it's Katie bar the door. The thunderstorms rage and within minutes the arroyos become frenzied rivers. Just about every year, some dummy drives into one and gets himself killed. Stupid way to die, drowning in Arizona.

The creek had a trickle of water in it, runoff from the snowfall up on the Catalina Mountains. It stays this way through the spring. Then the water goes underground again until the summer monsoons.

I passed several pairs of cows and calves including four large unbranded calves we'd missed in the last gather. In the valley, Brahma mamas munching the six-week grass while their little kids stretched out and napped or played with one another. The lush green grass is a mixed blessing. When the weather gets warmer, the grass will turn brown and head up with nasty foxtails that get into the animals' coats, ears and paws.

The Sutherland tanks came into view and I rode up to them, checking the ground for lion prints. There were none, but I spotted Sanders's tracks and followed them away from the creek up the ridge trail and finally topped out on Saguaro Mesa. The views from there were great. La Cienega to the north and Tucson to the south. With one of the county dumps in between.

I kept following the tracks up and down through several canyons until I hit the Grotto, a hidden canyon with a waterfall. This winter it had raged after an unusual two-week rain, but now it was merely a trickle. A two-hundred-foot trickle, but a trickle nonetheless.

It wasn't hard finding the slaughtered calf, since Sanders's tracks led me right to it. The lion had stashed its prey under a low mesquite tree and covered the carcass with dried leaves and soil. Mrs. Fierce darted up to the dead calf and then, smelling either the lion or death, beat a hasty retreat.

I dismounted and tied Gray to a tree several feet away from the kill before checking things out. Even without the clear, wide track, visible in the damp ground of the Grotto, or the covering over the calf, I could tell by looking that a mountain lion had killed it. Its neck was broken and the lion had begun eating just behind the rib cage. Cats always go for the organs first—the heart, liver and lungs—while coyotes eat their kills starting with the rear end, beginning just under the tail. The bright yellow tag on the calf's left ear read 217. It was a heifer; we never ear tag the steers, since they're sold every year.

As I stared at the calf, Valerie Higgins's autopsy pictures flashed through my head. Such senseless carnage. At least the mountain lion was killing for survival.

Walking back to Gray, I unzipped my cantle bag, pulled out my leather tally book and marked the number in it. When I got back to the ranch, I'd check my records and be able to tell just which calf had been killed and which cow had lost her baby.

Thankfully, we don't lose many of our cattle to mountain lions, as they prefer eating deer. Their appetites are healthy, though, since a lion in its prime can kill a deer a week.

It was still a three-hundred-dollar breakfast, any way you looked at it.

I headed the horse toward the saddle, a steep rocky climb out through prickly pear, barrel cactus and overhanging mesquite trees. When I reached it, I let Gray blow and catch his breath before heading down to the Sutherland Trail.

I stopped once in Cargadera Canyon and watched a family of Harris's hawks as they floated on the wind currents of the murky sky, hunting together as a family unit. The sun came out finally and warmed my back. Mrs. Fierce slept under a mesquite tree as I watched the birds. I turned Gray down the trail toward home.

The sun was still shining as I rode into the back pasture. I closed the gate and the first raindrop fell. Although I had a slicker on my saddle, I figured I could outrun it. Quickly I unsaddled the horse, threw the saddle in the tack room, turned Gray out in the pasture and ran for the house as the rain increased its tempo. It won the race. By the time I hit the screened porch, I was drenched and cold and my slicker was still neatly tied behind the cantle of my saddle.

After checking the record books and recording the calf's death, I took a quick shower, jumped into my gray sweats and put on water for cocoa. Throwing a couple of mesquite logs on the fire, I draped them with used candle stubs and lit the kindling. The fire sputtered but finally took.

The dead calf still troubled me, although there was no way I could have prevented her death. The Song Dog case was also nagging at me. It was as though I were caught in a game of tug-of-war. I'd taken the damned case as a favor to two women I'd known long ago, and now I felt guilty that my ranch responsibilities were interfering with my work. Before, with my other cases, no one had been killing people. I'd never felt this pressure. By taking the case, I'd put myself in one hell of a position.

As I dumped the cocoa mix into a Kentucky Derby mug, I decided to put off worrying about either the ranch or the Song Dogs for the night. I needed a break, so I debated my choices. I could either clean out the pantry, which really needed it, or watch *Lonesome Dove* for the third time. Naturally the cowboy saga won out, and by the time I fell asleep I was once again thoroughly in love with either Gus McCrae or Robert Duvall.

I woke in a cold sweat. I'd had a terrible dream. Charlene Williamson was trying to kill me. With a gun. She was swinging a hangman's noose at me and her dog was there, too, chasing me down. I ran from house to house, trying to escape her, and as people would let me in, I'd scream, "A gun? Do you have a gun?" They all said no, and I'd run out the back door just as Charlene and that damned dog ran in the front. The funny thing about it was that in spite of her weight, Charlene was having no trouble running fast. Very fast.

I woke up and lay completely still, letting my heart return to its normal cadence. Once I was settled, I rolled over and reached into the bedside table drawer. I patted the .38 that rested there and, feeling reassured, went back to sleep.

14

AFTER I GAVE THE ANIMALS THEIR BREAKFAST LATER THAT MORN-
ing, I grabbed a quick bagel and cream cheese and retrieved
my 20 gauge from the drawer.

Spreading newspapers on the kitchen table, I collected
my gun-cleaning kit and went to work.

I've got a few guns, most of which were my father's.
There's the .410 shotgun I used to hunt birds with my dad
as a kid, then there's a .38 long barrel revolver, a .22 rifle, a
.22 automatic and a Ruger 9mm. While the Ruger gets a bul-
let to its target quicker and is easier to reload, my favorite
gun is my Smith and Wesson .38. Make that Lady Smith
and Wesson. That's really the name for this particular gun.
The ad agencies for those firearm guys are no fools. First it
was lady electric shavers, now it's lady guns. Madison Avenue sells.

My gun, a five-shot snub-nosed revolver, is light and
compact. I bought the .38 for my personal protection, not
for work. I suppose if I were out on the streets like a cop, I'd
want something more. Then it would be foolish to be fum-
bling with five bullets to load, when I could just slip in a clip
with fifteen rounds in it. But since I'm not a cop, and not
usually chasing bad guys on the streets, I'm happy with my
pretty little Smith and Wesson that fits nicely in my purse.

And we used to worry about someone spotting a tampon in there.

Truth is, I'm not very good with the gun. I know I should go out and practice with it, but I never seem to find the time. It isn't entirely my own ineptitude. The short-barreled .38 isn't very accurate at any kind of distance.

The nightmare got me started on the gun cleaning. And the realization that I'd neglected the .38 for quite a while, just throwing it in my purse when I went into town at night. Usually I take it on trips with me, too, but I had foolishly forgotten it on my Luna jaunt. And regretted it. My first murder investigation already had me fixating on my gun.

After cleaning the revolver, I replaced it in the bedroom drawer and then dressed for Valerie Higgins's funeral.

Eleven o'clock found me in the back of St. Philips in the Hills, arguably Tucson's most beautiful church. A Swiss-born architect, Josias Joesler, had been on a world tour that stalled in California when a local builder named John Murphey hired him as a designer. The church was one of their most masterful collaborations. Resembling an old Spanish mission, the church has a spectacular window behind the altar that looks out on the majestic Catalina Mountains. After studying a view like that, any atheist would be tempted to convert.

Whether the church was full because of Valerie's popularity or the notoriety of the case, I couldn't say. But there were people standing behind me and spilling out into the aisles.

The service was one of those fill-in-the-blanks Episcopalian affairs that always amaze me. It was Valerie today, but tomorrow another name would be slipped into the liturgy, the pronouns changed, and the business of burying would go on. Seems to me that faith works better when it's a lot more personal than that.

Since I was in the back of the church, it was easy to slip out ahead of the family. I watched them and then the mourners file out.

Charlene Williamson spotted me immediately. She was

dressed in a long black caftan with a floppy black felt hat. I noticed her jangling bracelets had been replaced by a heavy gold manacle, I suppose out of deference to the quiet that funerals impose. She tottered over to me on thin high heels.

"Anything yet?" she asked.

I shook my head.

"Do you think he's here?" Her voice dropped to a stage whisper.

I shrugged, and ignored her eyes, as my own searched the crowd, even though I wasn't sure what I was looking for.

Jerry Higgins and the kids were surrounded by friends, and I saw no point in talking to him anyway. I'd hated intruding on his grief before, and from the looks of him today, he was having a tough time handling the condolences.

I felt a tug on my elbow and turned to face Uncle C.

"What are you doing here?" he hissed through clenched teeth.

"Paying my respects." I tried to sound innocent.

"Bullshit."

"We did go to high school together, remember?"

Charlene was paying close attention to our conversation and I wasn't eager to have her learn that my uncle, the police detective, did not want me involved in the Song Dog business. I certainly didn't need Uncle C launching into a diatribe about my playing little-girl PI.

"For chrissake, leave it alone, Trade," he barked, before turning and walking off.

"What was that all about?" Charlene asked.

I hesitated and then decided to play it straight. "The guy isn't keen on private investigators." I saw no reason to mention the fact that he was my uncle.

Charlene checked her watch. "I've got to run," she said, patting my arm. With that, she was off in a shroud of black cloth.

I stayed a little while longer but saw nothing out of the ordinary. There was no one walking around with KILLER branded on his forehead, so I finally gave it up. I dashed home and threw on my Levi's and boots before backing Priscilla up to the horse trailer.

Hooking up trailers to vehicles is one of those liberating things, sort of like walking around a shopping mall and having your money and credit cards in your pocket instead of carrying a purse. Men have had a corner on this market for a long time. They know how to fix plumbing, change tires, hook up trailers and handle chain saws. This isn't particularly sexist, just a fact of life. But I'm finding out the more I do this kind of stuff, the more independent I feel.

Anyway, there's no real mystery to hooking up a horse trailer and within a couple of minutes I was ready to roll. I loaded Dream in the trailer, picked up Sanders and drove to Clay's Arena.

He looked, as he always did, like he had just stepped out of the shower. His Levi's sported a clean crease down the front and he was wearing what looked like a new Brushpopper shirt.

On the way over, he began talking a little about his poetry, something he rarely does.

"I'm havin' a bit of trouble with something I'm working on," he began.

"Anything I can do?" I'm certainly no poet, but I was willing to give it a try if it would help.

"Well, I can't figure out a word that rhymes with *castration*," he joked.

"How about brain surgery?" I offered, laughing.

At the arena as we unloaded and saddled the horses, I noticed that most of the work had already been done. The cows, thirty of them, were already numbered. There were three sporting the number zero, three with number one and so on through nine. It was a relief to be here after the funeral.

Sanders went off to help sort cattle and Emily Rose joined me. We trotted and loped the horses around the arena, warming them up. As we slowed to a walk, her big palomino Hank fell in step with Dream. We discussed the surface of the arena. It looked good in spite of last night's rain.

"They think the car was a four-wheel drive," Emily Rose offered.

I looked at her.

"Are they sure?"

"No, it's just a guess. They've got to find a suspect car for a match."

I knew that would be easier said than done. If the car had been driven a couple hundred miles, no distance at all in our part of the country, then the tread wear would differ too much and a match would be impossible. Even checking cars at the reunion would be worthless, since it was still at least two weeks away, and that could account for a lot of miles. The car or truck had to be found soon for any tread-matching to work. Our conversation moved on to family issues, and Em told me she was visiting her mother in Globe next weekend and would be unavailable for team penning.

The mare in front of us was walking slowly, her rider slouched in the saddle, and as we came up behind them, the mare threw a fit. She kicked violently at Emily Rose's gelding, and when her rider tried to correct the horse by tapping her with a spur, she went ballistic, bucking and crowhopping.

We loped quickly away, giving the wreck room to happen. The little acrobatic witch broke in half several times, finally dumping her rider in the dirt as she continued bucking around the arena. The rider jumped up, slapped the dust off his Wrangler's and went to retrieve his horse. I doubted the mare had learned her lesson. A kicking horse is flat-out dangerous. Problem is, even when saddle horses are kicking at each other, it's easy for a rider to get his leg broken. Horses have spent thousands of years hanging out together, so they recognize the danger signals long before we do and usually turn away a split second before the kick lands, exposing the rider's calf as a target.

We kept riding around, even after the horses were warmed up. One of the interesting things about team penning is that anything can happen. Usually the real fun starts when the penning begins. Putting three people on three horses in an arena with thirty head of cattle is a psychiatrist's dream. Thirty-six different personalities with thirty-six different agendas. The burden is on the people/horse team: it's their mission to ferret out three head wearing the

same number from the herd and put them in a small pen at
the other end of the arena—all within a ninety-second time
frame. And without any of their friends coming along. More
than four head of cattle across the foul line, and you're out.

"Please clear the arena and we'll start penning," the an-
nouncer's voice came through the PA system as we rode out.

The cows were reasonably fresh. Clay had replaced his
old herd two weeks ago. The problem with any of the cattle used for sport, say for roping or cutting or penning, is after a while they get pretty smart. They figure out the
program, and then they want their team to win. They'll get
sour and duck out on you, or refuse to come out of the herd,
or some other aggravating thing that prevents you from
putting three of them in that little pen at the other end of
the arena. The problem and the joy of real fresh cattle is
that they don't have a clue as to what you want to do with
them, which makes the penners' task even more difficult,
but at least the cattle aren't scheming against you.

This probably sounds mean. And sometimes I have
trouble with it. I think: Why are we running these cattle
into that pen? What did they do to deserve this? But then I
think of all the cattle warehoused in stockyards with wet
manure slopped up to their knees, waiting to get big
enough for a hammer to drop between their eyes, and then
I think these guys have an okay life. It's kind of like Cow
Kindergarten.

For most of the week they're turned out on pasture
where they can hang out with their buddies, chew grass
and play with their cuds, have naptime and make cow pies.
Then on the weekends they have PE. At least it's a detour
from their eventual unfortunate destination. Besides, I
really believe some of them actually enjoy the game.

The first three teams had no times. The cattle won.

On our run, we were doing pretty good until Emily
Rose's cinch broke and her saddle slipped. She fell to the
ground. When Sanders and I saw she was on her feet, we
continued to try to pen the cattle. But two people on a fresh
herd just didn't cut it, so we joined the ranks of those who

did not pen. On our second run we got forty-five seconds on three cows. A respectable time, but with the no time in the first go-around, we were out of the average, and the jackpot.

Later we sat around having a beer together, mourning our bad luck. When Emily began talking about the Song Dogs, I ended up telling Sanders about my new case.

"Murder's not your style, Trade," he said, furrowing his forehead. "That's kinda like a blind dog knockin' around at the meat packer's."

"God, I hope not," I said, laughing, "or they won't be getting their money's worth."

"Well, don't go putting yourself in his sights," Sanders cautioned, and I knew it was the closest he was going to get to telling me he was worried about me.

I gave Emily the plastic bag with the rag doll in it before we finally called it a day.

I hit the Vaca Grande about five o'clock, and just as I cleared the front gate, I remembered. It was Thursday and I had a date with Daggett Early. Dates are a rare thing for me, so it was easy to forget. At my age finding a compatible fit, even for a casual date, is difficult at best.

If you go looking for one, it's next to impossible. It's like that evil greeting card where the front part has a hot photo of a bare-chested young stud with the first couple of buttons on his 501's undone. The caption says, "What we're looking for." You open it to find a picture of a fat guy with an NRA cap in his undershirt, scratching his hairy beer belly with one hand, while picking his nose with the other. Now the caption reads, "What's looking for us." Compatibility can be a bitch.

While I still believe that a woman without a man is like a fish without a bicycle, it's still nice to go out on some type of semi-romantic encounter occasionally, just to check to see if I'm still fluent. So, in spite of knowing better, I have to admit I was looking forward to my date with Daggett Early. Besides, there was a lot I needed to know about him. After all, so far he was very high on my suspect list.

As I put Dream up and fed everyone, I was already mentally searching my closet for something to wear. When I finally hit on the winner, I glanced at my watch.

If I didn't screw around too much, I'd even have time to squirt it before I left.

15

I MET DAGGETT AT ANTHONY'S IN THE CATALINAS. I DON'T think of myself as ultraparanoid, but for a first date I really don't like the guy picking me up at home. If it doesn't work out, it's just too personally revealing letting him know where and how I live. This system also takes the pressure off goodnights. And if the relationship starts to click later on, then I don't mind saving some wear and tear on Priscilla. I hadn't known Daggett well in high school, so even though I had lived at the Vaca Grande most of my life, there was really little chance that he knew where I lived.

Besides, this wasn't really a date. He was a suspect and as far as I was concerned, this was just a form of interview. Everything would be all right as long as I kept telling myself that.

Anthony's is one of my favorite restaurants in Tucson. In its original incarnation, it was owned by people from the Pennsylvania Dutch country who called it Las Campanas de las Catalinas. They offered real stick-to-your-ribs-type fare. Lots of borscht and pork roast and mashed potatoes. They also had an interesting gift shop, which saved my tail during more than one Christmas season, and a family of cats that lived in the belfry. The restaurant's been through several owners, each with a new vision and name, but it's been Anthony's for several years now, and I'm hoping it will stick around. Unfortunately, the gift shop and cats are gone.

The south side of the building has a long glassed-in porch with a full view of Tucson. The north side is equally spectacular, at least in daylight hours, with the Catalina Mountains looming through the wall of windows. Although seats on the patio are available year-round, tonight was cold so I knew that was out of the question.

I love alfresco dining but I haven't been as keen on it at Anthony's since the evening I saw a giant saguaro topple and crush one of the wrought-iron tables outside. Sounds like a Hollywood movie, *Revenge of the Giant Saguaro*. Although it was a freak accident, it was one of those images filed in my memory bank that I can't seem to shake, sort of like which restaurants get the best scores for roaches and mouse droppings by the Health Department. No sense courting trouble.

I was running a few minutes late, and since there were two Mercedes and a Porsche ahead of me in the valet parking line, I pulled Priscilla into the lot and parked her myself.

Daggett was waiting for me just inside the front door, and I have to confess I got a real charge when I saw him standing there. He was gorgeous. Even though it was February, he had a great tan. He was wearing one of those light blue oxford cloth shirts, open at the neck enough to show off a little skin. A navy blue blazer, gray slacks and black leather loafers completed his ensemble. Sounds simple enough, but he looked like dynamite.

"Trade, you look great." He came up to me and hesitated as though he were going to hug me. He didn't. Instead he cupped my elbow in the palm of his hand and lightly steered me toward the maître d'. "Black becomes you."

"Thanks." I felt good in my black suede skirt, a black knit top lined in velvet, my mother's old Navajo concho belt and black Stewart boots. While many Apaches still feel black is an evil color, I always feel safe in it. Black can be dressed up or down, makes you look thinner than you really are, and if you spill spaghetti sauce on it, no one can really tell.

My long, curly black hair was pulled back from my

face, showing off dangling silver and turquoise earrings. An etched heavy silver bracelet I'd picked up years ago at a pawnshop rode on one wrist, my Rolex on the other.

Our table at the end of the porch area offered a spectacular view of Tucson as well as privacy. I knew it was no accident that we had been seated there.

I ordered a Canadian Club and water, Daggett a dry martini. While our conversation was awkward at first, punctuated with long pauses, by our second drink we were chatting like old friends. He was good company. Bright and witty.

I discovered he was an investment counselor. Apparently he takes his business very seriously, because he talked for a good ten minutes about tailoring accounts to meet his customers' preferences, values and financial goals. I found myself saying, "Really?" a lot as I swallowed yawns. My reward came when I learned that most of his accounts are discretionary; he makes all the trading decisions for his clients. Very interesting.

On other fronts, I learned that he liked to hike, had his own airplane and is out of town a lot on business. That airplane business piqued my curiosity. It meant that he could easily travel without anyone knowing about it. He'd said that he'd been in Denver when Elaine was killed, but I couldn't help wondering how long it would take to fly from Denver to Albuquerque and back. Flying to Los Angeles to visit Deborah Chamberlain, the salmonella casualty, wouldn't have been much of a trick, either.

By the time dinner arrived, he'd found out about my horses and the Twinkies. When he ordered the wine, he also discovered that I didn't mind drinking red with fish. We were getting intimate fast. I was trying to give him just enough information to get him comfortable. That shrunken head still loomed in my mind, so in spite of his good looks and savoir faire I wasn't buying into his charm.

"So how long were you married?"

I played with my salmon. "Eight years. No kids. How about you?"

He nodded, and I waited for him to swallow his lamb. "Once. I've been divorced for years."

"Did you have kids?"

"One. A boy." He fumbled in his coat and withdrew his wallet, pulled out a picture and handed it to me. There was a young, good-looking, dark-haired woman with a small dark boy. She was kneeling and the boy was standing next to her, showing her some kind of flower. Both were happy and smiling. I turned it over, but there was no date on it.

"He doesn't look much older than six," I said, prompting him.

"It's an old picture. Softer times."

I'd never heard that expression before. I thought about it for a minute and decided I liked it. "She's very pretty," I continued. It was like priming a water pump; I wanted to keep things flowing, particularly information.

"Yes. But it didn't work out."

"I'm sorry."

He laughed. "I'm not. I wouldn't be here if it had. Maybe she and I were only meant to be together for a short time. I don't know."

His spiritual side caught me off guard. With the sketch I was beginning to draw of him, a hybrid demon seed of Ted Bundy and John Gacy, it was one of those *What's wrong with this picture?* irritations.

I handed him back the photograph, and he replaced it in his wallet. If she had left him, I figured he must still be in love with her to keep her picture. If he had left her, I wouldn't have expected him to carry the photo around with him, either. Unless it was the only picture he had of his kid. It was peculiar any way you cut it.

"You're probably wondering why I keep an old picture of them," he said, reading my mind.

"Oh no," I lied.

He poured some more cabernet sauvignon. "It's just a reminder to me to treasure each day. Scottie, my son, was diagnosed with leukemia the week after that picture was taken." His eyes clouded but did not overflow as his hands cupped his wineglass.

"God, I'm sorry."

"It was just one of those things. I guess some would call it God's will. Just damned bad luck."

My suspicion of him was suddenly clouded by empathy and compassion. I didn't know what to say, so as an alternative we ate in silence for a few minutes until the mood passed.

"So, tell me about Connie O'Hara." I was finally willing to break the spell.

"What's to tell?"

Was it my imagination or was there a momentary narrowing of his brown eyes?

"Well, you took her out a couple of times; have you seen her lately?" I watched him closely. Somewhere I read that if a person is lying to you, he'll look up and to the right.

"Nope." Daggett's eyes remained on me.

"Bobette said she had biology with you."

"Bobette?"

"Jarcik. She was a cheerleader." I didn't volunteer that I had driven to New Mexico and met with her.

His thin fingers played with the stem of his wineglass as he shook his head. "Sorry, I don't remember her. What's all this have to do with tonight?"

"I'm working on the case."

Understanding flooded his face. "Because we were all in school together."

"Something like that."

"Well, how's it going?" He seemed genuinely interested.

"Who knows? I'm spinning my wheels, but I don't seem to be getting anywhere. Why would anyone start killing them now, after all these years? I'm really having trouble with motives here. What's the link? I think the reunion is a key, though."

"I'm sure it probably is," Daggett said. "Dessert?"

"Only if they have chocolate mousse pie."

They did and I did.

We topped off dinner with Courvoisier for him, a

Golden Cadillac for me. I'd had enough to eat and drink that I was feeling warm and sleepy, not a good thing for a first date or an interview. I reached for my ice water and took a long drink. As I replaced it on the table, Daggett caught my hand. His hand felt warm and strong, and I was surprised that I didn't mind that he was holding mine. His dead child had definitely lowered my suspicion scale. I wasn't sure that that was a good thing at all.

"I've really enjoyed myself tonight, Trade." His fingers caressed the top of my hand lightly, and I felt the thrill of being touched by someone who you think you want to touch you, but who has never touched you before. There's nothing like that first rush.

"I've enjoyed it, too." There was no lying this time. He gave my hand a light squeeze before releasing it.

The waiter came with the bill. Daggett placed his credit card on the plastic tray and as he handed it up to the waiter, his shirt cuffs fell below his wrist, exposing deep scratches.

Suddenly I had that pasty lump back in my stomach. Remembering the defensive cuts on Connie O'Hara's arms and right palm, I impulsively grabbed his arm and turned it over, pushing up his cuff.

"My God, what did you do to yourself?" I asked, trying to keep accusation out of my voice.

He laughed. "Birds. Dumb things. I'm into falconry. Sometimes I screw up, and then I pay for it. Are you ready?"

We walked out and although the cool night air braced me, the shudder I felt came from remembering the long red scratches on his arm. While the falconry might make sense, since he was a wealthy man with very exotic tastes, I was not at all comfortable with his explanation. It was definitely something to check out.

"I'm in the lot," I said.

"I'll walk you to your car."

"It's all right."

He insisted.

We were at Priscilla. He held the door open for me. I rolled down the window before closing the door.

"Thanks, Daggett, for a nice evening."

He leaned in the window and cupped my face in his hands. I could have easily pulled away, but didn't. Maybe knowing how he kissed would be important to knowing him. Then again, maybe I just wanted to see if I still knew how, since it had been a long time. Whatever it was, I didn't fight it.

"You're beautiful," he whispered as he softly kissed me on the lips. He was a good kisser. Soft and tender, but in control. It was just enough. "Goodnight," he said, stepping back from the truck.

I cranked up Priscilla and drove slowly out of the lot. I was almost to the main road before I remembered to turn on my lights. My window was still down and a blast of cold air jolted me back to reality. What in the hell had I been thinking to let a man with a shrunken head kiss me? After all, where was it written that killers couldn't be good lovers?

16

THE RAIN RETURNED DURING THE NIGHT, AND MY ONLY FORAYS out in the stuff were my morning chores. Decked out in my black rubber Red Ball boots and yellow slicker, I managed to stay reasonably dry.

I love those boots. I put them on and it's like I'm a little kid again. You can splash around and stomp in mud puddles and never get wet. They're great. If I ever open a psychiatric institute I'm going to include Red Ball boots, along with apple pickers for manure, for every patient.

I checked the creek, but it hadn't risen, as far as I could tell. The water still barely covered the bottom of the bed.

Since it was too early to make any telephone calls and I was trapped inside, I had little choice but to tackle some of the household chores I had been putting off. My first stop was the pantry. I thought it might be nice to have drop-in company and not dive for the pantry door to seal it off from their inspection.

It was a wreck, soup cans commingled with the fruit, cereal boxes with only a few flakes in the bottom, bent cans of tomato sauce, spilled cat food, stale crackers. Definitely not a pretty sight.

The most exciting discovery came as I was cleaning the top shelf and pulled down the turkey roaster. No less than twenty-seven scorpions had made it their burial ground.

There were two larger scorpions, and then a host of teensy babies. Apparently the two adults had fallen into the pan, mated, had their progeny, and then all died of starvation. Or maybe they drank poisoned Kool-Aid, I don't know. It would have been a sad story if they hadn't been scorpions.

They must have been there for some time, since I know for a fact that scorpions can lose up to forty percent of their body water weight and still live. Humans aren't so lucky. Fifteen percent lost to dehydration, and we're goners.

I rinsed the dead scorpion clan out of the pan, down the drain, and turned on the garbage disposal for good measure. It never hurts to be safe. I believe in reincarnation.

Once the pantry was finally clean, I ran a load of wash and did a few other exciting household chores. Then I checked my Song Dog notes.

In Luna I had circled Vance Packard's name on my list. He had been Buffy Patania's six-week husband. It was after nine, so I picked up the phone and called her. After exchanging a few pleasantries, I asked about Vance and was told that the last thing she had heard was that he had taken a job with the Bechtel Corporation in Saudi Arabia.

"I don't really keep in touch with him, Trade." Buffy sounded irritated. "But I know MacKenzie does, so you might check with him."

I hadn't known that the *Javelina Journal* editor and the old quarterback had been friends.

"Did you do anything about getting a bodyguard?"

"Not really. I have the houseman who helps me out. And, of course, the security system and the dogs. I feel pretty safe here, really."

I wondered what the houseman did, but I didn't ask.

After hanging up, I spent another ten minutes on the phone trying to get the Bechtel phone number and then trying to get someone at their San Francisco headquarters to confirm that Packard worked for them and was indeed ensconced in Saudi Arabia. After being transferred a number of times, I finally talked to an officious secretary who, in a very inadvertent, you-couldn't-possibly-trace-this-to-me way, suggested that if I wrote to Packard care of the corporation, he would receive my communication. This was enough for me to scratch him off my suspect list, since he hadn't been a main contender anyway.

I pulled out the Javelina High yearbook and browsed through it, hoping to get struck with inspiration. None came. I looked again at the group picture of the cheerleaders and had trouble believing that any of us had ever been that young.

Then I turned to Daggett Early's senior graduation picture. *Ugly.* I looked up his name in the index. There were actually two Earlys listed. One was named Shannon. Did Daggett have a sister? I didn't remember her, but when I thumbed to her page I caught the family resemblance immediately. There was something familiar about her, but I couldn't quite place it. I'd probably seen her in the halls years ago.

Daggett had three other pages, besides his senior picture, listed for photos. On page 118 he was huddled around a glass beaker with some other goofy-looking guys. The caption identified them as members of the Chemistry Club. Page 134 was a co-ed shot with the French Club. And on page 163, I got my first look at him with most of his clothes off. He was vaulting over a hurdle with the track team.

I hadn't known he was even on the track team. I mean, who ever paid attention to those guys? I studied the picture for a few minutes, trying to imagine Daggett without his pants on. God, I hoped his legs look better than the scrawny pins in this picture. If they hadn't changed, I knew I never wanted to sit next to him in a pickup truck wearing my Levi's. My thighs would squash flatter and broader than his. I hate it when that happens. It was all moot anyway, because there was something very creepy about the guy. I didn't care how good-looking he was, there was no way I'd ever end up in bed with him. Or in a pickup with him, either, for that matter.

I listened to one of my cats scratch the kitchen door and tried to ignore it. They're so spoiled. All three of them. Wanting in and out at all hours of the day and night. I was trying to break them of the habit, but they know how to get to me. They extend their claws so that when they hit the glass it produces a sound not dissimilar to fingernails on a blackboard. Yechhh. After a few more minutes, I closed the yearbook and let the cat in.

It was Gorilla, my big black male cat. We left his testicles in the veterinarian's office a few years ago, and I'm not sure he's forgiven me yet. I know he hasn't forgiven the vet.

Anyway, Gorilla made his entrance and jumped on the cats' counter. One of the Mexican tiled counters hosts their water and the Gopher Breath bowl, which is usually filled with dry cat food. Gorilla was doing a pretty good job of inhaling the food. His routine was predictable; from there he would go in and take a nap on my bed until I kicked him out of the house again. Or until two A.M., when he wakes me up to open the door so he can go out. He has a pretty tough life.

The rain started waning in the late afternoon. I went out and checked the rain gauge. An inch. A heavy rainfall, when you consider our annual figure is only eleven inches.

The creek was up a bit, and now I could hear it from the pond. The ducks were in their glory as they stood on their heads trying to find something yummy to eat in the water. When they saw me coming, they zoomed quickly to shore and slopped across the mud in my wake, scolding me for not feeding them first. I felt like the Pied Piper.

Once chores were done, I threw some mesquite logs on the fire, zapped a couple of frozen green corn tamales in the microwave, tossed a quick honeymoon salad and poured a glass of burgundy. I sat at the kitchen table and read the current issue of *Time* magazine through dinner. When I finished with that, I grabbed the three previous issues, still unread, and threw them all on the back porch to take to St. Mary's Hospital in Tucson. I felt pretty virtuous that I was now caught up with the weekly news magazine. One less thing to nag me.

The rain gave me an excuse to steal some more time, so I sat in the living room recliner, always a mistake because it lulls me to sleep, and opened *The Bridges of Madison County*. I was probably the last person in the universe to read the overrated best-seller. Briefly, I wondered if there was a market for a sequel, *The Cattleguards of Pima County*. I was in the middle of the third chapter when the phone rang.

"Trade, it's Bobette." Her husky voice sounded as though she were right next door. "I thought I should call you."

"What's up?" I opened the pantry door while talking to her and admired my work. Only now I had to remember where the Twinkies were.

"Charlene and Binky came to see me."

That caught my interest. I closed the pantry door. "When?"

"They just left. They've been here for an hour."

"How did they find you?"

"I don't know. I thought you told them."

"No. I told Charlene I'd talked to you, that's all. I didn't give her directions or anything."

I could hear Bobette taking a drag on her cigarette. "Yeah. Well, it doesn't take much to find a person in downtown Luna."

"No, I guess not." I was betting they hadn't wasted any time with the Cookie Monster postmistress. I sunk back into the recliner. "What'd they want?"

"I think just to warn me. Charlene's pretty shook up by all of this."

I said nothing, but wondered why they hadn't talked to me before they made the trip.

"And Binky?" I asked.

"That asshole." There was a catch in her voice. I heard her take another long pull on the cigarette and exhale. But I could tell she tried to blow the smoke away from the mouthpiece of the telephone. "Do you know what he tried to do?"

I couldn't imagine and I told her so.

"Charlene leaves to go to the bathroom and that jerk's all over me like a dirty shirt."

"Shit," I said, both in commiseration and disgust.

"I shoved him off and told him to cool it. And then he said he always remembered me fondly. Fondly, can you believe it?"

Fondly was not a word I would have bet was in Binky Williamson's vocabulary.

"Anyway, I just thought I should call and tell you that they were here. I think it's pretty weird, considering Charlene never gave me the time of day in high school even though we were both cheerleaders."

"Well, maybe she's just running scared," I offered.

"She should be. Of that jerk she's married to."

"Is there something you want to tell me about him?"

There was a long pause on the other end of the line.

"No, not really."

"Be careful over there, okay?"

"I will, Trade. I didn't waste all that time in rehab to die. Not yet, anyway."

"Talk to you later," I said, and hung up the phone.

I collapsed the recliner, grabbed my book and went to bed. I had trouble reading, because my mind kept circling back to Bobette. I was sure there was something she wasn't telling me about her relationship with Binky. While she'd freely admitted that she'd slept with him, was there more to it than that? Why had he driven all that way to see her? More importantly, if something was going on, why would he take his wife? With his past record, could he be anything but unfaithful to Charlene?

Outside, a pair of great horned owls were carrying on a conversation in the creek. They were probably a couple hundred yards from each other, having a gay chat while the rest of the world was trying to sleep.

The ringing telephone awakened me in the middle of the night. There are a few things that are worse than being jarred out of a sound sleep by something as irritating as a telephone. I rolled over and grabbed the receiver. The bedside clock read three A.M.

"Long distance calling for Trade Ellis, please." The operator sounded like she was doing a takeoff on Lily Tomlin.

"Speaking." I couldn't imagine who would be calling me person-to-person. Someone who could afford it, I guessed.

I turned the light on and listened to a series of telephonic clicks as I reached for my glasses. I had taken my contacts out before bed and for some dumb reason I think better when I can see.

"Hello."

"Hello," I replied, still no idea of who my mystery caller was.

"Is this Trade Ellis?"

"Yes."

"This is Mina Arthur. An old cheerleader from Javelina High."

"Mina! Where are you?"

"I'm in Tokyo. I'm sorry about calling you in the middle of the night, but with the time change—"

"No, no that's okay. How did you get my number?"

"Buffy faxed me this morning." I could hear her rustling papers.

I fumbled for a pen and piece of paper, finally settling for one of the magazine inserts and a Magic Marker. I quizzed Mina about the rest of the cheerleaders and my list of most likely suspects.

She had lost contact with all of them, was married to a guy in the service, and hadn't been back to the States for two years. She had no plans to attend the reunion.

"Do you remember Bobette Jarcik?" I asked.

A light laugh came over the line. "Oh yeah."

Something in the way she said it told me that she was not one of Bobette's fans. "And?"

"Not a very nice person, Trade. Slutsville, in fact."

"Slutsville," I repeated.

"Of the universe," Mina continued, "and mean."

"Mean, in what way?"

"Oh, she didn't drown kittens or anything like that. She just had a really miserable temper. Remember Binky Williamson?"

"Yep." Our conversation was finally getting interesting.

"Well, I dated him a little our senior year."

Jesus, was there a Song Dog that Binky hadn't dated? Suddenly all my flashing neon signs were pointing at him.

"And?" I asked.

"She was not happy about that. In fact, she caught me in the parking lot and threatened me."

"How?"

"Said she's punch my lights out, trashy stuff like that."

"So did anything come of it?"

"No. He was a creep and I quit dating him right after that, so the whole thing was kind of moot. There was something else, though. About a week later I went out to get in my car and it was all scratched up. The insurance guy thought someone had taken a set of car keys to the paint."

"And you thought it was Bobette?"

"I couldn't prove it, of course."

"Did you know Daggett Early?"

"Early . . ." She rolled his name around her mouth like it was a diction lesson. "Early."

"Track team, whiz kid."

"Sorry, doesn't ring a bell."

We exchanged fax numbers, and I said I would send her a questionnaire in the morning. She agreed to fill it out and fax it back to me as soon as possible.

It had been a good call. I hung up thinking about Mr. Romance, Binky. Bobette's temper did liven up the mix and I felt some satisfaction in knowing that the last Song Dog had been found.

Alive.

17

SATURDAY MORNING, MARCH 1ST, THE CLOUDS CLEARED, AND the weather turned cold again.

In celebration of the new month, I treated myself to eggs Benedict at Rainbow's the next morning. This is my favorite morning meal if chocolate pie isn't available. Not only are they tasty, but I love the ultimate redundancy, eggs on top of eggs. Whoever Benedict was, she must have been a cardiologist.

The restaurant was fairly empty except for a couple of cowboys in the smoking section. They were lighting up, drinking coffee and coughing, but saying very little worth eavesdropping over.

Carter, our local stock and commodities expert and sometime scavenger, came in and took a table in the cowboys' room. His main claim to fame, besides having an uncanny ability to find anything at a bargain price, is that he is fueled by the displaced heart of an eighteen-year-old girl. I've overheard some of the guys wonder if she was a virgin, but as far as I know, none of them has had the courage to ask.

I sat and read the morning paper and devoured my eggs. Just as I finished them, Sanders came in and pulled up a chair. Rainbow brought him a cup of coffee, the real stuff. We talked about the rain and the cattle for a few minutes before he got down to business.

"You have company last night?"

"A couple of owls in the creek."

He drank his coffee. While I love the guy, he's one of the most irritatingly subtle men I've ever met.

"Did you see something?" I asked. I've found this direct approach an effective method to counteract his subtlety.

"Thought I heard something about midnight," he said at last. "May have been a car on the lane."

I knew his *thought* meant he knew damned good and well that there was a car on the road between our places, or he wouldn't have bothered mentioning it at all.

"I never heard it," I said, trying to draw him out. Before Mina's three o'clock phone call, I didn't remember anything except turning out the light right before I crashed. "Who do you think it was?"

"I don't know." He sipped his coffee and a worried look came over his tanned, handsome face. "Maybe something to do with that crazy case you got."

"I was pretty tired, but I guess I would have heard Mrs. Fierce."

"It probably wasn't anything."

We both knew it was. Shit.

"Maybe someone took a wrong turn," I offered hopefully.

"Maybe so," he said, draining his coffee. "Still, if you don't mind, I think I'll go have a look around."

"Have at it. I've got to stop at the office." Sanders has a lot of super qualities. Being my protector is just one of them. He is also the most observant person I have ever met in my life. Nothing escapes his attention.

We left the restaurant and headed back to the Vaca Grande. He passed me when I turned off at the old stage stop.

I had turned on the heater before going to Rainbow's, so my office was nice and toasty when I came in and settled down to work. I returned a call from Chester Littleton, an insurance adjuster I'd worked for. This time he wanted me to do surveillance on a suspicious workmen's comp claim. I took the case and jotted down the information on the claimant.

While it was nice to have a new case, I needed to stay focused on the Song Dogs. What linked them? The victims had to have a common denominator, besides being cheerleaders. Who did they all know who hated them enough to kill them? And why?

I pulled a legal pad out of one the desk drawers. Across the top of the first page I wrote "Victims" and entered the names of Elaine Vargas, Valerie Higgins and Connie O'Hara. Deborah Chamberlain was in her own column, since I still wasn't ready to chalk up her salmonella poisoning as murder.

Although Elaine Vargas had been shot, not cut, she was still a dead Song Dog.

I pulled the *Albuquerque Journal* article out of the file and reread the piece about her being shot to death at the mall. Her purse and jewelry had been taken. Valerie Higgins's wedding ring was also missing. The two women had missing jewelry in common, and I entered the words next to their names and circled them in red, while I wondered if anything had been taken from Connie O'Hara. Could the murderer be taking souvenirs?

As I recorded the names of the cheerleaders who were still alive—Charlene, Buffy, Bobette and Mina—I struggled with why any one of them would want to kill any of the others. Bobette's name still headed my list. After all, she'd just been released from prison after serving time for murder, and then there was that business with the doll.

What else did I know about Bobette? She'd been easy in school. What had she said? *Charlene never gave me the time of day.* The nice girls on the squad had not befriended her then. But was that a reason for killing them? And why would she wait twenty-five years to do so? Who sent her the reunion packet and how did that person know about her grandmother in Luna? Had he known her well a long time ago? None of the people I was considering had said anything about being close to Bobette. And what had Mina said? *Slutsville of the universe. And mean.*

I needed to know more about her incarceration. I remembered Emily was visiting her mother in Globe so I couldn't call her. I knew it would cost me, but I dialed a number and was put through to my uncle.

Although it was Saturday, I wasn't surprised when he picked up the phone.

"Morning, Uncle C."

"Trade, good morning, how are you?" There was real cheer in his voice.

"Doing great. Bea and I are getting together to do those tamales for Alicia." I felt guilty leading with this, but I rarely called him at the office.

"Uh-huh."

It sounded like he was drinking coffee.

"So, how's that Song Dog thing going?" I knew I had ruined his good mood.

"Why are you asking?" His voice was heavy with suspicion. "You're not still dicking around with it are you?"

Curious phrase, *dicking around*. I don't even have one.

I clearly hadn't thought this out enough and had to scramble for my lie. "Uh, I don't think so. One of the cheerleaders called me this morning. From Japan."

"The Arthur woman."

"Right."

"We've already talked to her. She didn't have much."

Uncle C obviously thought I was calling to tell him about Mina's call. I let him rest there.

"It'd help if we had a suspect car."

I bit my lip. It would help if he had a suspect who walked into headquarters eager to make a confession, too. I saw no reason to tell him I had a copy of the tire photos on my desk.

"Was anything missing from Connie O'Hara?" I was thinking about Valerie's missing wedding ring.

"Trade, you know that's inside information."

"I had dinner with Daggett Early the other night." I thought it would help if I offered him something in return.

"Yeah . . ."

"A guy we all went to high school with. You might want to check him out."

"We have." His voice sounded tired.

I decided to go for broke. "Uncle C, there's one other thing I was wondering if you could share with me."

"What's that?" He was sounding much more wary.

"Bobette Jarcik's arrest record." If I knew what Bobette had been in prison for, maybe some of the pieces would fall into place.

I heard him shuffle papers and I couldn't tell if he was stalling or actually going to give me the information. I held my breath.

"Why do you want to know?"

"I knew her and I just met her again. Mina thinks she might be mean." There, I gave him another gift, although I suspected Mina had already told him everything.

"It's public record, Trade. Murder. Second degree."

"Who'd she kill?"

"Let's see . . ." More rustling. "Maude Evans. Nine, almost ten years ago."

"Maude Evans . . ." I mulled the name over, but it didn't ring any bells. "Was she from here?"

"No. San Francisco. Jarcik came in on her unexpectedly, a fight ensued."

"What do you mean, 'came in'?"

"They were lovers, Trade." I could hear the discomfort in his voice. He really wasn't comfortable discussing lesbian relationships. "Jarcik found her with another woman. They fought and Jarcik killed the Evans woman."

What was it Bobette had said? *Self-defense, but they called it murder. Someone tried to kill me and it didn't work out.*

"She stabbed her, didn't she?"

"With a kitchen knife. Right through the fucking heart," he said.

I thought of someone else who'd been stabbed through the heart. *The cause of death was penetration to the left anterior chest wall, which avulsed the pulmonary artery.* Connie O'Hara.

"She said it was self-defense, Uncle C."

He laughed. "The prisons are full of innocent people, Trade. Just ask them."

My head was spinning. I kept thinking of the wisp of a woman that I had found in Bobette Jarcik. She was so eager, in a used sort of way, to find herself, to get on with her life. For some reason I had trouble believing that she was killing women from her past. What had she said about the reunion? She needed to *exorcise demons*. Was she exorcising them by murdering Song Dogs? By stabbing them through the heart? Like she had stabbed her lover?

"She's high on our list, I can tell you that," Uncle C admitted. "Stay out of it," he warned again before hanging up the phone.

I reached for a red felt-tip pen and added two checks to Bobette's name. She was now more than Number One on my Hit Parade. Suddenly I realized she might actually be the murderer.

Continuing down my list, I wrote Daggett Early's name and wondered why he would wait twenty-five years. And risk losing everything he had made. Besides, Bobette had told me he had nearly fainted dissecting a frog. How could a guy who fainted with a formaldehyde frog cut the arms off a woman? I wrote down, "Nerd in high school, wants revenge," followed by, "Deep scratches—defensive?," "Airplane, easy travel," and "Macabre." He had told me I was beautiful. It's hard to put a guy like that on your shit list. But that's where he landed. Smack at the top. Just below Bobette Jarcik.

I couldn't overlook Binky Williamson, either. In high school he had dated both Elaine Vargas and Mina Arthur, had slept with Bobette Jarcik and was now married to Charlene Carlton, who, because of his history, was also a strong suspect.

I played with the list awhile longer, hoping revelation would strike. But it was hopeless. After putting it off as long as I could, I picked up the phone and made an appointment to meet with Mrs. O'Hara, Connie's mother, later that afternoon. After my experience with Jerry Higgins, I wasn't relishing further contact with the recently bereft.

Immediately after hanging up, Julie from Darrell's Hardware called to tell me my fax from Mina had arrived.

Darrell's is one of those catchall places that you find in small towns. It makes a valiant effort at supplying just about anything a person would need, thus saving a couple of thousand people needless trips to town. Nickel copies, books on the Southwest, film processing, chain saw sharpening, floor wax, a fax machine, and the occasional used packsaddle are only some of its many attractions.

I picked up my fax and headed into Tucson, thinking it would be a good idea to return to square one. I needed to know more about the woman who had hired me. Charlene Williamson.

18

I'D NEVER BEEN TO THE WILLIAMSONS', BUT I KNEW FROM THEIR address that they lived in the Catalina Foothills, an exclusive stretch of real estate that boasts great views of Tucson and gated communities that keep the riffraff like me out.

I had no reason to think that Charlene would not pass me through when the gate man called, and she did just that. While I would have preferred a totally unexpected visit, a five-minute warning was the best I could get.

Priscilla got several haughty looks from matrons driving Mercedes station wagons and Range Rovers. I figured a pickup truck as classy as the Dodge was an uncommon site around here. Most of the gardeners were in shot Chevys with rusty license plates, Gott water coolers bolted to the sides and rakes sticking up from their truck beds.

Charlene's house was a surprise. It was long and lean, a modern ranch style with two front windows barred with wrought iron. Beyond the iron, closed curtains sealed off any view of the interior. The grounds, perfectly manicured, were done in xeriscape landscaping. The cement circular drive in front of the house hosted not one speck of engine oil as far as I could tell. I hoped Priscilla would maintain the tradition.

The red dirt in between the cacti in the front garden had been recently raked, narrow tines furrowed across the soil in a pattern that begged me to go stomping through it. Resisting, I headed for the front door through a courtyard harboring a couple of Chilean mesquite trees. A spitting lion, set in a stone fountain on one wall, taunted me as I rang the bell.

"Trade!" Charlene's bulk filled the threshold. "Come on in."

"Sorry to drop in on you," I lied, "but I was in town and thought I'd come by."

I stared at her. She was sporting one of the most magnificent black eyes I'd ever seen.

Aware of my appraisal, one of her bloated hands flew to the right side of her face.

"Isn't it awful? That's what I get for getting up in the middle of the night and not turning on the light."

I thought it curious that she had answered my question before I'd even asked it.

"That's a pretty good shiner." I was sure Binky'd had something to do with it, but I said nothing.

"Oh, no problem. Come on back."

I followed Charlene through the living room. If a house could be schizophrenic, this one was. While the outside was modern and Southwestern, the inside was done in something close to French Provincial. Laura Ashley was very much in evidence, with overstuffed sofas filled with fat flowered cushions and chintz everywhere. Needlepoint pillows littered the room with cute little messages on them like, "If you haven't got anything good to say about anyone, come sit by me." Fabric-draped tables sported cliques of silver-framed people and little enameled boxes.

Porcelain figurines, the kind that look cheap but cost a mint and are a pain in the ass to dust, were grouped on every available surface. Antique baskets filled with dried flowers sat on the floor and all the windows had those ballooned things that always remind me of clown pants. As I walked across the carpeting, a plush blue that cushioned every step, I found myself wondering if the conflict between the architecture and the interior design extended to Charlene and Binky. And where had the money come from?

In high school, anyway, neither Charlene nor the Rodeo King had big bucks as far as I could remember. The house must have been a recent acquisition. Then there was the matter of the black eye.

We passed through the dining room with its Chippendale table, chairs and china cabinet. Gilt-framed pictures of two grim-looking people, I presume married ancestors, glared out at the room. Judging from Charlene's girth, their disapproval had not been a deterrent at dinnertime.

Charlene led me to the kitchen via what could be described as a breakfast nook. Only this one wasn't used for eating. A computer station lined one wall and piles of paper were scattered everywhere.

"Sorry about the mess," Charlene apologized as we walked through.

In the kitchen, more dried flowers cascaded out of baskets on top of whitewashed oak cabinets complemented the white tile floor.

A long wrought-iron rack hosted copper and stainless steel pans. The range was restaurant quality and a Sub-Zero refrigerator tried to hide its bulk next to the double stainless sinks. Everything about the room signaled Serious Cook, and I remembered that Charlene had listed cooking first on her biography under hobbies.

A long butcher block, scarred with heavy use, served as an island in the middle of the kitchen. Fresh bell peppers, onions, celery, cucumbers and tomatoes sprawled across it. It was the only old thing in the room. Everything else looked brand-new.

"I hope you don't mind if I work while we talk," Charlene said. "We're having company for dinner, and I want to get the gazpacho done so it can chill."

"No problem," I said, wondering where she had found such plump bell peppers. The tomatoes also looked pretty good, not like the anemic-looking ones I usually find in the markets in March. I guess if you're a serious cook, you'll hunt up the good stuff.

"So, what's up?" she prompted.

"Well, I just thought I'd drop in and see how you and Binky are doing."

"Fine. We've been looking into getting a burglar alarm."

"Great." I looked at the French doors leading to the patio and thought a burglar alarm might give them ten seconds, if someone really wanted in. "Is that the piddler?" I pointed to a big black Labrador retriever on the other side of the glass doors, whose mouth held a Happy Face Frisbee.

"Pardon me?" Charlene stopped her chopping and gave me a funny look.

"Your bodyguard."

"Oh, Duke." She nodded toward the patio.

"I thought you were going to leave him in."

"Well, I usually do, but God, Trade, he's a mess. He's got some kind of ear infection, a yeast thing, and he really smells. He's always in at night, even though he still piddles," she said in a placating tone.

"Well, that's great if the killer comes at night," I said, curious if a dog with an ear infection could even hear anything.

"And Binky's still got that damn gun. It's next to our bed."

"Well, let's hope you never have to use it."

"Is there any news on the Song Dogs?" Charlene asked, reaching for a bell pepper. She took a boning knife and deftly stripped off long pieces of the membranes.

Mentally, I admired her dexterity with the blade. It also reminded me not to discount the fat woman as a suspect. Not that I needed another one, with Bobette and Daggett vying for first place.

"Why don't you use the Cuisinart?" I asked, thinking about Valerie and Connie.

"I like doing it this way," she said. Her face was flushed and I had the flash that Charlene had something sexual going with her vegetables. Kind of like me and the Twinkies.

"Is Binky here?"

"No, he had a few errands in town." She reached for the tomatoes and began chopping.

Charlene was reaching for a long, fat cucumber when

our conversation was interrupted by the telephone. As she snatched it from its cradle on the wall, I noticed that she had streams of tomato juice running down her right arm. A healthy scratch meandered through the tomato design. Maybe she put up a fight when Binky slapped her around.

I heard the flap of rubber as Duke bounded into the kitchen. I guessed he'd gained his ingress through a doggy door somewhere. He carried the stupid Frisbee in his mouth. Dropping it at Charlene's feet, he nudged her fat calf with his nose. She ignored him.

"Well, I don't know why not," she was speaking into the phone. "We've been through this before. Any fool can see they're the same."

She tapped the boning knife impatiently against the telephone as Duke continued nudging her to throw the toy for him.

"Not now, Duke," she whispered through gritted teeth.

His response was to begin barking.

"Fine. I'll have my lawyer be in touch." She slammed the receiver back into its wall holster, put the knife on the butcher block next to the green pepper and grabbed the cucumber.

"Sorry, business thing," she said.

"I didn't know you worked."

"Just some wrap-up on my sister's stuff."

I remembered Laverne Carlton from the biography she'd given me. "I was sorry to hear about your sister's death," I said, although I hadn't known her.

"Don't ever have anyone die on you, Trade, it's a real pain." She pointed the cucumber at me.

As she did so, Duke launched himself off the floor and, in one graceful leap, snatched the cucumber out of her hand and ran off with it.

"Duke!" She shrieked at him, but he didn't return with the vegetable. "God, it serves me right. I've spent hours teaching him to play Frisbee. Binky was a champion in college and I wanted to teach Duke something that he and Binky could do together. Now he thinks everything's a Frisbee."

It looked to me like she had some more training to do, since the dog was snatching non-Frisbee things out of her hands.

"We just put in the doggy door because of the murders," she added.

"That looks like a nasty scratch." I pointed to her arm.

"Stupid dog jumped on me." Duke clearly was not on her most favored list.

I still wondered if it had anything to do with her black eye, but she wasn't talking, so I changed the subject. "You've got a beautiful house here." It was a fishing expedition. While I'm naturally curious about such things, I wanted to know everything there was to know about all of the cheerleaders.

"Thanks." She retrieved a fresh cucumber from the refrigerator and replaced the boning knife with a vegetable cleaver. The dimples in her hands winked at me as she rocked the blade over the new cucumber. Chop, chop, chop.

She never missed a beat as she scooped up the cucumber and dumped it in the blender. "Binky's doing good."

As her hand dropped to the side of the butcher block to remove yet another knife, I leaned over and looked at the collection.

"Holy cow, Charlene, you are serious about this, aren't you?"

"If you're going to cook, then it's important you have the right equipment," she sniffed, somewhat defensively.

Right equipment she had. She had enough knives to earn her lifetime mailings from both Sabatier and Chicago Cutlery.

"Each one has its own specialty," she said with obvious pride.

Right. A knife for every occasion, I thought. I wondered which knife a person would use to stab someone through the heart. A serrated one? A boning knife? Was there a heart blade? Shit, now she gets another red check. I was looking at Charlene in a new light. She was a big woman with a blade fetish, but there was still a soft, timid look about her. I had trouble believing she was strong enough, physically or mentally, to overpower anyone, much less murder someone.

I waited until she began chopping onions.

"Why'd you go see Bobette?"

The rhythm of the chopping never faltered. "I was going to tell you," she said casually. "It was just a spur-of-the-moment thing. We were watching the basketball game on TV and the score was a runaway. Binky thought maybe we'd learn something if we went to see her."

"A five-hour drive in bad weather on impulse?"

"Well, we do things like that. Sometimes." There was a whine in her voice. "It wasn't worth it, though. She couldn't tell us anything, and we're both exhausted today."

"I imagine," I said. What I wanted to say was, *How goddamn stupid is your husband that he takes you along so he can hit on an old flame?*

"Binky's not used to feeling so helpless. He's used to being in charge of things."

"I can understand that," I said, reaching for a piece of bell pepper. I was getting hungry. "Bobette and Binky used to date in high school, huh?" I was stretching it a bit, since Bobette had told me that they hadn't dated. Still, in my book, screwing sort of counted as a date.

The knife clattered against the wooden chopping block.

"Where'd you get that crazy idea?" Charlene's high voice broke and squeaked. She hadn't a clue.

"I don't remember," I lied easily. "I probably have it wrong."

"Oh, I think you definitely do. Binky never took Bobette out."

I quickly changed the subject again. "How are the reservations coming along?"

"One hundred forty-three as of Friday." Charlene reclaimed her knife and her composure and went back to work. "We're having another meeting this Thursday. Do you want to come?"

"Probably not." I'd already gone that route and what

little time was left to me would be better spent delving into my suspects.

A thud against the French doors startled me. Duke was jumping up on them and barking, his tail wagging in cadence with his yelping.

"Binky must be home," Charlene said quietly.

I glanced at the kitchen clock. One-fifteen.

Binky's body filled the glass frame of the doors. He had a grocery bag in one hand and dropped the other to pet the excited Duke. The dog tilted his head a funny way when Binky scratched his ears.

"Good boy, that's my dog," he said as the animal wriggled in ecstasy. Somehow I felt it was more attention than he ever gave Charlene.

He came in the kitchen. "Hi Hon, Trade."

He set the bag on the counter and gave Charlene a quick kiss. His eyes were open, and he was looking at me as he kissed her. What a sleazebag—always looking for his next opportunity.

He came around to my side of the butcher and hovered. He was one of those people who crowd into your space, somehow making you feel dirty for their invasion. He was close enough that I could detect a bad odor, faintly familiar.

"What's up?" He scooped up a handful of green pepper strips before finally retreating.

"Trade just stopped in to see how we're doing."

Binky reached in the Sub-Zero and withdrew a Bud Light, perhaps a concession to watching his weight. I noticed he didn't offer me one. "So what's new?"

"Not much, I'm afraid. We were just talking about your visit to Bobette Jarcik."

"Trade thought you dated her in high school, can you imagine?" Charlene chimed in. It sounded genuine, not like the kind of subtle hint a woman would give her husband as a warning to watch what he said.

"You're barking up the wrong tree, Trade." Binky said, not answering his wife's question.

Why hadn't I ever noticed that the Rodeo King had

such sinister eyes? They seemed to narrow every time he looked at me.

"We drove up there thinking maybe Bobette would remember something," he said. "She didn't, though."

"Do you get to L.A. much?" I directed my question to Charlene. "To see your boy?"

Binky and his wife exchanged an intense look.

"No." Did I detect a heaviness in Charlene's voice? Was there a problem with visiting her son? I'd thrown the question to shake things up. Visiting her son at Pepperdine would have also given her an opportunity to visit Los Angeles and, maybe, Deborah Chamberlain. Although no one was calling her a murder victim yet.

"Look, Trade, are you forgetting who you're working for here? What is this shit?" Binky took a long pull on the Bud Light.

"Hey, no offense." I held up my hands. "I was just curious."

Charlene's eyes were shiny, as though she were on the verge of tears.

"Well, remember the cat," Binky said, threatening me.

I stood. "Well, I've got to get going." I was pretty sure the longer I sat here, the more unpleasant he would get. There was something about me that set him off, and I didn't want to aggravate him any more than I had to. He seemed pretty damned defensive and hostile for a guy who professed to be concerned about his wife. He was already a strong contender, and our exchange had only elevated him on my list of suspects. Still, right now I had no reason to push him. Besides, Charlene was going to have to live with his bad mood after I left. Was there a connection between her black eye and their trip to see Bobette Jarcik in Luna?

Charlene saw me to the front door and thanked me for coming by.

As I walked out of the courtyard onto the driveway, I found Priscilla blocked. Binky could have parked behind me, and I could have driven straight out, but instead he parked nose to nose. Insensitive prick, I thought. Then I laughed at myself. There was nothing insensitive about it. He'd done it on purpose.

Although the tan Ford Explorer looked fairly new, it was covered with mud, probably from the Luna trip the day before.

I got in Priscilla and started backing out. As she rolled a few feet backward, something clicked in my head. I stopped the truck, jumped out and walked back to the Ford.

In contrast to the mud on the body, the tires looked new. Brand-new. In fact, clean white chalk marks still adorned the sidewalls. Tilting my head, I was able to read the manufacturer and tire model. Yokohama Super Diggers. I was willing to bet that getting new tires had been the errand that Binky had gone on. While I've never been good with cars, suddenly I found myself interested in this one. How old was it? Old enough to have gone the thirty thousand to thirty-five thousand miles that would warrant new tires?

As I walked back to Priscilla, I caught some movement out of the corner of my eye.

I turned to the barred window, but no one was there.

19

AFTER LEAVING THE WILLIAMSONS', I MADE A SLIGHT DETOUR and wound up on Magee. You make your own luck, and I had, for the alternate route took me to Eegee's, one of several fast-food healthy restaurants in town that were started by a couple of young local entrepreneurs years ago. Driving a couple of miles out of my way meant that I was able to indulge myself with a hot Vegetarian Grinder. This is one of my all-time favorite meals, crunchy vegetables, melted mozzarella cheese and pickles on a whole wheat submarine bun zapped in the microwave until the juicy Italian dressing oozes out all over. It's an absolute mess and to kill for.

I tried to concentrate on my driving as the dressing dripped down my chin. Catching it with a napkin before it violated my shirt, I steered Priscilla with one hand in an attempt to stay in my own lane.

Fast food should probably be outlawed. I'm sure eating and driving has probably caused at least as many accidents, in quantity if not severity, as drinking and driving and talking on the phone and driving.

The diet Pepsi was cradled between my legs, and other than the first initial poke of the straw through the plastic lid, it seemed to be behaving itself. Sometimes they can get out of hand, too.

Connie O'Hara's mother lived in the Fountains, one of those nice enough residential living places for older people on the northwest side of town. I rang the bell on the first-floor unit and was surprised when an elderly woman in a wheelchair answered the door.

"Mrs. O'Hara, Trade Ellis."

"Oh yes, please come in." She rolled the chair deftly away from the door, allowing me to enter. She looked like she was pushing ninety—a lot older than I had imagined.

The living room was furnished in an eclectic style that reminded me that Connie's father had been a career Air Force officer. A Japanese folding screen hung above the sofa and was flanked with lacquered black tables. A Turkish brass tray served as a coffee table and it was laden with dated copies of the *Smithsonian* and *National Geographic*. I suspected most of Mrs. O'Hara's traveling was done these days through the pages of the magazines.

"Please take a seat." She gestured to the couch.

I sat and instantly felt more comfortable now that we were at eye level.

"May I get you something to drink?"

"Oh no, I've just had lunch." I hoped my onion breath wouldn't overpower her.

We exchanged a few niceties before I brought up the reason for my visit.

"Mrs. O'Hara, what did Connie do in Denver?" I asked gently.

"She had her own business, a travel agency. She was very proud of that." The woman reached for a burgundy box of Kleenex, grabbed one and dabbed at her eyes. "She also had some investments."

A little bell went off in my brain as I remembered a particular investment counselor. "Did she know a man by the name of Daggett Early?"

"Hmm, no, that name doesn't mean anything. Should it?"

"No, we went to high school with him and he's an investment counselor. When you said *investments*, his name came to mind and I thought that their paths might have crossed." I saw no need to tell her Daggett and Connie had had a couple of dates in high school. I then tried a different tack. "Did she live in Denver a long time?"

"Oh, for years. She liked it there. Said she was tired of the heat."

"But she came home frequently?"

"A couple of times a year. And then we'd trade off at Christmastime. Sometimes I'd go there, you know. She was coming this last time for my birthday. She'd planned a little party for me here at the Fountains."

"But she never came," I said as softly as I could.

"No." More pink Kleenex to the tired gray eyes. "She never made it."

"What were your plans in conjunction with her visit? Were you going to pick her up?"

"Oh no, I don't drive anymore. Clarence, the maintenance man, does little errands for the residents here. I told Connie that he could pick her up, but she said not to bother, that she'd probably just rent a car. You know usually she wouldn't do that for such a short visit, and she was only coming for the weekend. I don't understand why she rented that car."

"Did she have bags?"

"Only the ones she would have had on the plane with her. She never checked her bags. She couldn't stand to wait for them."

"Did her bags turn up?"

"One. The police still have it. They're running some kinds of tests." The pile of Kleenex was growing. I hated to ask her all the questions the police had already covered, but I needed to know, and they'd probably be back to talk to her again, anyway. So far, I hadn't uncovered anything earthshaking, but then I was building up to what I really wanted to know.

"Mrs. O'Hara, did Connie talk about any of her friends from high school? Was she still friendly with any of them?"

"I told the police this already. I told them everything I know."

"I know, I'm sure you did. But as I explained to you on the phone, we think that the person who killed your daughter may have been someone we went to high school with."

Mrs. O'Hara gave me the names of three people that Connie had kept in touch with. None of them sounded familiar, but I jotted down their names.

"Did your daughter ever date a man by the name of Binky Williamson?"

"Williamson . . ." she sounded the name out slowly, drawing out each syllable. "No, that doesn't sound familiar. I don't think so."

"Did Connie have a yearbook?"

"Yes. In fact, it's here. She never moved all of her things to Denver. I guess all of it will come back here now."

"Do you mind if I take a look at it?"

Wordlessly she wheeled the chair a short distance and pulled the Javelina High yearbook from the bottom drawer of a china cabinet. She rolled back and handed it to me.

I didn't know what I was looking for, but I started at the beginning and began reading the inscriptions. Most were typical dopey high school stuff. "Don't do anything I wouldn't do," "Chemistry class was fun," "Call me over the summer," and other banalities were scrawled across the pages.

The inside of the rear cover hosted a long love letter from a guy who had apparently been Connie's squeeze in high school. Although it was incredibly mushy, at least he'd had the guts to sign it: David Eberlein. I couldn't remember anyone with that name, so I checked the index. No listing. Again in the senior pages. Still no David Eberlein.

"This was her boyfriend, this David Eberlein?" I asked.

"Oh yes, such a nice young man. They dated that last part of her senior year. I think she still talked to him from time to time."

"Do you know how I can reach him?"

She shook her head. "No. He lives here in Tucson, though. I thought maybe I'd hear from him after it was in the paper."

I made another note on my pad. It was bad enough intruding on Mrs. O'Hara, but at least my visit resulted in some new information.

Connie's mother was clearly very lonely. We chatted for another fifteen minutes, and as I left I accepted an unspecified future date for lunch.

On the drive back to La Cienega, I kept thinking about David Eberlein. Who was he? If he hadn't gone to Javelina, where did he know Connie from? Why hadn't he called her mother? Was he still around and did he have anything to do with Connie's death or the other Song Dog murders?

I drove past the turnoff to the Vaca Grande and on into La Cienega. I passed through town before turning off on the County Line Road. Asphalt quickly turned to unmaintained dirt, and I bounced and jostled across it until I came to the third dirt driveway on the left. A pack of mongrels greeted me, all yipping and barking at the truck. I blasted the horn a few times before Charley Bell stepped out of his double-wide.

"What's happening, Ellis?" He hollered. No one has a first name with Charley.

Now that their owner was outside, the dogs returned to the space Charley had made for them under the trailer.

"Need you again, Charley."

"Hope you never stop." He winked at me.

Charley is about seventy, mostly bald with some fluffy white fringe on the sides and loves dirty jokes. He's a retired railroad engineer who has fallen in love with the computer industry. Now he can program anything and can fix just about any computer ever made. He belongs to dozens of bulletin boards and has friends on all of them, which translates into a very large resource network. Which makes him a dandy friend for a one-woman PI firm.

On top of all that, he can tap into almost any computer system. Computer wizard, hacker extraordinaire and a nice guy. And a generous one.

"Come on in." Charlie's voice always sounds a little scratchy, as though he's coming down with a cold.

I followed him into his trailer. The living room and dining area have been taken over by computers. If there had ever been conventional furniture in his place, it had long been displaced by the electronics. What isn't a computer is a modem, interface cable, mouse, monitor, scanner, printer, manual or printout. Software programs and circuit boards are scattered around Charley's house the way the rest of us toss magazines. A few years ago he had to have his entire trailer rewired to accommodate his new toys.

"I need to know if a woman made a car rental reservation in Tucson a couple of weeks ago," I said.

"Okey-dokey." He grinned, thrilled as always to have someone drawing on his vast expertise. He sat at one of those funny-looking stool-type chairs and began punching buttons. "Name?"

I gave him Connie O'Hara's name and the date she was supposed to come to Tucson. His brown-splotched hands moved rapidly across the computer keys.

"Let's see. We'll start with the big boys first." He continued tapping the keys until both sides of the split screen were filled. "Avis, Budget, Hertz, National, Thrifty. Nope, nope." Tap, tap, tap.

"Dollar, Enterprise, General, nope." Tap.

"Let's try Ugly Duckling, nope." He continued through a few of the minor agencies, but found no car reservation for Connie O'Hara. Apparently she'd made other plans for getting to her mother's that night. Had the killer given her a ride?

"Anything else?" he asked hopefully.

I shook my head. Even with all of this modern technology before me, I couldn't think of how to utilize it.

"Then let's have a drink!"

Charley poured us a couple of stiff Jim Beams and water. While it wasn't my drink of choice, I nursed it to be hospitable.

"Say Trade, did you hear about the couple in their eighties who decided to have children?"

"No."

"Well, they go to the doctor and the doctor says, 'Well this is unusual, but modern medicine has come a long way, so it might be possible.' So he gives them one of those little specimen jars and tells the man to fill it and return it the next day."

This was a new one for me. I could always count on Charley for having the latest dirty joke.

"So did he?" I knew my cues by heart.

"Well, he comes in the next day with an empty bottle, and he says, 'I'm sorry, Doc. I tried with my right hand, then I tried with my left hand. And the missus, she tried with her right hand and then she tried with her left hand."

I groaned and took a big hit on the Jim Beam.

" 'And then she tried with her teeth in and then she tried with her teeth out.' "

A warm flush came to my face, and I was praying the punch line wasn't far behind.

"And we still couldn't get the cap off the bottle!" Charley bent over laughing as I joined him.

"Charley, there's one more thing. Could you check out a man named David Eberlein?"

"Give me a spelling, Ellis."

I spelled it out for him and told him a joke about a leprechaun who makes love to a penguin, thinking it's a leprechaun nun. Then I thanked him and said goodbye.

The elusive David Eberlein kept intruding on my thoughts on my way home. Who was he? How could I find him? And, most importantly, had he picked Connie up from the airport that night?

20

BY THE TIME I PULLED INTO THE VACA GRANDE, THE SUN WAS starting to set. Mrs. Fierce ran behind the truck on the way in and was followed by a canine friend. As I climbed out of Priscilla, both dogs were wagging their tails.

"Who's your new bud?" I asked.

Mrs. Fierce's answer was a whole body wiggle and one hump of my leg.

The stranger, a female, looked like an Australian cattle dog, a blue heeler with a hint of something else thrown in. I petted her and felt around her neck for a collar and some identification, but there was none. As my hands brushed over her back and ribs, I could feel that there wasn't much flesh covering her bones.

"Well, little girl, you could use a square meal," I muttered. I picked up one of her front paws and saw that it was raw. The dog had obviously done a lot of traveling.

I fed both dogs before doing the other chores. If the visitor hadn't been so thin, I wouldn't have fed her and encouraged her to hang around. Sometimes well-intentioned people do that and end up alienating a dog from its owners. Besides, I had enough animals.

Once inside, I checked my calls. When I heard Sanders's voice, I knew it must be important since he hates talking to the answering machine.

"We're gathering in the morning." He'd kept his message to a minimum.

Shit. With all of the Song Dog business I had completely forgotten that we were supposed to gather the cattle in the north end of the valley. Some boss I turned out to be. I couldn't even remember when my own cattle were going to be picked up. While many ranches only gather twice a year, in the spring and fall, I do it more frequently. I like to check out my herd, and, since I run bulls with my cows year round, there's always work to be done with the calves. I'd been seeing a few large calves we'd missed, so, with Martín off in Mexico, I'd asked Sanders last week to make the arrangements with the Mexican cowboys, no small feat, since most of them didn't have telephones.

And this was no honk-'em-up outfit like folks in some parts. That's too easy: A cowboy drives his pickup to a pasture, lays on the horn and the cows come running for their feed. We don't gather with four-wheelers or helicopters, either. Not our style. We're old fashioned that way.

Gathering means working cattle to us. We'd push the cows and their new calves into the north pasture. Once they've all been gathered, and separated, we inoculate, earmark, castrate, tag and brand the new babies.

Gathering wouldn't help solve my case, but it's a great way to spend the day. Plus, I'm a dirty shirt cowgirl. Definitely hands-on. I don't like sending a group of cowboys out to gather my cattle without me, no matter how busy I am. Besides, with Binky, Bobette, Daggett, Charlene and now David Eberlein forming a crazy cat's cradle in my brain, maybe the riding would help clear the cobwebs out.

There was also a call from Emily Rose.

"Why couldn't this maniac have been into Barbies?" she asked. "Nada, zilcho, nothing on the rag doll."

While I was disappointed, I wasn't surprised. While some things hold fingerprints well, cloth isn't one of them.

I had just settled in to watching the *NewsHour with Jim Lehrer* when the phone rang. It was Daggett Early.

I was relieved to hear his voice. It had been days since

our date, and I was beginning to think I'd lost my touch. Not that I was trying, but still . . .

"Hi Daggett."

"What have you been up to?"

I shared just enough about the investigation to make him think I wasn't withholding information, which, of course, I was. I saw no harm in mentioning meeting to Mrs. O'Hara. I neglected the part about my visit to Charley Bell's.

"So how's the investment business?" I asked in a weak attempt to keep the conversation going. It's hell talking on the phone when you've been on just one date with someone and don't yet have a lot of common ground to cover. And even harder when you suspect that person of murder.

"Busy. In fact, I'm leaving town tomorrow afternoon and I was wondering if you could have lunch with me before I go."

"I'm sorry, I can't. We're gathering cattle."

"Cattle." Daggett repeated. He'd probably never had a date turn him down for cows before.

"How about a rain check?" Of all my suspects, he was the easiest one to get close to, so I wasn't going to let an opportunity slide by to keep an eye on him.

He invited me to dinner at his house the following Wednesday evening. I looked at the calendar on the inside of the pantry door. That would be ten days before the reunion. I accepted, and we hung up.

Suddenly Jim Lehrer didn't seem quite as exciting. I was too busy congratulating myself on Daggett's having called for another date. It was a pretty stupid thing for a woman in her forties to be doing, but I loved the affirmation. If he hadn't been such a strong suspect as a serial killer, he sure would have made good fantasy material. I could probably still use him for that. At my age, the daydreams are frequently better than reality, so they're worth savoring. A vivid imagination is a wonderful thing.

Mrs. Fierce lay near the front door, a strange place for her to choose. When I opened it, I found the heeler curled up on the other side. It was a cold evening, dipping into the thirties, so I threw an old blanket on the front porch. The dog pawed at it, curling it up into a little nest before settling in for the night. I sure wasn't doing much to discourage the beast from hanging around, but I felt sorry for her.

When I closed the door, Mrs. Fierce once again lay down in front of it. She wasn't about to let her new friend get too far away. I went into the kitchen and made a note to myself to call the paper and place a "Found" ad if the dog was still there in the morning.

Four-thirty A.M. came quickly. I tried to go back to sleep but Gorilla pinned me to the bed, his huge black body plopped on my chest. His wet nose kept creeping under my folded hands as he insisted on being petted. The good thing about sleeping with a cat is he doesn't care if you've brushed your teeth or not. I rolled over and ran my index finger under the sheets, pretending it was a mouse. Gorilla took the bait and began stalking the lump. His instincts were faster than my finger, unfortunately. I never would have dared to play the game without the protective sheet; my finger would have been shredded. Finally, tired of playing bait, I rolled out of bed and got dressed.

Mrs. Fierce and her new friend, who I found myself calling Blue, followed me to the corral. Blue followed Mrs. Fierce as she ran out in the pasture and nipped at the horses' heels in an effort to bring them in faster. Gray and Dream always take a dim view of this encouragement and kick out at the dogs. I was pleased to see that Blue, like most heelers, could flatten her body to the earth and avoid being kicked. Mrs. Fierce, of course, learned long ago how to avoid the lethal hooves.

I returned to the house and ate cold chicken enchiladas with sour cream for breakfast before heading back outside.

I checked the barn thermometer before saddling Gray. Twenty-four. I was ready for it, though, bundled up and feeling a little like Humpty Dumpty. Most of the layers would come off, stuffed in my cantle bag or tied to my saddle, before noon. Early March in Arizona can sometimes be cold, but when I think of the eastern cities buried under snow, I feel bad griping about it.

I met Sanders at the east gate. He was also bundled up, his Stetson low on his head to protect his ears from the cold. It must have been all those years in South Dakota, but the cold here never bothers him the way it does me. He also never seems to need as many layers as I do.

We rode up on the mesa where we joined up with the rest of the cowboys. After talking it over, the young guys, Diego and Ramon headed down the valley in a broad swing, Memo and Al covered the mesa, while Sanders and I took the upper reaches to the National Forest boundary.

We were all working in tandem, making a gigantic sweep of the terrain, gathering any cows, calves and bulls we found. Our rendezvous point would be the holding pens at the north end of the valley.

It was a beautiful morning. Coveys of Gambel's quail scattered as Sanders and I rode by. Midmorning we jumped a herd of mule deer, who bounded up the hills with stiff-legged bounces, a noisy escape that scattered rock and broke brush.

Most of the cattle were grazing. With the mother cows staying on the same range, they know the routine by heart. I've had some of these cows for ten years, so when they see us coming, they know we mean business and they start to move north. They're a lot easier to work than steers, who are in a pasture for just one year and then sold. You go to gathering steers and half the time they don't know where they are, much less where they're going.

We took our time, not wanting to chouse the cows. Racing after them and working them too fast isn't very effective. There's an old saying, "Wild cowboys make wild cows," and it's true. You go to chousing them and pretty soon they're on the run and hard to control. Going slower actually gets the job done faster. It's not at all like in the movies.

Sanders and I came to the edge of a canyon, and, looking down, we could see mamas grazing while their babies nursed or played with one another. Two coyotes sat patiently on the hillside, hoping for breakfast. When opportunity knocks, they hamstring the little ones. Luckily, with the long-horned Brahma cows watching out, that doesn't happen very often. Some outfits shoot lurking coyotes, but we don't have to do that here; the mother cows do a good job of defending their calves. Polled cattle have a harder time, since they don't have horns.

It was a noisy morning with the cattle calling to one another. Farther ahead we could hear a bull bellow. As we gathered the cattle together, several bulls joined the herd. They threw sand with their front feet in a great show of bravura that was followed by butting heads and locking horns. A couple of the Hereford bulls had bloody pink smudges across their white curly foreheads. They'd already been battling that morning.

We met the rest of the cowboys at the north corrals. The job of building the butane fire fell to Ramon, who at twenty was the youngest of the cowboys.

I nodded to Sanders. It was his cue. Although I was the boss of the outfit, today I was abdicating and he would sort the cattle. My mind wasn't on the business at hand anyway. It was still racing with all of the Song Dog combinations.

Alfonso was on foot with a lariat and Diego, Memo and I stayed on horseback guarding the gate as Sanders separated the calves from their mothers. The mothers were pushed past the corrals into the holding pasture. Occasionally a calf would dart around or under Sanders's horse and past Al, and the rest of us would ride like hell to retrieve it and then push it back into the pen. There was a lot of bawling back and forth, as both cows and calves were eager to mother up again.

Once the cattle had been separated, the cowboys got to work branding, ear tagging and castrating. I inoculated. When we finally finished, we threw some tinfoil-wrapped bean burritos on the edge of the fire to warm them for lunch.

It was late afternoon by the time Sanders and I rode

through the back pasture of the Vaca Grande; both dogs came running to greet us.

"New dog." There wasn't a question in his voice.

"She showed up last night. Might be a keeper."

"You could use another dog."

I kept quiet. I knew something was coming.

"Someone may have been here the other night," Sanders said.

"You saw tracks?"

"I didn't recognize the tires and it looked like someone stepped out of the car. Probably nothing."

I knew he'd been waiting all day for this conversation. There was no point in saying anything more. When Sanders wanted to share something, he would. That much I had learned in our years together.

We said our goodbyes, and by the time I had unsaddled, put Gray up, and gone inside, it was after four. I called Ortega's Market on South Sixth to see how late they were open. If I hurried, I could make it before closing. I needed to pick up the dried corn husks for the tamales Beatrice and I were supposed to make on Tuesday. Deciding I'd rather screw up one late afternoon with a trip to town than ruin a whole day, I hustled. The Song Dogs could wait.

Ortega's Market might just as well have been in Sonora. Located in an old mud adobe building with a wooden porch barely propped up with rotten four-by-fours, a trip inside was like stepping back in time. With its scarred plank floors and old-time cash registers, there were no UPC symbols or magnetic scanning devices in sight.

Ristras of red chiles hung from the beams and the spice rack held plastic bags filled with essentials: cumin, whole pequín and tamarind pods, corriander seed, cinnamon sticks, saffron, oregano, cilantro and chiltepins. Blue cornmeal and panocha flour settled on the shelves next to snow-white blocks of lard, with big wooden vats of loose pinto beans below.

The vegetable section included piñon nuts, nopales, jicama, plantains, tomatillos, chayote, pomegranates and cane sugar. Goat cheese, *queso anejo* and head cheese graced the cold case. In the meat department pigs' feet, strips of venison jerky, tripe for menudo and oxtails vied for space with more standard fare.

While I would have liked to look around, it was near closing time and I didn't want to impose on the help. I found the dried corn husks, filled my basket and checked out.

Ortega's is in the heart of South Tucson. This is still a fairly depressed part of town and a lot of food stamps go with the territory. The residents are a mix of hardworking people, drug dealers, prostitutes and the homeless, some of whom have been very helpful in my previous investigations.

South Tucson is also notorious for its authentic Mexican restaurants. The anglicized versions in the trendier parts of town can't hold a candle to the food offered here. The L & L Restaurant, one of the most famous, is directly across from Ortega's parking lot. I threw the corn husks behind Priscilla's front seats and climbed in. As I was fastening my seat belt, I noticed a familiar car pull into the L & L parking lot. I pulled my visor down and fumbled in the console.

Because of the business I'm in, I always keep a loaded camera in my car. I grabbed the Nikon, one of those self-focusing ones designed for idiots, hit the zoom button and focused on the Ford Explorer as it found a parking space.

I watched through the lens as the man let himself out, walked around to the passenger side and opened the door for the woman. As she exited, she threw her arms around his neck, rubbed her chest against his and gave him a long lingering kiss.

I got the shot.

If it turned out, I'd have a perfect photograph of Binky Williamson and Buffy Patania in a compromising position.

It was something I neither wanted nor had counted on.

As I closed the lens cover, I looked across at the parking lot again. I could have sworn Binky was glaring right at me, but then he turned away and walked into the restaurant.

21

I SPENT A PRETTY FITFUL NIGHT. MY DREAMS WERE CHASE SCENES, with me starring as the prey. I never like those. Then, when I woke up, which seemed almost every hour on the hour throughout the night, I tried to make sense of Buffy and Binky.

The whole thing was ludicrous and sounded like a fourth-grade taunt: "Binky's banging Buffy, Binky's banging Buffy." I wondered how it would play to a game of hopscotch.

At the least the affair revealed some inappropriate behavior. Binky, married to Charlene for a little over a year, should have still been lusting after his wife. That's usually true for the first year or two of any marriage, then things settle into "comfortable." At least that was my experience. Problem with my marriage was that "comfortable" then evolved into "roommates," which eventually deteriorated into "cohabiting with a rat." But that's another story.

Still, I wasn't surprised at Binky's being unfaithful. He was a jerk. The real surprise to me was that he'd found a woman to be unfaithful with.

Which brought me to Buffy. Okay, maybe she hadn't listed Charlene as her best friend on her form, and as a matter of fact she hadn't listed Binky at all, who was obviously a much closer friend, but she made the top of Charlene's list. Kind of a crummy way to treat an old friend and another woman.

The other thing that didn't make any sense was the combination itself. Buffy was downright beautiful. She was thin, intelligent and rich, and could probably fool around with most of the men on the planet. Why would she pick Binky?

While he'd been hot stuff in high school, the intervening years had not been kind. Now he was spreading out, married, and in love with a dog with a yeast infection in its ear. He also clearly had a mean streak lurking beneath his surface. While the Labrador loved his master, Charlene had seemed almost afraid of him. And then there was the black eye.

I finally got up for good about five. It was still dark out. I brewed a pot of decaf and wished for the hundredth time this year that I had the morning paper. They won't deliver to the ranch. They'll drop it off at the long string of rural mailboxes, which means I have to go out and retrieve it. If I'm going to make that effort, I might as well go on up to Rainbow's and read it with company.

Remembering tomorrow's date with Bea, I retrieved four roasts from the freezer and threw them on the counter to thaw.

Mrs. Fierce ran to the kitchen door and whined. I opened it and found Blue on the other side. The two dogs greeted each other like long-lost friends. Mrs. Fierce dropped her front end down to the ground as she coaxed Blue into a game of tag. Mrs. Fierce must have taught Blue the game in my absence, because Blue took off like a shot through the door and the game was on.

I had just settled back into my kitchen chair when Christmas the cat ran her claws against the door. I let her in, and she jumped up to the cat counter, sniffed at her empty bowl and whined. As I opened the pantry door to retrieve her food, a field mouse scurried across the floor, presenting an alternative breakfast. Christmas chased after it and it disappeared behind the refrigerator. She sat there patiently, waiting for it to screw up and make another appearance. I hoped the cat would take care of it before I had to deal with a trap.

At first light I did the morning chores and took off for Rainbow's. I stuck my change in the newspaper machine out front and fumbled for the third paper from the top, while trying to make the top two look like they hadn't been messed with.

Although it was just after six, the cafe was starting to fill up with the Good Old Boys. Sometimes I wonder how Rainbow makes any money at all; most of the tables in the smoking room are filled with guys just wanting to shoot the bull. They all drink coffee, cup after cup of it, but rarely order breakfast. I guess it works out. In downtown La Cienega, the information that comes out of the smoking room is priceless, the small-town equivalent of insider trading on Wall Street.

I ordered the Early Bird Special, sort of an ersatz Egg McMuffin, Rainbow style. This one came with a garnish of two orange slices and one of the first strawberries of the season, red bottom and green on top.

Opening the morning paper, I turned to the classified section first. At the top of the "Lost and Found" column was a notice telling me I could place a "Found" ad for free.

I scanned the "Lost" column and found no dog matching Blue's description. Because it's hard to stop once I get started, I went ahead and read the "Found" section, then "Farm Equipment," "Livestock" and the "Personals." After screwing around in this manner for ten minutes or so, I finally tore off the top section of the classifieds, where the number was listed, and put it in my pocket. Now, with the important things out of the way, I reluctantly went back to the front page.

Same old gruesome stuff. People waging war against one another, terrorists blowing things up, flooded towns, lawyers shot to death, police shortages. The paper was filled with stories I didn't want to read, and did.

Buried in the Metro section of the newspaper was an 88-CRIME story offering a twenty-five-hundred-dollar reward for information leading to the apprehension of the murderer of Valerie Higgins. No mention was made of Connie O'Hara's killer or that the two might be related.

I dawdled around until seven, when I knew the hardware store would be open.

I entered Darrell's under the pretext of getting some rubber washers for a leaking faucet and ended up in the Pet Care section, where I picked up a red dog collar for Blue. I also dropped off the roll of film that had been in my camera.

I stopped at the string of mailboxes and collected the mail. When I finally got to the stage stop, I turned the heater on first thing. The concrete floors are scattered with Navajo rugs—great to keep clean, but cold in the winter. I made a pot of coffee and checked the answering machine. There were several messages, including one from Beatrice reminding me about our tamale date tomorrow. There was also a message from Chester Littleton, the insurance adjuster who had given me the new workmen's comp case. I played it twice, to make sure I'd heard it right.

"Trade, this is Chester," he began. "I hope you haven't done too much on that new case. The claimant was in a car accident last night and broke his back. Looks like we're screwed ducks. Bill me for what you've done."

Since the case had been in my office for a grand total of two days and I hadn't started on it, unfortunately there would be no bill.

I was half surprised to find nothing on the machine from Binky. Maybe he hadn't seen me after all.

Going through the mail, I found another check from Buffy Patania. Curious, since I hadn't billed her on any additional hours and was still working on the original retainer Charlene had given me. I might have thought it was payoff money to keep my mouth shut about what I had seen in the L & L parking lot, but it was postmarked the day before I'd seen her and Binky. Briefly I wondered if Charlene was paying her share of the freight. From what I had seen of her house, she could certainly afford it.

There was also a note from Bobette Jarcik telling me she was coming to Tucson the following week for her grandmother's open-heart surgery. She didn't know where she would be staying but promised to get in touch when she hit town. I hoped she hadn't advertised her visit to too many people.

Another highlight of my mail was the envelope from Carol Wright. We're intimate friends. Although our correspondence is a bit one-sided, she's been faithfully writing me for about ten years now. And so thoughtful. She always encloses the nicest coupons.

I run hot and cold with coupons. Sometimes I go apeshit and clip like crazy and throw them in an envelope. In a good week I might remember them when I go to the grocery store and save five bucks. Then there's the time I spend going through, checking the expiration dates, and trashing the coupons that I forgot to use.

I debated about Carol this morning and ended up deep-sixing the entire envelope, feeling only mildly wasteful as I did so. The attention I give my junk mail is in direct proportion to the degree of boredom I'm suffering. And with this case, I had no frigging time to be bored.

I worked at composing my "Found" ad and discovered it was taking me much longer than I thought it would. I had mixed feelings about placing an ad at all. If someone had lost Blue and loved her, then they deserved to have her back. But if she had left home looking for a square meal, there was no way I wanted to return her.

I finally compromised my conscience with my desire by writing, "Found female dog." When I got around to calling the newspaper, the ad-taker argued with me. She wanted me to describe the dog in more detail to cut the number of calls I would receive. I held fast. The way I figured it, if these people really wanted their dog back, the least they could do was to tell me what she looked like.

I was mildly depressed when I hung up the phone, and I knew that Mrs. Fierce would be heartbroken if her new friend was claimed. I said a prayer to the spirits that things would work out all right.

I was filling out the deposit slip for Buffy's check when the phone rang. It was Emily Rose.

"Trade, I caught you. Have you heard about the shrine?"

"Shrine?"

"That trash bin where the arms were found. Rumor here is it's been desecrated."

I could almost see the faded geraniums and chipped votive candles in front of me. *Pay attention, a life was taken here.*

"What happened?"

"Well, people have been writing on the sides of that thing all along, but the business guy's just left it, thinking it'd run its course. The university kids are still lighting candles down there. It's almost become a cult thing, though I doubt a single one of them knew her."

"A cult." I mulled that over.

"Just thought you'd want to know. Gotta go, 'bye."

I wanted to know more and although it pained me to do so, I called Uncle C. He wasn't pleased with my call.

"This ain't graffiti, Trade. Even though we're treating it as a 10-59, it's vicious. The police photographers are down there now. We're painting over it this afternoon and the goddamn thing's coming down."

I heard his coffee cup hit his front teeth.

"This is getting really ugly and I want you out of it."

There it was. Uncle C's demand again. I said nothing.

"I mean it, Trade. You're in way over your head on this thing."

"I know, Uncle C." I could concede that. After all, I wasn't promising anything, just acknowledging what he told me.

Then I remembered Bobette. I told him she was coming to town. He asked me to have her call the Sheriff's Department when she got here. I decided to gamble on a theory.

"The tire prints, Uncle C. The Williamsons have a Ford Explorer. It's a four-wheel drive and they just changed all four tires."

"Don't jump to conclusions, Trade," he said by way of chastising me.

"I just thought you might want to know." I hate it when he does that to me. It's like he's seeing me as a child again. Poor Uncle C tried to fill in after Dad died, but it didn't work out too well, since by then I was a teenager and not eager to listen to anyone.

"We know." He sounded exhausted. "The tire shop already shipped them all out to their yard at the airport. We're checking on them, but they're probably gone for good."

Shit. How many fastidious tire shops could there be in Tucson and why did Binky Williamson have to choose one? Was it just coincidence? Would they ever be able to find his tires?

"Out, now," Uncle C said, as though he could read my mind.

"Right, Uncle C." I couldn't get off the phone fast enough. There was no way I was giving up the case. As if I didn't have enough problems already, now I was going to have to dodge my own uncle.

I grabbed the truck keys. I'd had another critical errand scheduled for this morning, but it could wait until I checked out the shrine before it was dismantled.

There was a small crowd gathered around the dumpster by the time I arrived. Yellow crime-scene tape cordoned off the area and two uniformed policemen, their arms crossed, stood guard, keeping the curious from getting too close. While I know quite a few cops, these were strangers. At least Uncle C might never know I made this visit.

The so-called shrine, never pretty to begin with, was a mess. The fake geraniums had been pulled out of their pots and shreds of them were scattered all over. Broken glass and melted candle wax littered the street. Scraps of paper were enmeshed in the chain-link fence behind the trash bin. In addition to the gang graffiti and sexual suggestions, a pentagram spray-painted in red had been added, and the number "666" was written below it in letters half a foot high.

The saying was untouched. "Death cancels everything but the truth."

It mocked me. I was trying to uncover the truth, but where in the hell was it?

The most horrifying part of the desecration was a partially covered black dog. Judging from the stiff body, he'd been dead for a while. He may have died of old age, but he sure didn't climb up there on his own—he was missing his front legs.

"What's that mean?" I asked the friendlier-looking of the two cops as I pointed to the dog.

"Some sicko," he said.

"Do you think it has anything to do with the murder?"

He looked at me as though I were something that belonged in the dumpster. "I'm not a detective. They don't pay me to think about those things."

A police car drove up, and a man and a woman wearing white lab coats exited. They ducked under the tape and then proceeded to the dumpster, where they started retrieving the contents.

As I walked away, I wondered if they would find the dog's legs in the trash bin. And what that would mean.

I shuddered.

Nothing here reminded me of anything, or anyone, I'd known in high school.

22

Buffy Patania lived in the Tucson Mountains in one of those huge white houses that could be seen for miles around.

Sometimes when people build in the desert, they are a little solicitous after they have mowed down the native plants and forced the animal residents to seek new neighborhoods. Their concession, after such violation, is to camouflage their homes in colors like sandstone and terracotta and desert rose. At least they sort of blend in.

But Buffy's house allowed no such compromise. A great monolithic structure, it looked as though it belonged on a Greek isle somewhere, not in the middle of the Sonoran Desert.

I drove up a hill to reach the manse, and as I got out of Priscilla I had to admire the view. Downtown Tucson spread before me. I bet it was beautiful at night. I also bet Buffy had lived here long enough to take it for granted.

I rang the bell and a small Filipino man let me in. I waited in the cold marble foyer while he sought out Buffy. A macaw in a black wrought-iron cage ignored me. At the other end of the foyer, a floor-to-ceiling arched window framed the patio and swimming pool—one of those negative-edge jobs where it looks as though the water falls off the end of the world.

I walked over to the birdcage and tried to engage the

macaw in conversation. He was having none of it, and I was still making a fool of myself, trilling my tongue and making kissing noises, when the houseman returned.

"This way, Miss Ellis, please."

He led me down a wide hallway, past a library and out the French doors onto the patio. Buffy was kneeling over a flower bed, surrounded by empty pony packs of flowers. She stood as I approached and tucked her trowel under one arm while she brushed the soil from her hands onto her worn Levi's.

"Trade! What a surprise!"

"I wasn't sure it was going to be," I said, carefully looking at her face.

"Oh." She knelt again and stabbed the sharp end of the trowel into the petunia bed. "Come sit down." She motioned to the patio furniture. "I'll get us some lemonade."

"I'm fine."

But she was up again, retreating back into the house. Briefly I wondered if she was taking the opportunity to call Binky. Within minutes, however, she was back with a pitcher of cold lemonade and two tall plastic glasses. She poured each of us a drink and then sank into one of the chairs.

"So," she said cautiously, "how's the case going?"

"Well it's getting more interesting every day."

She stuck one of her long thin fingers in her glass and whirled the ice around.

"Did you get my check?"

"Yeah, thanks."

"Charlene's been keeping me up to date." Buffy looked me in the eye. "She told me someone found Bobette and sent her a notice."

I wondered if Binky had told her that he had also found Bobette. And groped her. Before we got down to adultery, I remembered something else. "Did you know a guy by the name of David Eberlein?"

"David Eberlein. I don't think so. Did he go to Javelina?"

"He dated Connie O'Hara in high school. I don't know where he went to school."

"Beats me. I can't place him. Is he a suspect?"

They were all suspects in my book, but I didn't want to share that, so I just said, "He may have picked Connie up from the airport."

I waited. With a lot of people you can do that. They can't take the silence and will fill it with anything. Often incriminating things.

Buffy didn't take the bait, so we sat quietly for a few minutes listening to the bees hum around her plants and to the Kreepy Krauly chug around the pool gobbling up algae. Buffy took the opportunity to flick dirt out from under the fingernails of her left hand with the fingernail of her right little finger.

"I went to see Charlene yesterday. She's sure got a nice house. Binky must be doing well in the insurance business."

Buffy laughed. "Bink didn't have much to do with all that. The money's Charlene's."

"Where'd she get it?"

"Her sister's estate was settled last year. She left everything she had to Charlene."

"She must have been well off," I said. That explained all of the new things at the Williamsons' house. They'd obviously inherited a bundle and weren't having trouble spending it.

"Rebecca De Ville."

Now I was impressed. And I remembered Charlene's biographical form. "Laverne Carlton was Rebecca De Ville? *The* Rebecca De Ville?"

She nodded.

Rebecca De Ville's books filled the romance section of every major grocery store and bookshop in the country. In a few short years she had had a stellar career. She had been a household name until she died not long ago.

I remembered her death. It, too, had been spectacular, making headlines everywhere. Vacationing with an ecological study group in Norway on the Arctic Ocean, she ventured outside her tent one night and was knocked down and killed by a marauding polar bear. The bear swam off with her body, and it was never recovered.

"There are a few problems with it, though."

"With what, the estate?"

"The *literary* estate."

"Like what?"

"I can't really say. I don't know much about it, there's just a few problems, but I'm sure it will all get worked out."

We sat in silence a few more minutes. Finally I decided that if I left it up to Buffy we'd be sitting there all day, so I jumped in.

"Why Binky?"

She traced the rim of her plastic glass with the tip of her finger and then dazzled me with her smile.

"Who?"

"Come on, Buffy. I was in South Tucson yesterday. At the market across from the L & L."

She went back to stirring the lemonade with her finger. "Bink said you saw us."

"Why him?" I repeated.

"We had a thing in high school, and when I ran into him last year, we just sort of picked up where we left off."

"Was that before he married Charlene?"

"No, after. I was in Europe so I didn't see him again until after they were married."

"Does she know?"

"Charlene?" She looked at me absently, as though she were trying to place her. "No. She doesn't know."

"I thought you were friends."

"We are. This has nothing to do with her."

I disagreed but said nothing.

"It's just a thing, a physical thing between us. I mean, I'm not in love with the guy or anything like that."

"But you're sleeping with him."

"That's different. It's an arrangement, that's all."

I was thinking of Binky in a new light. He obviously had more to offer than I had thought.

"Look, I know this doesn't make much sense." Buffy's eyes were clouded as though she were worried about what I thought. "But it's easy. We've known each other since high school. It's just sex. It's like finding a good doubles partner."

"And you're tournament players," I said, thinking the whole analogy pretty dumb.

She ignored me. "It's different, I know that."

"But safe."

"Safe?"

"He's married. Unavailable. You don't have to make a commitment."

I watched her mouth fall slightly open, as her tongue flicked her perfectly white teeth for just a second. Whatever else she'd told me, I knew I'd hit home with this one. She was a conqueror, not a nester. A scalp hunter. The beautiful Buffy Patania had been married once. For six weeks. Whatever had happened during her marriage had soured her on commitment. Now she was in a relationship for what she could get out of it. Period.

"Does Binky feel the same way?"

"He isn't asking for a divorce, if that's what you mean."

It wasn't. I wondered, if Binky and Buffy had connected before he had married Charlene, if our conversation would be any different.

"He's pretty happy with her," Buffy continued. "As happy as Bink can be with anyone." She laughed. "And he keeps me happy because he doesn't pressure me."

"Why'd he marry Charlene?"

"Money."

Apparently there were no secrets between the two of them. She also wasn't into protecting him.

"And you've got money." It looked like Binky had a strong motive for knocking off his wife. If he could get her out of the picture he might inherit the De Ville money and then turn around and marry Buffy's fortune. But what was his motive for killing the other Song Dogs? An elaborate cover-up? I decided that when I returned to the office the Rodeo King was going to get another going-over with the red pen.

"Look Trade, I'd never marry the guy, if that's what you're thinking. Ever. I'm into occasional safe recreational sex and that's it."

"And you've discussed this with Binky?"

She laughed again. "As much as anyone can ever discuss anything with him, yeah. He's happy with the arrangement."

Was he really? As he crawled into bed with his overweight wife every night, didn't he ever dream about a lifetime of curling up next to Buffy's sylphlike body?

"You're not going to tell Charlene, are you? I mean, she doesn't need to know. It would only hurt her."

"Right." I was seeing Buffy Patania in a new light and decided I didn't much like her. The soil under her fingernails wasn't the only dirt she was carrying. She was one of those women who have never had blisters on their hands. Everything had been handed to her all her life, including other people's husbands.

I said my goodbyes and left.

As I hit Silverbell Road and headed north, I glanced in my rearview mirror and saw a Ford Explorer turning up Painted Hills Road.

23

I WAS HOME BY NOON. ALTHOUGH THE DAY HAD STARTED OUT cold, it was now kissing eighty. It was one of those beautiful days when the cardinals hover in groups around the bird feeders and the color of the sky is something that could never find its way to an artist's palette.

I'd made plans to meet Sanders and just in front of the tack room door I noticed a snake track. It was fat, wide and straight, not curvy like a bull or king snake, so I knew it was a rattler, and a good-sized one at that. Seeing it didn't exactly make my day.

A lot of people take great pride in the number of rattlesnakes they kill in a season, keeping track of their kills from the previous years and collecting the rattles much the same way old-time gunslingers used to notch their guns. I'm not one of them.

When I see snakes out in the desert I try to leave them alone. I figure I'm invading their territory and that makes me the trespasser. If I find them around the ranch buildings, though, it's a different story. A snake here can cause a lot of problems. During the summer they come out at night and if you step on one, you've given him a pretty good reason to bite you. Plus, the dogs or cats can get bitten. Horses are larger and snakes hate to waste their venom, so the horses are fairly safe, unless there's a rattler curled up in the grass.

Most snakebites to horses are on the nose when they're grazing. This can be fairly serious, since a horse can only breathe through its nose.

We get a lot of rattlesnakes on the Vaca Grande. Last summer, early one morning I was squatting down to clean the chicken water and I found a sleeping diamondback about six inches from my leg. Scared the shit out of me and I sent him to Rattlesnake Heaven.

Sometimes I think I should learn how to handle them with one of those long sticks, so I can relocate them safely. But, when they're on the property, I'm ashamed to say I shoot them. The poor snake has to die because I'm too cowardly to do things differently. This sets me a bit apart from my Apache ancestors, who refused to kill rattlesnakes within their camp. They respected the rattler's power to kill, although they were not above asking a visiting stranger to do the coup de grâce.

Since I just had a track and not the actual snake, I decided to negotiate. I spoke to the track. "Grandfather, if you're around here, you better head on out. I don't want to shoot you, but I can't have you hanging out where there's people and animals. So go on back to the desert." I was being kinder than the Old Ones. They would have admonished the rattlesnake to get back in his evil hole and take the evil world with him.

Maybe my request would be honored, and then again, maybe it wouldn't.

Apaches weren't alone in their conversations with unwanted creatures. Last year I read a book by some guy named Boone. He became friends with a fly. Started to swat it because it was bothering him, but instead struck up a conversation with it and suddenly had a great new friend.

I've tried his system before with things I would normally annihilate, like little red ants in the kitchen. It's pretty cool. You go up to an ant and ask if he's the head ant. Now, I can't tell you for sure that I have ever actually talked to *the* head ant, but I always ask the guy to at least deliver the message to the head honcho.

My conversation usually goes something like this: "Listen, please tell your leader that I don't want to kill you guys, but I can't have you in the kitchen. You've got twenty-four hours to get out of Dodge. After that, you're history." If they choose not to leave, say some of them want to be martyrs, there's always Raid. But sometimes they take the warning and leave. Honest.

This talking-to-ants business was one of the problems with my marriage. My ex-husband was always running for the bug killer instead of trying to negotiate with them. He thought I was crazy.

I saddled Dream and met Sanders up on top of the mesa. He was waiting for me, slouched down on his horse looking like the Marlboro cowboy when the Marlboro cowboy was cool. When he opens his mouth he sounds like the legendary Rex Allen. He'd tracked two bulls down the Sutherland Wash to Catalina State Park, and we were out to retrieve them.

The park gets a lot of traffic, most of it hikers who sometimes forget to close the gates in spite of the signs urging them to do so. Now the two Herefords were hanging out around the group use area, having a ball scaring the hell out of the campers and day users. Unless provoked, the bulls are really pretty mellow, but they are big and they do have horns. It was time to bring them home.

Since Sanders had tracked bulls down to the creek, I thought it peculiar that we were meeting on top of the mesa. But with Sanders, I knew there must be a good reason, so I kept my mouth shut. I'd find out soon enough.

We rode in silence for a while before Sanders pulled his horse up. Without a word he dismounted, walked a few feet and then squatted on the ground.

He ran his finger over something on the earth and then walked over to the overgrown jeep road that rimmed the mesa. He looked at the road and walked down it a ways before coming back to me.

"I want to show you something." I heard the worry in his voice.

I dismounted and followed him. He squatted again and pointed to a footprint in the dirt. It wasn't real clear; the desert air had sucked the moisture from our last rain out of the ground. While most of the sole had meshed into the tiny rocks that comprised the surface, the heel print was barely distinguishable with a noticeable, faint NB. I recognized it as the logo for New Balance tennis shoes.

I put my foot, size eight, next to the track. It was larger and wider than mine.

"A man was up here. A hunter?"

"Maybe." He stared below and I followed his gaze. Just to the north, I could see the ranch. Tall cottonwoods were beginning to leaf out, the morning sun was picking up the sheen of the pond. A white shape that I knew was Gray was in the south pasture. The rest of the ranch horses had been turned loose, and I could see a cluster of color up near the stage stop. I suspected they were grazing, although from the distance I really couldn't tell. Farther north, I could see Sanders's spread, his barn and willow trees and a few specks that I knew were cattle in his south pasture. The view of both our ranches was always good from up here, and on more than one occasion we'd stopped to admire it.

I looked at the footprint again. It was directly in line with my place.

"You didn't just stumble across this, Sanders."

Still squatting, he picked up a mesquite twig and started scratching in the dirt.

"No. I thought I saw someone up here this morning when I was working in my garden." He drew circles on the ground before tapping the twig next to the heel of the track. "I think this is the same print I found next to your place last week." I knew that Sanders hadn't been watching my place per se. He always noticed tracks. It didn't matter if they belonged to man, beast or vehicle; if something was out of place on the ground, he'd notice it.

Chills numbed me as I remembered the hanging doll. "You didn't tell me."

"I wasn't sure it was anything."

"But now you think someone was up here watching the ranch, watching me?" I tried to keep the anger out of my voice. If he thought I was in danger, he should have told me before now. But I knew saying anything would do no good. Sanders only shared things in his own time.

He nodded.

I looked at the ranch again. Anyone with powerful binoculars would have a bird's-eye view of the Vaca Grande. The driveway, cars coming and going. It would be a perfect vantage point for a burglar. Or a murderer. I shivered. Suddenly the afternoon felt much colder.

I led Dream and followed Sanders over to the jeep road. His early years of trapping, coupled with his time with the Border Patrol, have made him one of the best trackers in our part of the country. We were following faint tire tracks and he suddenly stopped beside the clearest print. It was faint, but some tread was apparent. A hot burn galled my stomach.

I couldn't be sure, and probably wouldn't be, even with the photograph of the tracks in front of me, but the tread pattern was remarkably similar to the one that had been found with Connie O'Hara's shredded body.

My mouth went dry and I began to shake. I took a deep breath. I was quickly learning that the stakes are much greater in murder cases than they are in the run-of-the-mill PI work. Briefly I thought about saying nothing, because I didn't want Sanders to worry. Then I decided the hell with it, because I was scared to death and needed all the help I could get. If I could call in the cavalry to save me, I would.

"This tire track looks like the one that was found next to one of the bodies," I finally gasped.

"I kinda figured it might," he said. He placed one of his hands on my shoulder and gave me a reassuring squeeze.

I looked down the jeep road. If someone knew the area, he could have come up through the National Forest to the road, and then connected up to the power line road and down through the valley. It would take a four-wheel drive, and it would be slow, but it could be done.

I glanced down at the Vaca Grande again. The view was no longer quite as appealing. I squinted, trying to imagine what a person with binoculars would be able to make out. Who the hell had been up here spying on me? And why?

"Let's get those bulls," I said, trying to sound as normal

as possible. There was no need for Sanders to know how scared I was. I mounted Dream and we dropped off the mesa to the south. As I rode, I mentally went through my suspects. Unfortunately, it could have been any one of them.

When we hit the Sutherland, we tried to stay out of the water as much as possible. And with the winter storms there was a lot of it. The normally dry creeks can really rage, the water roils and four-foot waves begin to rise. These create bogs, trapping the water underneath the sand. The bogs can be there even when the ground on top is dry, which it wasn't.

When a horse or cow gets bogged down, it can be pretty frightening for the animals. They can get buried all the way up to their withers. Most of the time they flounder around and finally hit solid ground and lunge out. Sometimes, though, they sull up and refuse to move, and then you have to do what you can to get them motivated again. Most of it wouldn't pass muster with the animal rights folks, but it can save the animal's life.

We crossed the water where the cows had. This is usually a sure bet, because cows won't cross where they feel it's boggy or where one of them has gotten bogged down.

We followed the fat, wide bull tracks down the Sutherland straight to the group use area, where we came upon two hikers resting on a large rock. Because of their shorts, hiking boots and very pale skin, I guessed that they weren't Arizonans.

"Have you seen a couple of bulls?" I asked.

"Bulls?" The woman's New York accent was thick. I thought she might be having trouble with mine because she repeated it. "Bulls?"

"Hereford bulls. Red and white. We're looking for them."

"Bulls." She repeated it to her male companion. "My God, bulls."

"They won't bother you if you just leave 'em alone," Sanders said reassuringly.

The woman began collecting her water bottles, camera and backpack. "We're going back to the campground."

"They really won't hurt you," I said, but to no avail. The woman was quickly trying to pull on her backpack and urging the man to do the same. I didn't have the heart to tell her that the bulls were probably in the middle of their campground.

We had just started down the trail when Sanders reined his horse around to the couple.

"And ma'am, be careful there. That cowpie"—he pointed to a coiled circle beside the trail; to the untrained eye it looked like a pile of mud—"is a rattlesnake. He's asleep right now and he won't hurt you if you just kind of sneak by quiet-like."

I stuck my gloved hand in my mouth, stifling a laugh. Of course he was right, it was a rattlesnake. But who would have thought being helpful could be so damned funny?

"Oh my God," the woman said as she collapsed back down on the boulder.

I was willing to bet her next winter vacation would be to Florida.

We finally found the delinquent pair. They were bedded down together under a big mesquite tree and didn't appear to be thrilled at having been found.

"Well, at least there's two of 'em," Sanders said with relief.

I knew what he meant. Pushing one bull is a chore. It's much easier if he's in a herd of cows; then he'll go along with them. But a bull alone can be a real pain. He won't want to move very fast, or at all, and he'll hide out every chance he gets under trees and in the brush. It's always a mystery to me how something that big can hide so quickly and disappear. And we're not talking hardwood forest here—I mean, this is the desert.

We checked their ear tags. The numbers on the tag of the larger bull were faded beyond recognition. For this rea-·son, we'd taken to calling him Faded H. His partner in crime was 100.

It's funny how you get to know your cattle. While we don't have names for every one of them, we recognize a lot of them as individuals and give them descriptive tags. Kind of like Apache names. Where an Apache might call a bald man "boss with a high forehead," we'd refer to a cow as the "cow with one horn," or "that cow who lost her calf last spring."

We'd pushed Faded H and 100 before. For some reason this pair seemed more interested in hanging out around people than dating any of the cows. One thing was for sure, they weren't doing the job they'd been hired to do by terrorizing campers.

"Looks like we got the San Francisco boys," Sanders offered as we rousted them out from under the mesquite and started pushing them north.

It was a slow trip as the bulls plodded across the desert, lumbering through prickly pear cactus, with only an occasional foray under a mesquite tree. These bulls are around people often, and they have been worked enough so they aren't flighty. They also aren't mean. Their degree of resentment at being pushed during nap time was restricted to an occasional swish of the tail and a dirty look over one massive shoulder.

As we rode, neither Sanders nor I said much. I was racking my brain, still going over my suspects. Who'd been up there? I suspect Sanders was wondering the same thing. Sometimes it's just easier keeping your thoughts to yourself.

While the Williamsons were the only ones I knew who had a four-wheel drive vehicle, it could have been anyone on my list. Even if I could prove who was up there, so what? There was no law against taking a Sunday drive, even if it was on a ridge above *my* ranch. I was thankful, though, that Sanders had seen someone up there, because it strengthened my resolve to watch my back.

After pushing the bulls to the Sutherland tanks, we parted company. It was past five by the time I rode Dream through the back pasture gate.

Juan was in the garden planting when I rode in.

"Tomatoes." He held a pony pack. "Curly had them."

"Great. We're gambling again, huh?" I yelled.

He laughed. It was a debate we had every year. When to plant the tomatoes. Some people believe in that stupid

Pennsylvanian groundhog as a seasonal prophet. Out here, the mesquite trees are the real harbingers of spring and the last frost. Horses can shed, cottonwoods can leaf out, snakes can emerge from hibernation and fruit trees blossom, but spring has not arrived until the mesquite trees start putting out their fragile green leaves. So far they hadn't, so Juan's tomatoes might be in trouble. It was a roll of the dice.

After unsaddling Dream, I watched him roll in the sand.

I had just opened the screened porch door when Mrs. Fierce and Blue came charging around the corner, slow to discover my arrival home. They wiggled and squirmed as though I'd been gone a week.

Thinking about the mesa intruder, I retrieved my .38 from the bedroom drawer and walked through the house checking things out. Nothing had been disturbed and there was no evidence of anyone having been in my home. Thus assured, I returned the gun to its resting place and checked my messages.

The little red blinking light on the answering machine was going crazy, marching all the way across the track and then repeating its journey. Today was a red-letter message day. As I pushed the play button, I cringed, remembering the "Found" ad I'd placed.

I could just hear the classified ad lady—"Nah nah nah-nah nah, I told you so"—as message after message described a lost dog. There was a poodle, a cocker spaniel and a rottweiler. Two German shepherds. A black and tan hound and a husky. And that's just the identifiable breeds. All of these calls were punctuated by hang-up calls. And a call from Bea saying she'd be out at eight the next morning to make tamales. Plus one from Charley Bell apologizing that he hadn't uncovered anything yet on David Eberlein.

The roasts I'd put on the counter in the morning had thawed, so I began seasoning them. As I rummaged in the pantry for the pressure cooker, I decided that I didn't want to give anyone false hope—I needed to return the calls of the lost dogs' owners.

My first call was to the paper to cancel the ad. I had to save my answering machine. I'm going through one a year as it is, and with today's volume we were now on an accelerated aging program.

I cradled the phone between my neck and shoulder, always a mistake to do for very long once you're past forty, and fumbled with the pressure cooker. I squished in two of the roasts and went to work peeling carrots and making salsa, all the while talking to a string of disappointed pet owners. I was beginning to feel guilty for placing the ad.

I interrupted my frantic kitchen work to do chores, and then came back in and hit it again. The kitchen was a mess. While I'm relatively neat and tidy in most areas of my life, I've always viewed the kitchen with the same degree of affection that Frankenstein must have felt for his lab. This is my labor-a-tory, and I can trash it in no time flat. Empty crushed tomato cans, strewn flakes of peeled carrots stuck to the counters, cilantro stems dropped on the floor, onion tailings piled in the sink, along with scraps of green peppers, meat slime on the salt and pepper shakers—the desecration was endless. And this was nothing compared to what Bea and I would do the next morning.

After listening to the pressure cooker groan for an hour, I pulled it off the burner, let it cool, and retrieved the now shredded meat, replacing it with the remaining roasts.

My lab experiments were punctuated by telephone calls with still more reports of lost dogs. Although my neck and shoulder were starting to cramp, I tried to listen patiently to each caller and explain that Blue was not their dog.

It was after ten by the time I got the kitchen put back together. The calls had finally stopped. I kicked off my shoes and curled up under an afghan in the La-Z-Boy. The living room curtains were open, and I thought about closing them, but I had just settled in so I reached for *Bridges* instead. I'd barely read two pages when the phone rang yet again.

When I answered it there was no greeting. I repeated my hello and a man with a muffled voice began speaking.

"I lost my dog," he said.

"Yes."

"You found a dog."

"Yes. What kind of dog did you lose?"

He went into great detail about the male dog he had lost. Before I could stop him, he was giving me explicit details of the dog's anatomy and sexual preferences. I hung up.

I'd forgotten that about classified ads. Years ago, I'd advertised some hound puppies and gotten a slew of obscene phone calls. Then there was the gold bracelet I lost. Stupidly I advertised that one, too. That ad had uncovered a pervert who was willing to trade out for the bracelet.

I put the answering machine on and went back to my book. As I settled back into the chair, I was haunted again by the tracks up on the mesa and the hanging doll.

Jumping up, I closed the living room curtains and retrieved my .38 from the bedroom drawer.

I suddenly felt very vulnerable.

24

BY ELEVEN THE NEXT MORNING THE KITCHEN WAS A WRECK. THE counters were covered with all of the ingredients for fine tamale making—a huge crock filled with water to soak the corn husks, stainless steel bowls loaded with the beef and red chile sauce, smaller ones hosting slivers of carrots, an old pottery bowl holding the masa—and then there were the olives.

The olives were always a bone of contention between Bea and me. Like all tamale makers, we had our preferences. They were always green, but the argument centered on pits or no pits. Bea was of the Pit School, and she had her stash of intact green olives off to her side of the kitchen. I don't like eating things that you have to spit out of your mouth. It seems so counterproductive. So the pitted warriors were on my side.

We'd already decided that to keep the tamales from commingling would be too difficult, especially since they were all going to San Carlos for Alicia Cassadore's Changing Woman ceremony. So the tamale eaters would just have to guess.

As I worked, I kept thinking about the stupid rag doll and the tracks up on the mesa. Someone was definitely trying to get to me. The doll was an overt threat, but the mesa? I could only assume that the spy was, in fact, casing my place. I didn't like that idea at all. Twice during the night I'd awakened, thinking I'd heard noises. I'd grabbed my glasses and gun and walked through the house, checking every door and window to make sure they were locked and unviolated.

It was safe to say that my mind wasn't on tamale making at all. I'd been dropping things on the floor since I'd started cooking and had nicked my finger with a knife. But I'd promised the tamales long before Buffy and Charlene had hired me. And just being jumpy was no reason to renege on my pledge to the Cassadore family.

We'd been working all morning assembling our little treasures, grabbing a soaked corn husk, spreading it with masa, slapping the meat and sauce on top, sprinkling it with carrots and polishing it off with the aforementioned green olives. Then it was a quick folding and crimping of the corn husk.

Two huge tiered steamers, each with three shelves that held nine tamales rattled away on the stove. After the tamales had steamed for an hour, we retrieved them and lined them up on the tile counters, letting them cool before putting them in Ziploc bags for freezing.

Tamale making is always a big production. We do the same thing at Christmastime, only then we pull in more people and make a really big deal out of it. It's a lot of fun. Everyone shares the labor, and the results, and it works out very well, depending upon how many margaritas we consume while we are in production.

Today, though, our assembly line put General Motors to shame. And people laugh at the title Domestic Engineer. Most of our success was due to the fact that we hadn't started on the margaritas yet.

I was gratified to see plastic bags taking over the freezer. From past tribal celebrations, I knew that maybe as many as three hundred people would attend Alicia's ceremony.

Bea and I chatted all morning. She wanted to know how I was doing with my investigation and I brought her up to date.

"There's a lot of pressure on this one," she offered.

"Why does that not surprise me?"

"It's amazing how many forty-year-old women are running scared. The station's even been getting calls."

"From women who went to Javelina?" I asked.

"A few. Most just want to know what's going on and why we aren't giving it more coverage. Then we explain that it's not getting coverage because we aren't getting anything."

We both knew the statistics. The longer this dragged on, the less likely the police were to solve it. My chances were probably slimmer.

By early afternoon we had started on the frosty drinks.

"I forgot to tell you, I'm coming to your reunion," Bea said.

"How're you going to do that? You're not in our class."

"Got a hot date." She grinned.

"Imagine that," I said. Bea and I are opposites in that regard. While I do get asked out, guys hit on her all the time. In fact, she can hardly go to the grocery store without being recognized. She dates a lot and goes out with practically anyone who asks her. She says she hates to hurt anyone's feelings. I think she sees herself as the Florence Nightingale of the Dr. Ruth set, sans sex—well, sometimes sans sex. I consider myself more discriminating. "Who's the pigeon this time?"

"Peter Langley."

"The real estate guy?"

"Uh-huh."

I hadn't known Peter Langley in high school. Now I saw a lot of him. He was always in the newspaper in those multimillion-dollar producer ads put out by his real estate company.

"I thought he was married," I said suspiciously.

"Getting divorced," Bea assured me. "Anyway, I think it should be fun. And this reunion has added suspense."

"Oh yeah. It'll be a real game of Clue."

"So, is everyone coming?"

I knew she was talking about the cheerleaders. "As far as I know. Mina's in Japan and won't be over. The other three that are left are all coming," I said. "I've been meaning to ask you, did you ever know a guy by the name of David Eberlein?"

Bea grabbed one of her olives, popped it in her mouth and shook her head. "Why?"

"Just curious. He was Connie O'Hara's boyfriend and wrote some mushy stuff in her yearbook. I think she had some kind of a relationship with him right up until she was murdered, and he hasn't turned up. No one seems to know who he is."

"I met some guy she was with a few years ago in the Tucson Mall. I don't remember his name, but he acted like he was her boyfriend."

"But you don't know who he was?"

"Trade, I can't remember which video I rented last night."

I love it when Bea affirms my own shortcomings. Baby Boomerism is wonderful. If getting old isn't exactly blissful, at least it's not lonely.

"Well, if it comes to you, let me know."

She assured me she would, and we continued with the tamales.

By four o'clock I thought I would never look at another tamale or drink another margarita again.

Bea helped me clean up our mess and finally left around six. I fed the horses, collected eggs and fixed a cheese omelet and salad for dinner. The aftereffects of the margaritas were beginning to hit, so I drank a lot of water, settled into my chair and read until shortly before ten. I turned on the television, hoping to catch the news, but fell asleep and didn't wake up again until the middle of sports. Finally, I stumbled off to bed, exhausted.

When I got to the stage stop the next morning, I should have known right away that something was amiss. While my intuition was nagging me, my mind was racing with the minutiae of the case and I wasn't listening. By the time I was really aware of danger, I was inside, and the surprise was revealed.

I pulled my .38 and studied my trashed office. The roll-top desk had been plundered, all of its contents dumped onto the floor. Three of the desk drawers had been thrown down on the cement and the dovetail joints of at least one of them looked busted. All of the cubbyholes were empty and a carpet of paper littered the polished concrete. The desk chair and wastebasket were overturned in the middle of it all. With relief I noticed the Navajo rugs were still there, so the vandal was apparently not a thief.

Two of the filing drawers had been similarly violated, and empty file folders were tossed upside down on the floor, their contents now in a pile with the rest of the papers. That alone sent my blood pressure skyrocketing, since I knew it would take hours of work just to sort through the papers and get everything back in place.

This case was not only dangerous, but now was hitting too close to home. Two days ago someone had been watching the ranch, and today my office had been burglarized. This was nothing at all like catching an errant husband en flagrante delicto.

Briefly I thought of leaving. But my office was small, and I could see everything except for the bathroom. That door was shut, which was the way I always left it, and I took that as a hopeful sign. I knew I had to check it out before I settled in to clean up the mess.

With gun raised, I snatched open the bathroom door. Empty.

Carefully I crossed the room on my way to make a pot of coffee, which I quickly realized was impossible, since the burglar had emptied the can in a pile on the floor. I wondered what he had been looking for that would be small enough to fit in a coffee can. As I picked up the can I was assaulted with an awful odor.

And then it hit me.

Duke, the Williamsons' dog.

The smell was the same as the nasty one that I had smelled in Charlene's kitchen when Binky Williamson had hovered over me. One of the Williamsons had been here and I was guessing it was Binky.

And his quest? It could only be the film that I had taken

of him and Buffy at the L & L. Unless he was the murderer. Then it could be everything I had on the case, which wasn't much. My main contribution so far seemed to be a list with a few names circled and checked with red pen.

One of the casement windows was wide open. I walked over to it and looked out. The screen had been pried loose and was lying on the desert floor. Next to it was a faint footprint. Other than looking about the same size as the one up on the mesa, the sole of the shoe was different; this one had no lettering on the heel. I took little comfort in this, thinking of the several pairs of tennis shoes in my own closet. Had Binky been watching my house to plan this little surprise?

I went outside and retrieved my camera from Priscilla before going around to the window. I studied the print for a long time. Finally, I stashed my gun in the waistband of my Levi's and began shooting photographs.

That done, I went back inside and called Sanders. On matters of such importance as tracks, a second opinion is always valid.

He answered on the third ring.

"Sorry to bother you," I began, "but there's been a break-in at the stage stop."

"You okay?"

"Yeah, I'm fine." Now that I knew that no one was there, I was no longer frightened, just pissed. I suppose it was good that the burglar was gone, for in my state of mind, I would have happily shot him without a thought to the consequences.

"Are you packing?" Sanders asked.

I looked at the gun clutched in my hand. "Oh yeah."

"I'm on my way," he said. His voice seemed to drop an octave from its already low range, and I knew that he was concerned. I also knew he'd waste no time coming to my rescue.

Rummaging through the mess on the floor, I retrieved a Twinkie from the coffee grounds and unwrapped it. Maybe it would cheer me up, I thought, as I broke it in two. As I stared at the white goo, I quickly discovered I was too up-set to eat. I righted the wastebasket, dropped the uneaten Twinkie into it, then laughed at the futility of my actions.

After clearing a path from the front door to the desk and setting the desk chair upright again, I quickly began shuffling through the piles of papers and putting my office back in order.

"Howdy Trade." Sanders's steady voice came through the front door before he did. He should have been born an Apache. He always appears without warning. "Looks like you could use some help."

He walked over to the open window and looked out.

"I'd like to send this son-of-a-bitch hoppin' straight over the coals of hell," he offered.

And that's about all he said.

Suddenly it occurred to me that I never even thought about calling the police.

25

THAT NIGHT I DROVE MYSELF TO DAGGETT'S FOR OUR EN-
counter. I was definitely thinking of it as just another interview, not a date. While he'd offered to come out to the
ranch to pick me up, I still wanted some distance between
him and myself. My intuition was telling me that there was
no way I wanted this guy to know where I lived, although I
had no problem with taking another look at his house, especially the stuff in that curio case.

He's said seven, and it was just after when I rang the
bell. He opened the door immediately.

As I stepped into the living room, I could smell something wonderful cooking.

"You look great." Daggett gave my hand a quick
squeeze. "Let me take your coat."

I handed over the black suede jacket. I was wearing
Levi's, my best pair that had actually gone to the cleaners
and were now sporting a center crease down each leg. My
black turtleneck did a pretty good job of showing him that I
was a girl. I wanted his guard down. If he was thinking of
me as a date, why disillusion him?

I followed him to a niche off the living room that held
his wet bar.

"Drink?"

I didn't spot any Canadian Club, but there was a bottle of VO, so I settled for that.

"It's just us, I hope you don't mind," he said.

"That's fine. Smells good."

"Beef bourguignonne. One of the few things I know how to make."

We sat across from each other on two matched love seats that overlooked his patio. His outside lights were on, and in spite of the cool weather, water trickled down a stone fountain. A tall block wall sealed the yard in privacy and oversized oleanders that had probably been planted when the house was first built stood as sentinels outside the wall. Overall the effect was one of seclusion and privacy, even though Daggett's home was in the heart of the city.

We made small talk for a few minutes while I warmed him up, hoping to eventually steer the conversation to the Song Dog case. I talked about the tamale making with Beatrice and then on to the Changing Women ceremony set for the following weekend.

"You know, in high school I didn't realize that you were Indian," he said.

While I thought his approach a bit insensitive, I ignored it. "My grandmother is actually a full Apache."

"That's where you get that great hair and those beautiful cheekbones."

"Right." I laughed. He was hitting on me. Maybe his guard *was* down. "But I think I have to give my father some credit for the curls." It was going to be a long night.

"Do you go to the reservation often?"

"Not as much as I should. I'm really looking forward to this weekend." Suddenly I realized that it was true. I hadn't been up to San Carlos for a couple of months, and I needed to get away. I was becoming obsessed with my murder case, and the change of scenery would do me good.

I was eager to detour the conversation away from me, but it was too early to drift into the Song Dogs.

"This is a beautiful room," I said inanely. I wasn't really lying. Although it had a cold feeling and there was not a comfortable chair for reading anywhere, it was beautiful. Like something out of *Architectural Digest*. I was willing to bet that the Berber carpeting had never seen real dog vomit.

"Thank you. I had a good decorator. I think he did a great job. Will you excuse me? I need to check on things in the kitchen."

As if on cue the doorbell rang.

Daggett crossed the room to answer it, and a tall good-looking kid stepped into the living room.

"Hey! I'm sorry man, I didn't know you had company."

"No problem, Andy. Come on in, there's someone I'd like you to meet."

While I was clearly older than the newcomer, I can never remember all that stuff Mrs. Wright taught me back in dance class about who's supposed to stand for whom or how the introductions are supposed to be made, so I stood. The young man came over and extended his hand. "Andy Presley," he said.

I introduced myself and stared at Andy. There was something very familiar about him, although I was sure I'd never met him before.

"Want a drink?" Daggett asked. I wondered if he meant alcohol, because the kid sure didn't look legal.

"No thanks. Listen, I'm really sorry to butt in like this. I didn't know you had company." He emphasized the word *company* and gave Daggett a knowing look. Daggett, to his credit, ignored the leer. "Some guys and I want to go to the lake this weekend, and I just stopped by to see if I could borrow the truck."

"I trust you'll be more careful this time."

"Hey man, I'm sorry about that."

Daggett turned to me. "Andy thinks my truck is indestructible."

My antennae were up. Interesting. Daggett had a truck? Maybe a truck that could get into remote places, like where Valerie Higgins's body was found? That piece of information was worth the price of dinner. Finally, I'd gotten some worthwhile information from him.

"We're just going to the lake this time," Andy continued. "No cross-country, I promise."

Four-wheel drive, no less. I wondered if there was any way to discreetly get into the garage and check it out.

Daggett laughed. "All right. It's yours."

Before Andy left, they made arrangements for him to pick up Daggett's truck on Friday. As he was leaving, Andy turned back. "Mom says you're due for dinner."

"I'll call," Daggett promised, as he pushed Andy out the door.

He turned back to me. "Now I really do have to tend to the kitchen."

"I'll join you," I said, scooping up my almost empty drink from the glass coffee table.

He noticed it immediately, and we made a detour back to the bar, where he refilled it, conceding to my request to make it light.

The kitchen was all sleek and modern, one of those space-age things where everything is white and polished stainless with granite countertops and invisible cabinet openings. The kind of place where if you didn't know where to look, you'd have trouble finding things—like the refrigerator. I finally spotted it hanging down from the ceiling in three sections.

"Laundry room?" I pointed to a door in the far wall, wondering if it led to the garage.

"Pantry."

A covered teakettle on the commercial range was the only evidence that the kitchen had been recently used, much less for dinner preparation.

While I was too suspicious of Daggett to ever consider him a serious prospect, his kitchen was yet another clue that things wouldn't work out between us. While he was gorgeous and rich and reasonably good company, he was also too damned neat. That in itself was more of a burden than I wanted to bear. This was not the kind of man who would drop an ice cube on the floor and put it back in his drink. But this was an investigation, not the rehearsal dinner.

"What can I do to help?"

Daggett nodded toward the refrigerator. "The salads can come out."

I found them in the second door. The refrigerator was also spotless. The neck of the catsup bottle looked clean, and I couldn't see any of that white mold that grows on strawberries. He was incredibly structured and neat. I wondered how comfortable he would be chopping off someone's arms.

I put the salads—escarole with hearts of palm—on the counter while Daggett dished the bourguignonne and pencil-thin asparagus onto plain Wedgwood plates.

"If you can take these and the bread, I'll get the salad and wine."

I grabbed the dinner plates and tried reaching for the bread, but decided that was a mistake. One of my regrets has always been that I never worked as a waitress. I think it would be handy to be able to line up all those plates on the inside of my arm with total confidence that none of them would crash. Remembering past disasters, and having a reasonably high regard for fine china, I left the bread on the counter.

The sleek dining room clearly fit the rest of the house. The table was long and mirrored and flanked with rounded chrome chairs with black leather seats. Another Taber-Borcherdt painting adorned one wall and a crystal nautilus shell rested on a hanging granite buffet. A beveled mirror covered the wall above the shelf. I caught Daggett's reflection in the mirror. His face was very intense, like he was concentrating fiercely on something. Was he that wrapped up in dinner? Or was he caught up in something else?

The table was set for two, directly across from one another on the width, a more intimate arrangement than if we had played "mother" and "father" against the length. He was really pushing the date element here.

Daggett pulled out my chair and then poured the wine.

The beef was delicious. While beef bourguignonne is hard to screw up, he had done a superlative job with it. The asparagus was also perfect, al dente, and the salad had a tangy lemon dressing.

"God, it's nice to take a break from that damned case," I said, leading him easily into the conversation I wanted to have.

"Oh right. Is there anything new on that?"

I told him about the break-in at the office and how I had spent the day cleaning things up, hoping to get him to volunteer his whereabouts.

His interest was apparent as he leaned across the table. "Do you have any idea who did it?"

I cut the tips off two more asparagus, trying to be as dainty as possible. If I'd been eating alone at home I would have picked them up with my fingers.

"No," I lied. Daggett's four-wheel drive vehicle had quickly propelled him to a position near the top of my list. But there was no need to give him any clue to his ascension.

"Do you think the killer broke into your office?"

I thought about the pictures I'd taken of Binky and Buffy. "I don't know," I said truthfully.

"God, you don't think they'll break into your home, do you?" He was staring at me. A little too intently, I thought.

I shrugged. "I have guns and know how to use them." I wanted him to know that there would be some danger involved should anyone try something that foolish.

"Andy seems like a nice boy." I abruptly changed the subject, wanting to know more about his relationship with the kid, especially since his own was dead. I also wanted to know more about the truck.

"Andy?" He said absently. "Yes, he's a nice boy. He hasn't been a problem at all. We've been lucky."

"We've?"

"Oh God, I'm sorry. He's my nephew, my sister's kid. I should have told you." He laughed, a deep baritonal rumble that was not unpleasant. "You must have been wondering what was going on."

"Oh no." Another lie. Remembering Shannon Early from the yearbook, I said, "Oh right, you've got a sister, don't you?"

"Shannon, she was behind us in school."

"But she doesn't have a truck." I gave him my best smile.

He laughed. "No, and unfortunately I do."

"Do you do a lot of four-wheeling?"

"Not much. Say, how about some more asparagus?"

I didn't press the truck issue. Instead, I started playing with the stupid anthuriums sitting between us. They're so saucy with those yellow things sticking out. I was sure the sensual flowers were not an accident.

"It looks like you're healing." I nodded to his arm, where the falcon had got him.

"That was nothing," he said. "Unfortunately, it happens more often than I'd like."

"I'd love to see your bird. Is he here?" I asked, hoping I wasn't being too obvious.

He shook his head. "I keep him at a friend's house out in the country, a fellow falconer. There are other birds, and I think he's happier there."

Right. No bird shit to clean up, I thought. *If* there was a bird. Or maybe it was just a great creative cover story for the scratches Valerie gave him as he murdered her.

Dinner went well, for the most part. The food was great and Daggett was gorgeous. He still had that wonderful spark in his eyes, but I was beginning to notice that it came and went at will and was not a steady thing. That bothered me. I like steady sparks, not the intermittent kind.

My instincts had already checked in, and I knew there was something wrong with Daggett Early. Maybe it was just eccentricity, but on the other hand, maybe he was my killer. My pride was also slightly wounded, as he didn't seem quite as mesmerized by me as the first time we'd met.

Dessert was a fresh fruit tart. I was relieved when Daggett told me it had come from Reay's Ranch Market. A baking falconer would have been just too much.

Over espresso I tried to focus our conversation on the reunion.

"Will you go with me?" he asked abruptly.

He caught me by surprise.

"What?"

"Will you go with me to the reunion?"

From the moment that little tilting sailboat had arrived

in my mail, I'd been thinking about the reunion. Frankly, I wasn't looking forward to it. Much less going to it by myself.

"Sure." It would be much easier to keep an eye on Daggett if we were together. But maybe he was thinking the same about me.

"Would you like a Courvoisier or something?" was his response. He still wasn't showing much enthusiasm. Maybe I'd been wrong about his viewing this evening as a date. Had he also been interviewing me?

"No." I glanced at my watch. "I really need to be going. It's been a long day."

As we rose from the table and walked back through the living room, I remembered one of the reasons I'd come. Gravitating toward the lit case that held the shrunken head, I realized that it had been replaced. So had the glass sculptures and the ivory carving. Cards and a pair of antique-looking eyeglasses had been added to the gambler's shelf. The antique hideout gun was still there.

"A traveling exhibit?" I asked.

"I change it now and then. It keeps my interest that way. Otherwise I just get used to everything and take it for granted."

"I'm ready for the new tour," I said, studying the shelves.

The top one held a pearl choker with an antique gold clasp. The pearls were draped in a circle and in the center was a gold cameo locket with the portrait of a woman.

"My mother's," Daggett explained, pointing to the jewelry. Then, "Shakespeare, seventeenth century," as he indicated a small leatherbound book on the next shelf.

His sudden animation told me he was really into his collection. It was the most enthusiastic he'd been all evening.

"Gambler's cards?" I pointed to the old deck.

"Right. They're called readers." He opened the case and handed me the pair of blue-tinted spectacles. I put them on, and as he fanned out the cards, I could now make out a pattern of marks on the backs.

"Phosphorescent ink."

I handed him the glasses and asked the question that had been bothering me since my first visit to his house.

"Isn't it dangerous keeping a loaded gun in an unlocked case?"

He put the cards and glasses back.

"No. There aren't any little kids coming over. I live alone. Why not? Besides, I'm not even sure those old bullets would fire."

I didn't think it was worth the risk, having a loaded gun out in the open, but it was his choice.

"And that?" I pointed to the bottom shelf, the one that had originally held the shrunken head. The gruesome thing had been replaced with something black and shriveled that resembled a dried prune.

"It's an ear."

"An ear. What kind of an ear?"

To my horror he opened the cabinet and took out the glass box. He took the dome cover off and held it under my face. Thankfully, there wasn't a strong odor, only a faint musty one. "A very old ear. It's human."

I couldn't control the shudder that went through me, and I was sorry I'd walked over to the damned cabinet. What kind of a sicko was he?

"This is from the mid-1800s," he explained, without noticing my unease. "It came from a necklace. The Mexican government hired scalp hunters to eradicate the Indians," he said, now watching me intently. "This ear came off a scalp hunter's necklace. They cut off ears and kept them as souvenirs, after taking the scalps for ransom."

My stomach roiled, and I was sure I was about to throw up. I didn't need to ask which tribe of Indians; I'd grown up hearing all of it. The effect his treasure had on me did not go unnoticed. Had he hoped for my reaction?

"Oh God, I'm sorry," Daggett said too late, his hand grabbing my elbow. "Forgive me, I forgot."

But it was much too late for that. I just wanted out of that house, away from him and especially away from the ear, and all the evil it represented.

"I have to go," I said, surprised at how strong my voice sounded.

He walked me to Priscilla, and I thanked him for the evening. It was now halfhearted and he knew it.

"Trade, I'm really sorry about that. Please forgive me."

"It's all right," I said, faking a sincerity I certainly didn't feel. "But it's late and I have to go." I was relieved when he didn't try to kiss me goodnight.

Every time I thought about the ear on the drive home, I tried to force it from my mind. But it kept coming back to haunt me. Had he done that on purpose? But why? Anyone with a penchant for such dreadful things could surely consider murder.

I wrestled with how to get out of my reunion date with Daggett. I'd find a way to keep a close eye on him without making myself sick.

As I turned into the Vaca Grande, I realized something else was bothering me.

The cameo locket.

26

WHEN I GOT HOME BOTH BLUE AND MRS. FIERCE WERE WAITING in the driveway. Somehow I found that comforting.

Blue had now been elevated to resident dog status, so I let her in the house with Mrs. Fierce. I spent a few nervous minutes wondering if she was housebroken as she sniffed at everything, but luckily she seemed to be taking her new surroundings in stride.

I fixed a cup of Sleepy Time tea, hoping it would give me a good night's sleep. That awful shriveled ear kept intruding on my peace of mind. Usually I'm pretty good about sending negative thoughts on their way, but tonight I was having trouble.

I also felt pretty damned stupid about trusting Daggett, even for a minute. It's funny how Mommyisms come back to haunt you when you've done something foolish. The one I was remembering now was, "Pretty is as pretty does."

And Daggett didn't. He was a hunk with a counterfeit spark, and although he was rich and a good cook, his choice in knickknacks was for the birds. Behind his slick salesman veneer was a penchant for horrible shriveled dead things. I thought about giving him two checkmarks to go along with his red circle—one each for the ear and the shrunken head. The circles and checkmarks were a pretty ineffectual way to run an investigation, but the truth of it was just about everyone in this case was a suspect and I needed some way to prioritize the bad guys.

Daggett had been a geek in high school, but why would he want to kill the cheerleaders? Had he asked them out on dates and they'd all turned him down? So had he killed them to avenge slights he'd endured in high school? I laughed at myself. I was beginning to sound like a horror novel—*Bad Seed Arises from Depths to Slaughter Town*.

By the time I finally went to bed, I decided Daggett deserved his red checks. My list was getting colorful. Two red checkmarks for Bobette, Binky, Charlene and Daggett. While the list was balanced, mentally I was favoring my male suspects, which caused me to doubt myself. Why was I buying into the killer being a man? I needed to rethink the women.

Charlene had that great knife collection and knew how to use them. At least on cucumbers. And Bobette had slept with her husband. And his cucumber. Buffy was currently sleeping with him. Jealousy could be a powerful motivator. But what about the other dead cheerleaders? What motivation would she have had for killing them? Then I remembered that Elaine Vargas and Binky had been a hot number in high school. Bingo. Three of the four dead women had slept with the Rodeo King. But why would Charlene care after so many years? And was that enough of a motive to kill them?

Buffy, in spite of her assurances to the contrary, might want Charlene out of the picture so she could have Binky to herself. A revolting thought. But why would she kill all the others? To cover up a planned murder of Charlene? Had she had problems with the other cheerleaders?

Bobette, on the other hand, by her own admission was out to exorcise demons. And she had stabbed poor Maude Evans through the heart. But if she was out to settle old scores, why tell me? And why use a method of killing that would easily implicate her, since she'd done time for it? Were the Song Dogs her demons?

I had another fitful night. This time I was pursued by scalp hunters, eager to take my long black hair. Even if it was curly, I wanted to keep it. I awakened around two in a cold sweat and shrunk under my covers until my heart stopped thundering.

When I finally realized that I was home, safe in my own bed in the twentieth century, I was able to get up and walk through the house checking all the doors and windows to ensure that they were locked. I didn't care for my new habit, but only then was I able to go back to bed and sleep.

It was after seven by the time I woke Thursday morning, very late for me. When I went out past the pond, I found myself studying the ground for strange tracks, but there were none.

Juan was there with the Weed Eater, annihilating more of the green invaders. He did a good job, but there was just too much to be done by one person. I fired up the old Toro gas lawn mower and attacked some of the wild mustard and skunk cabbage.

It was a tricky business, but the lawn mower and I were old friends. I talk to her, encourage her to keep on running. It's sort of like the ants, talking to machines. It works. Must be the Apache in me. If we talk to trees and rocks and feel they have souls, why not lawn mowers?

Miss Toro and I did a fine job, clearing the areas around the chicken coop and pond, which made me feel much better about the snake situation.

Some of the trees around the pond needed trimming, so I ran the long orange extension cord out from the screened porch and hooked up the twelve-inch chain saw.

That is power.

It isn't as impressive as a heavy gas model, but that baby will still cut and slice through thick limbs in nothing flat. And I used to think an electric carving knife was slick!

It felt really good to work. I'd been shaken by the tracks up on the mesa, the break-in at the stage stop and my visit to Daggett's last night. Now, working with the chain saw, I felt as though I was somehow coming back into balance.

The work was going well as limbs gathered around my feet and the hum of the saw resonated in my ears. I looked up to see Juan in a pantomime before me. I shut down the saw.

"I'm going up to Darrell's for some more line," he pointed to the Weed Eater. "Do you need anything?"

"No thanks," I yelled.

He gave me the thumbs-up sign and walked to his ancient pickup and drove off.

I kept working on the trees, pausing only long enough to sip on a blended drink of lemonade and tea. My shirt was damp with sweat and my arms were beginning to ache from the work, but it was a good ache.

A big privet limb had just fallen when a huge shadow fell across the dirt. Startled, I whirled with the chain saw still running and faced the form who had cast it.

Binky Williamson stood before me, with Blue and Mrs. Fierce barking at him. With the noise of the chain saw, I hadn't heard their warning. I saw his Explorer parked under one of the cottonwoods.

I shut the saw down but continued holding it in front of me.

"Nice of you to call first," I said with a bravado I didn't exactly feel.

"Cut the crap, Trade."

"Excuse me? You're on my property, Binky."

He looked at the chain saw and sneered. "You think you're pretty tough, don't you?"

Clearly, Binky was not accustomed to seeing a woman on the business end of a chain saw.

"Me? Nope, I'm just trying to get some work done here, that's all. What can I do for you?"

"I want the pictures."

"Pictures?"

"Goddammit Trade, you know what I'm talking about. Those pictures you took of me and Buffy at the L & L. I want them."

"Well, they're not here. I took them in for processing, and I haven't picked them up yet."

The Rodeo King's brain went into stall while he pondered this new development.

"Well, when do you get them?"

"I guess the next time I'm in town." I neglected to tell him they were just up at the hardware store.

He shifted from one foot to the other, as though uncomfortable in his own skin.

"I can have duplicates made for you," I said sweetly.

His face flamed red, and I knew I was pushing it.

"Duplicates," he repeated furiously. "What is this shit?"

The saw was getting heavy, so I put it down. "I have to admit it was a surprise seeing you and Buffy together. It was something I never considered."

His piggish eyes narrowed. "You're not going to tell Charlene."

It was clearly not a question, more a statement of fact. A threat. I looked around for the dogs, but they were busy playing hump dog down near the chicken coop, oblivious to the little drama unfolding at the duck pond.

"No," I conceded, "I have no intention of telling her."

He took a step backward, moving out of my space. "Good."

"She's not in love with you, you know." There, I was back in it. When will I learn to shut up?

"Who?"

"Buffy."

He snorted. "What do you know?"

"I know she told me that she didn't love you."

A black look crossed his cratered face.

I kept at it. I wasn't trying to be cruel so much as trying to get the lay of the land. Buffy had told me that Binky knew the score. That was fine, if true. If it wasn't, I needed to know. It could definitely be relevant.

"Buffy would never tell you that," he said.

"Okay." I shrugged, feigning disinterest.

"We love each other." He almost sounded like he was whining. "And it's going to work out."

"But there is that matter of the little woman," I said. "It'd be a lot easier if she was out of the way."

"I'm not the one killing them, if that's what you're thinking."

We stared at each other for a long minute.

"What about Elaine Vargas? You guys were pretty hot in high school."

"I haven't seen her since senior year. You're blowing smoke, Trade."

"Well, let's see, then there's Bobette"—I began ticking them off on my fingers—"and Mina."

"You're full of shit."

"And you're not a burglar, either, are you?"

"I don't know what you're talking about."

"Really? I could smell Duke in my office." It was kind of a long shot, but I had smelled what I thought was Duke at the stage stop.

"You can't prove jack shit," he snarled.

I looked at his feet. They weren't as large as I would have guessed for a guy his size. He was wearing Nike tennis shoes. I walked closer to the pond where the ground was damp and hoped he would follow me. He did. Aggressively.

"The cops won't believe you." He got a smug look on his face. "And you better have damned good proof, or I'll sue your ass so fast it will make your head spin."

What a guy. Charlene and Buffy were *so* lucky.

"The police don't even know about it, Binky." I walked back to where I had left the chain saw. He followed me.

"What?"

I had him there. He was sure that I had called the police about the break-in.

"I never bothered calling them. What would be the use? I knew it was you."

He leaned over, close into my face, clearly pissed off. "And how does that make you feel, Trade, to know that I can come onto your ranch, get into your office anytime I want, that I can take what I want?" He looked across the pond to the house. "Even your house, Trade. You can't stop me. You're not man enough."

A pasty lump threatened to congeal in my stomach, but it was quickly overrun by my anger. This creep had a lot of nerve coming on my property threatening me with invasion and violation. "Don't count on it, Binky."

He laughed at me.

I picked up the chain saw and flipped the switch. It started right up, and I took a step toward him. "After all, a woman with a chain saw can do anything, can't she?"

I was glad I had a long extension cord. As he backed up, I stepped forward. I wasn't really *threatening* him, just evening things out a bit, and it felt good.

"Crazy bitch!" He yelled, loud enough to be heard over the buzz of the saw. I could tell by the way he said it that *woman* and *chainsaw* had never before been linked in his vocabulary.

I returned to my trimming. As far as I was concerned, our conversation was over. He apparently agreed, since he turned and walked back to his Explorer.

When his dust had disappeared from the driveway, I shut down the saw and walked back over to the edge of the pond. I didn't need verification for the office burglary, but the tracks from the shoes looked like a match. They were not the New Balance pair he had worn up on the mesa, if he'd been up there. Had he been up there today waiting for Juan to leave?

With the case back in the forefront of my mind and only eight days to the reunion, the rhythm of my yardwork was gone. I went into the house and zapped two frozen green corn tamales for lunch. I knew I was feeling stressed when I chased them with three Twinkies. I only overdose when I'm feeling real pressure.

After lunch, I saddled Dream and rode over to the office, passing Juan on the lane. I waved at him. I had kept quiet about the entire Song Dog business, because I knew that it would only worry him. At seventy-two, what was he going to do to protect me? At best he could play night watchman, and I knew that because of his age he was getting little sleep as it was.

At the stage stop, I loosened Dream's cinch. I always ride with a lightweight halter under the bridle, so after slipping the bridle off I tied him to one of the mesquite trees.

He was used to the routine, and immediately drifted off to sleep, resting his right rear leg. I threw his bridle over the saddle horn so that, if he woke up, he couldn't chew it.

Once inside, I checked my phone messages. The first was from Daggett, apologizing again for last night. He said he was leaving town this morning but would get back to me later in the week. He sure was casual about his trips, I thought. I'd spent the previous evening with him and he never mentioned traveling at all. I hoped he wasn't headed for Japan and Mina Arthur.

Just hearing his voice reminded me about the damned ear again. As far as I was concerned, Daggett Early was responsible for my nightmares. It also bothered me a lot that someone who looked so normal could be so frigging weird. Those were the kinds of guys that lured women and little children into their unmarked vans and then carved them up.

I was pretty uncomfortable about it, but decided to postpone canceling the reunion date until I was entirely sure what would be best for the case. Who knew what might come up?

At the next blink there was a message from Shiwóyé asking about the tamales and telling me she was looking forward to my visit. Apparently my cousin Top Dog, an Iron-man contender, had returned from a triathalon in Hawaii and would also be at the Changing Woman ceremony. That was good news, since I hadn't seen him in over a year. Our schedules were always at odds. Top Dog's also a firefighter, and every time I visited the reservation, he was off on a trip somewhere, either competing or fighting forest fires.

A call from Emily Rose and one from Bobette Jarcik finished the recordings.

I returned Emily Rose's first. She answered on the first ring and began talking fast.

"They've made the tires from the O'Hara scene. Yokohama Super Diggers."

I remembered Binky's new tires, but Emily Rose beat me to it.

"They checked the shop where the Williamsons got their new tires. Same brand, Yokohama Super Diggers. Same as their old tires. They've checked the stats and the tires have the right aspect ratio and fit the photographs of the tread. We need the actual tires to fit the personality."

"Personality?"

"The rock bruises and cuts, the wear and tear. These things are like fingerprints, they're that exact, *if* you've got the tire."

Judging from the sound of the thousands of tires out at the airport, that was a big *if*. At least I wasn't imagining things. The tires on the mesa were similar to the photographs Emily Rose had given me.

"Well, they drove to Luna."

"We know. They also traded in a spare and a patched tire. That Williamson guy told the dealer they'd had two blowouts on the trip."

"Shit."

"Exactly. Those people had a pretty good reason to get new tires."

"How many people replace their tires with the exact same kind?" I asked.

"More than you'd think." She sighed.

"So we're back to square one?"

"Not exactly. They've assigned a few deputies to the tire disposal yard. They're sorting through to try and find them."

"Needle in a haystack?"

"Oh, there are only a couple of million tires down there. It's gonna take some time."

"Well, at least they're looking at Binky Williamson. Have you heard anything on the dog at the shrine?"

"Not much. A few of the locals reported that it may have been a stray down there on Fourth Avenue. The legs were inside the trash bin."

That surprised me a little. If there was any connection to Valerie Higgins's murder, the legs should have been found at another location. Even a copycat would have made the parallel.

"They don't think there's a connection," I said, as much to myself as to Emily Rose.

"They're not saying."

I briefly told her about the break-in and Binky's visit.

After hanging up, I tried Bobette. The number that she left was a bed and breakfast down near the University Hospital. The woman who answered the phone told me that Bobette was at the hospital with her grandmother and promised she would give her guest my message.

As I left the stage stop, the slamming door startled Dream. I had to check the cattle, so I put his bridle back on, tightened his cinch and we headed north, through the cedar breaks and into the National Forest. I counted eight new calves, thankfully all healthy. After riding in a big circle, I rode back down through the Cottonwoods, a part of the Sutherland Creek that is shaded in the summer by ancient cottonwood trees.

As I came out of the forest I stopped at the North Tanks and gave Dream a drink.

The Brahmas were there, licking the large white salt blocks that we periodically left for them. Although it was after three, it was still warm and sunny and the calves were stretched out napping.

In the distance I could hear a bull bellowing.

I watched one of the old Hereford bulls listen to the traveler's roar. He cocked his massive head and snorted in response.

The visitor let out another bellow, and the resident bull began pawing the ground furiously, throwing huge clumps of dirt over his powerful shoulders.

His quiet fury was accompanied only by low snorts.

But the newcomer was not so shy. He was screaming his head off as he got nearer to the group.

I sat on Dream and listened as the roars got closer and the visible bull threw more and more dirt over his shoulders. The ground beneath him was torn up, with divots of grass scattered far and wide.

I decided to stay for the impending fight.

The newcomer approached the herd. He was smaller than the old Hereford, and the cows ignored him as he walked across the pasture.

And what did Mr. Dust Storm do after all of his fierce prelude?

He walked away, leaving the cows to the noisy carpetbagger.

As I rode home, I got to thinking about the bulls. And threats. And fights. And that led me to thinking again about Binky, and I wondered if he was like the old Hereford, all bluff.

Time would tell.

27

FRIDAY MORNING I PACKED PRISCILLA WITH THE TAMALES, MY clothes, the .38, Mrs. Fierce and Blue. Since Shiwóyé didn't mind dogs in the house, and since the Changing Woman activities would be outside, I knew the girls would be welcome.

I headed up Highway 77 through Winkelman and Globe, turning east on 70, until I finally hit the San Carlos Reservation. As I drove, I kept thinking about the week I had left until the reunion. I was sure the killer would be there next week, but which one was it? Seven days . . . not much time.

The land stretched out in front of me, and I thought about my ancestors. The Apache people were "removed" by the federal government in 1872 and have remained here ever since. The old San Carlos Reservation is now buried under the lake of the same name, a victim of the Coolidge Dam, which was completed in 1928.

Spread over close to two million acres, the San Carlos Reservation today covers long flat stretches next to running water as well as tall mountain peaks. The Gila and San Carlos Rivers gently snake through the land. The San Carlos is frequently dry, although it's been known to flood, jump its banks and create havoc for those living along the waterway. A broad variety of plants thrive here, from the pines, spruce, aspen and oak of the high mountain ranges, down to the lowland prickly pear and ocotillo. Deer, bear, javelina, elk and turkey are plentiful, with hunting fees a major part of the tribe's revenues.

This may sound like heaven on earth, but what is not readily apparent is the poverty, the high rates of unemployment, alcoholism and diabetes, and the undereducation of the Apache youth. Dreams die early here as the ancient culture struggles to survive in a modern world.

On the way into town I passed a sign warning, DON'T LET ALCOHOL BE YOUR LAST TASTE OF LIFE. The town of San Carlos was as bleak as I remembered it. I had to remind myself that it was the people that made San Carlos a special place.

Shiwóyé's house, a very modest slump block home, the result of some governmental project to provide adequate housing to the rural poor, was at the west end of town. White cotton sheets hanging on the clothesline flapped in the breeze as I drove into the yard, scattering my grandmother's chickens, who had been pecking at invisible bugs in the dirt.

The door was open even though it looked like Shiwóyé wasn't home. I don't remember a time when any of her doors were ever locked.

The wonderful smell of fresh bread greeted me, but other than that everything was exactly as I had left it. Floor-to-ceiling bookshelves, holding an eclectic collection of fiction ranging from Jane Austen to Mark Twain, plus an equal amount of broad nonfiction, filled one wall. An overstuffed sofa in danger of losing its innards sat in front of the wood-burning stove, the source of heat for the tiny house. Looking at the couch, I could almost see the indentation of my grandmother's body resting there, for she spent many winter evenings huddled before the stove, reading. A long, scarred plank table made years ago by Top Dog in wood shop rested in front of the sofa, its surface piled high with assorted magazines and periodicals. A basket next to the sofa held still more.

In a corner cabinet was an old black and white television, hooked up to a satellite dish outside. An elderly cedar rocker and a down-filled easy chair with broad arms completed the picture. In this house, there were plenty of places to sit and read.

I brought in the box with the tamales and put them in Shiwóyé's ancient refrigerator, then threw my suitcase in the spare bedroom and went outside to check on Blue and Mrs. Fierce. They had made two new friends, brown long-legged dogs typical of San Carlos and poor towns everywhere. The four of them were happily engaged in a game of doggy tag.

I felt the cotton sheets hanging in the yard. They were dry, so I took them off the line and buried my face in them, reveling in the clean smell of sun and heat. I took the sheets inside and was folding them when Shiwóyé walked in.

Without a word she crossed the living room floor and gave me a strong hug.

"Hello Shiwóyé," I said.

We gravitated to the kitchen where she poured us each a tall glass of iced tea. We folded the sheets and then she put them away. She returned to the kitchen and watered the herbs sitting on her window sill.

At least ten minutes had passed, and my grandmother had not said a word. I knew it was up to me to begin, so I started to speak endlessly about La Cienega and the ranch. I went on nonstop for twenty minutes. Since my visit was going to be short, I wanted to get this over with right away.

Still Shiwóyé did not speak, which is not that unusual for an Apache. She was following a custom handed down for generations.

I began to prattle on about my case.

Finally she spoke.

"Shiwóyé, shichoo."

The dam had broken. Through my prattling, I had given her time to analyze whether or not my exposure to the outside world had changed me. While it would have been considered rude for Shiwóyé to interrogate me, by my own words I had enabled her to see if my attitudes or views had altered. It was a ritual we went through every time I returned, just like countless Apache parents welcoming their children home from boarding school.

"Pretty Horses, are you hungry?" she asked.

She called me by my Apache name, one she had given me when I was a small child. It's an Apache custom for grandparents to give their grandchildren names. Usually they wait until the child grows and develops, so that the Apache name reflects a characteristic of the child. When I was three, I was fascinated by horses and the words "pretty horses" often fell from my lips; now they came from hers, reclaiming me.

My grandmother never changed. I suppose she was shrinking, but she had never been over five feet tall anyway, and I didn't notice any further diminution. Her face was the color of weathered leather, like an old treasure map with the cracks and crevices giving it history and character. Not once in my life had I ever heard Shiwóyé speak of makeup or sunscreen or moisturizers. Yet she was the most beautiful woman I knew.

We spent the next hour getting caught up.

Years ago, when Shiwóyé was a young girl, the elders took her up to Mount Turnbull. Left alone, she had to find her way back. She passed this test, and others, and is now a powerful medicine woman in San Carlos.

Apache medicine women are specialists. My grandmother is known for her social medicine; she's like a psychiatrist. A lot of what she does these days is counseling for drug and alcohol problems.

The noted Apache warrior Cochise was also a social medicine man.

When I told Shiwóyé about the Song Dogs she didn't seem surprised. Unlike Uncle C, if she was concerned about my ability to handle this case, she showed no sign of it. I've always treasured her confidence in me.

"Gordon Jarcik," she mused.

"Bobette?" I asked, pretty sure I had never discussed her with my grandmother.

"Her grandfather." Roots were important to Shiwóyé

and she always remembered them. "He taught with Duncan in Window Rock. Jarcik was a man with a bad temper." Interesting. My grandfather had taught with Bobette's grandfather. I wondered how hereditary bad tempers could be.

Briefly I told her about Bobette's murder conviction and her time in prison.

"Sometimes it is difficult to change crops in a field," she said.

It was all she would offer in warning me about Bobette.

As the sun set in the west we ate beef stew and dill bread she had baked that morning. We did the dishes, huddled around the stove talking, and finally went to bed about ten.

Although I was up early the next morning, Shiwóyé beat me to it. The coffee was brewing as I walked into the kitchen and she was reheating my tamales in an old Westinghouse roaster.

"Top Dog's eager to see you," my grandmother began.

"Where is he?"

"He's camping out in the meadow where Alicia's ceremony will be. He knows you are coming."

I ate breakfast quickly and then drove out.

There were a few people on the south end of the field as I pulled in. The San Carlos River was along the far side. A wood fire had been started to ward off the morning chill, and people unloaded boxes of food from two pickups and an old station wagon.

I recognized a few members of the Cassadore clan and stopped to pay my respects. When I asked about Top Dog, they pointed to the far end of the grassy clearing.

The morning dew lapped my Levi's as I walked across the meadow. It was another flawless San Carlos day, without a single cloud to mar the bright lapis of the clear Arizona sky.

As I got closer, I waved and Top Dog returned the greeting before looking up to the heavens. Overhead on the wind currents, a hawk circled.

I gathered my cousin in my arms. His body was hard and strong from all of his training. He was also a member of the elite Apache firefighting crew, the Geronimo Hotshots, and he was wearing a long-sleeved black T-shirt with an image of Geronimo incorporated into the logo over his heart. The pager on his belt would alert him to report for duty if his crew received a call. He sported a heavy gauntleted leather glove on his left hand.

"Welcome home," he said.

"It's good to be here. How'd you do in Canada?"

"All right. That stuff's for the young guys."

"What's with this?" I tapped the leather glove.

"Something new. I'm trying to teach that bird to hunt when I tell her to." He pointed to the sky where the hawk was still circling.

"You're into falconry?" I couldn't believe it. First Daggett and now my own cousin. What were the odds of that happening? Was this a new trend?

"Whatever." He shrugged. "It beats the cockfights."

I knew what he was talking about. In southern Arizona some of the Hispanic men were into cockfighting—a brutal sport that usually left at least one of the contenders dead.

"This is better, more spiritual," he said.

The hawk was drifting lower in the sky, but suddenly his wings started pounding furiously against the wind, and his strong wingbeats returned him to the higher altitudes.

Just as he regained his height he closed his wings and dove straight down in a power dive.

"God, look at that." I said.

We watched as the hawk swooped onto another smaller bird and snatched it in his talons. The lesser bird never knew what happened as the hawk took him.

Top Dog signaled with his glove, and on cue the hawk returned to him and settled on his gloved fist, dropping the dead bird at his feet.

"Hand me that rufter, will you?" He pointed to a soft leather hood on the ground. I handed it to him, and he smoothed it over the bird's head.

"I'm impressed," I said. "What makes them do that?"

"Instinct and training. They're killers by instinct. All we have to do is train them to kill selectively. And return to us."

"That's all." I laughed.

"Well, there's some patience involved. And time."

It made me think of the patience the Song Dog killer must have had to wait so many years before killing his prey. Assuming it was someone from their past—so far, I could find no other connection.

"How long have you been into this?"

"About six months. I'd like to start training them—this one's my first."

The hawk seemed quite content to settle on my cousin's hand.

"He's a beautiful bird," I said.

"She. Most of the trained ones are."

"Female?"

"Right. They're larger and bolder. Make better hunters."

A question was nagging me, but I couldn't figure out what it was.

"I just interviewed a guy for a case who's into falconry. In Tucson." Unlike with Uncle C, I never have trouble talking to Top Dog about my cases. Like my grandmother, he's always respected my work.

"Maybe I know him. What's his name?"

I gave it to him, but in spite of falconry being such a small sport in Arizona, it rang no bells with him.

"But hey, I'm just getting my feet wet here." It was an apology for not knowing Daggett.

"I'd say you're doing a bit better than he is. His bird gave him some pretty nasty scratches on his arms."

Top Dog gave me a surprised look. "What is he, a dumb shit or something? Hasn't he heard of gloves?"

"Maybe not," I said, wondering myself about Daggett.

I spent an hour or so talking with Top Dog, and then returned to Shiwóyé's where I picked up the tamales. Before leaving for the celebration, my grandmother had wrapped them in tinfoil and insulated them with layers of newspaper.

When I returned to the clearing, there were at least fifty people there. After a few minutes the ceremony began, as six old Apache men tapped a primal beat with their gnarled hands against drums more ancient than they. As they played, a medicine man, Posit Lupe, began to chant a song of creation. Thirty such prayerlike songs would comprise the ceremony.

Alicia Cassadore, on the verge of her womanhood, was resplendent in a white, yellow and green dress with a tunic of heavy white beaded buckskin over it. The Apaches were never wasteful, and when the white man came, we made good use of their discarded tin cans. The legacies of those ancient endeavors were now visible in the small tin cones jangling from the buckskin. Alicia's straight, waist-length hair, black and shiny, was caught by the sun and reminded me of a raven's coat.

I found Top Dog, Beatrice, Uncle C, Josie, Shiwóyé and the rest of our clan, and I sat with them as we watched the ceremony begin.

Alicia began dancing with a ceremonial cane decorated with eagle feathers that represented long life, as well as the crutch she would someday need as an old woman. She danced in place on a piece of buckskin, tapping it with the cane in time to the beat of the drums.

"Alone she dances," Shiwóyé said aloud, identifying this part of the ceremony to no one in particular.

As Alicia knelt on the buckskin, her godmother, Darlene Peaches, stood by. Both Darlene and Alicia had a long day ahead. During the six-hour ceremony Darlene would be the young woman's mentor.

As the singing began, Alicia raised her hands shoulder level and stared into the sun as she swayed from side to side.

The medicine man sang on, giving a litany of Apache history and belief. Gloria Steinem and that bunch would probably not be happy here—the men always do the public speaking and prayers.

Darlene Peaches was now carrying the ceremonial cane, and she and Alicia danced together.

I love coming to these ceremonies because they are an affirmation of my heritage. The spiritual messages and prayers were performed in essentially the same way a hundred years ago. Then, however, the ceremonies ran for four days. Now, economics are such that they usually only last one. Food has to be provided for all the guests, the ceremony participants are given gifts, and, of course, the medicine man has to be paid.

After a few more songs, we all moved to a ceremonial site nestled among the low hills close to the river. More and more Apaches came as the ceremony continued through the morning. It looked as though there were many more than the three hundred people I had expected.

"They're doing it," Bea whispered, drawing closer to me. And I knew what she was talking about; it was one of my favorite parts of the ceremony.

Posit Lupe walked up to Alicia and took her cane. Walking a short distance east of the buckskin, he planted it in the earth. As she began the first of the four chants, Alicia ran to the cane, circled it and then returned to the piece of buckskin. Then Darlene Peaches followed the same path. Lupe then picked up the cane and handed it to Alicia, who finished the chant dancing in place. The medicine man took the cane again and turned to a spot farther out than the last one and planted it in the soil. Again Alicia ran around it, followed by her godmother. This was repeated for the four chants, each trip signifying a stage of an Apache woman's life: infancy, adolescence, womanhood and finally old age.

The drums kept beating as she finished the fourth chant. Posit Lupe continued chanting, not unlike a rabbinical cantor, his voice as hard and strong as when he had begun earlier in the morning. If you're going to be a medicine man, it helps to have a good set of lungs. Lupe's invocation was calling for the power of Changing Woman to enter Alicia's body. Years ago, this power would stay in the body for four days. Now, I suppose, Changing Woman knows the rules have changed and probably only hangs around for six hours.

Just before noon, we all lined up and dipped our hands into a basket of yellow corn pollen. We each sprinkled the pollen over Alicia and blessed her. She was now Changing Woman, and some participants stopped to ask for a healing touch from her.

Throughout the day my thoughts kept coming back to

the dead cheerleaders. At one time we had all been as young and innocent as the twelve-year-old Alicia. Would death stalk her, as it had the dead Song Dogs, before she needed to walk with a cane?

The festivities ran through the afternoon, and around five we finally began feasting. I sat with my relatives and dug in. Unfortunately, I got one of Beatrice's tamales with the stoned olives.

"I love coming back," I volunteered to no one in particular.

"You might think about moving back permanently," Top Dog offered in response. It was an old argument we had; he couldn't understand why any of us chose to live anywhere other than the reservation. Right after high school my cousin had joined the Marines to see the world. He had come home three years later with a general discharge, his body and mind in ruins from heroin addiction. It had been a long struggle back, but once returned to the living, he now refused to live anywhere other than San Carlos.

Uncle C's voice was cold. "Don't count on that. Trade's hit the big time down in Tucson. She has her first murder case."

I knew he was trying to provoke me, so I said nothing. I didn't want to get into it with him and lying to him here, at Alicia's ceremony, seemed terribly inappropriate.

"Did Bea tell you she's coming to the reunion?" I asked, determined to throw his concern and his attention elsewhere.

Aunt Josie rolled her eyes and went back to fill her plate.

"And unless I change my mind, I'm gong with Daggett Early." I watched Uncle C closely, but there was no indication that this news meant anything to him. Maybe Daggett wasn't as high on his list as he was on mine. But then he probably hadn't seen Daggett's glass case, either.

I remembered something else I'd wanted to ask him about. "How thoroughly did you all check out Deborah Chamberlain's death?"

I gave Bea a knowing glance, and she picked up on my cue.

"Who's that?" Bea asked.

"The broad that died of food poisoning out in L.A.," Uncle C said. "We're just treating it as a coincidence. Two million people die from it every year; she just happened to be one of them. Couple of other people got sick at the same function. She was just unlucky."

"Charlene Williamson has a son that lives with his father in L.A.," I volunteered. The Williamsons would have a good reason to go back and forth to California. Had Binky dropped in on Deborah and somehow killed her and made it look accidental?

"TV movie stuff," my uncle commented dryly, eager to drop the subject.

But Bea was primed. "So, who did it?" she asked.

Uncle C was used to her questions and found it easier to talk to his daughter than his niece. He directed his answer to her. "That Williamson woman could have killed the others. We've had a few expert opinions now on the stabbings. Turns out from the cuts that either a man or a woman could have done them."

I blushed, thinking of my own stupidity. While Bobette had been an early suspect, it was only recently that I had considered the other women in that role.

"It sure keeps that Jarcik woman in the race," he said as he stood and stretched. "There's something about her that really bothers me."

I waited, but he said nothing more.

"Have you heard from her?" I risked the question.

"Nope." He patted his belly.

I kept quiet. There was no use muddying the waters.

"Dad, what about that dog thing?" Bea asked.

"We got the three kids who did it," Uncle C said, "They were locals, nothing to do with it." With that he headed back to the food.

The dancing and partying were now in full swing, so of course I stayed too late.

I slept in the next morning, until seven, and then went on Shiwóyé's rounds with her. We visited a few teenagers and a man who had just gotten out of the state prison at Florence. Dusk found us eating beef stew again for supper. We watched the ten o'clock news and went to bed.

The next morning I put the dogs in the truck and drove home. Somewhere around Globe, I remembered the question I'd had for Top Dog. He'd said that most falconers preferred female birds. They were more aggressive and made better hunters. Yet when I'd had dinner with Daggett, I was pretty sure that he had referred to his bird as "he." I jotted down a note to myself to check it out.

As I thought about the females being better hunters, a vision of Bobette Jarcik stabbing Maude Evans intruded on my mind.

Try as I might, I couldn't shake it.

28

When I reached La Cienega I could see a plume of thick black smoke south of Tucson. Judging from the dark cloud, something impressive must have been on fire. I fumbled with the radio dial, finally lighting on my favorite country music station, but the reception was so lousy I couldn't make anything out, much less a breaking news story.

It was early afternoon when I drove into the ranch. Mrs. Fierce and Blue were slobbering against Priscilla's windows all the way down the lane. I guess they were happy to be home, too.

Juan was in the garden when I drove in. I thought about honking the horn, but I knew that he wouldn't hear it any more than he had heard Priscilla's throaty diesel engine.

I pulled around back, and he finally looked up and waved.

"¿Bien viaje, mijita?"

"Great trip. How's everything here?"

"Bien. Do you need help with the truck?"

When I thanked him and declined his offer, he returned to hoeing weeds.

I threw my overnight case on the kitchen floor and was greeted with my diligent, ever-blinking answering machine. In spite of my being gone on a long weekend there were only four messages. If I'm out for just two hours I'm bound to get at least ten calls. One of the four was from Daggett Early, one from Mrs. O'Hara—a hang up, and finally what sounded like a frantic call from Bobette Jarcik, who was staying at the La Posada B & B. I scribbled their initials down on a scrap piece of paper to remind me to return their calls.

Because Bobette sounded so upset, I tried her first. But the number she left rang and rang.

I was hoping that I'd get Daggett's machine, but no such luck. He answered his phone on the third ring.

"Trade, I'm glad you called me back. I was afraid you were really mad at me."

"I'm not mad." Even as I said it, it came out leaden. I wasn't angry, just sure that I didn't want to get any more involved with him than I had to in order to resolve my case. As a potential love interest, he was totally creepy. At this point I couldn't care less if he saw me with no makeup, dirty hair and unshaved legs.

"Listen, I wanted to ask you if you'd go with me to The Cork Friday night."

I'd forgotten about that. Saturday night, the big reunion night with dinner and dancing at the Tanque Verde Guest Ranch, had been my focus. The Cork, a local restaurant and watering hole, was the Friday night prelude to all of the reunion festivities.

I thought about it. I needed to check everyone out on Friday as well as Saturday to carry out some sort of surveillance, so it probably wouldn't do any harm to go with him. I was sure that Saturday night would be my last night with him anyway. Since I'd decided I wasn't interested in him, it had taken the pressure off me. I could probably get by with the squirt bottle and not have to iron anything either night.

"All right," I knew I sounded reluctant at best.

We made plans to meet, and hung up quickly. I had a bad feeling, but did my best to ignore it. Not a good sign.

The next call I made was to Mrs. O'Hara. She had looked through Connie's things from Denver and had found something missing.

"What is it, Mrs. O'Hara?"

"An opal ring I gave her for her thirtieth birthday. It was a family piece, a pretty thing, a big bluish opal in the middle surrounded by smaller stones."

It rang no bells with me. "Could she have been wearing it when . . ." I paused, thinking of a way to be gentle.

"Maybe. She didn't wear it very often. But I've looked and looked and can't find it anywhere. I just thought it might mean something. I've also talked to the police and they've double-checked their inventory."

The way she said *inventory* made me think that Mrs. O'Hara was a tough cookie. She would survive the death of her only child.

"Thanks for calling, Mrs. O'Hara. If I find out anything, I'll let you know."

I went out and checked on the horses and chickens and ducks. Everyone was fine. I really wanted to get into my grubbies and do some more trimming, but instead I decided to go into Tucson and try to track down Bobette.

La Posada in Tucson is one of those long rambling adobes in the center of town. It was a holdover, an old-time ranch house from a time when the now urban core had been a working cattle ranch. The main house of La Posada hosted several guests rooms, and there were four guest houses, or bungalows, as the brochures called them, at the back of the property. The grounds were in perfect order—the rye grass mowed, palm trees trimmed, petunias in full spring glory.

I stopped in at the office in the main house and lied to the innkeeper. I told her Bobette was my cousin, and that she'd called me to come down to see her, but had forgotten to give me her room number.

"I'll buzz her, dear," she said.

I gave her my most innocent smile. "Oh, I'd really like to surprise her. We haven't seen each other for a year."

The way she mulled this over told me Bobette had not shared with her the need to be discreet.

"Oh, how nice. She's in Coyote, through the patio on the right end." Her quick acquiescence left me feeling cold.

If I could fool her so easily, who else could get to Bobette? She pointed across the courtyard to a small adobe house with a mission tile roof.

The irony of a Song Dog being in Coyote bungalow was not lost on me, either.

I was walking up her pathway when I heard two people arguing. A man and a woman. I couldn't hear what they were saying, but the conversation was heated.

Damn! I'd left the .38 locked in the truck. Who'd figure you'd need a gun in the middle of Tucson on a bright spring day?

I veered off the path and went around the side of the bungalow. A tall adobe wall separated the property from the back alley. Just nosing past the edge of the wall was a tan truck. I recognized it.

The Williamsons' Explorer.

The redwood gate in the wall was open and I stepped through it. The argument was louder now. I heard a sharp crack and ran for the sliding door.

Binky and Bobette were inside, her hand clutching her cheek. I banged on the glass, and they both turned to me.

"Trade, thank God you're here!" Bobette opened the door.

As Binky sneered at both of us, I noticed that his eyes were red and wild. He wiped his nose on his shirtsleeve as he shouldered his way past me and out of the house. Within seconds he was gone.

"What's going on?" I asked.

Bobette dropped her hand from her face and I could see Binky's print there.

"He hit you?"

She held a tea towel under the open faucet and then pressed it to her flaming cheek.

"Some things never change," she said dully. Her eyes were puffy and her face blotched—I knew she'd been crying. "You want some lemonade?"

I didn't—I wanted answers—but I said yes.

"Let's sit outside," she suggested. "At least it's pretty there."

We sat in old-fashioned redwood furniture among the blooming pansies, geraniums and petunias, watching the tiny hummingbirds feed on red sugar water.

"How'd he find you?"

"I screwed up, that's all." She sipped her lemonade. "I thought I could handle things and I was wrong."

I waited.

"I just wanted to clear the air between us. I knew he'd be at the reunion and I thought if I could get to him before that it would be easier on me. That maybe I could get him on my side." She laughed coarsely. "Boy, was I wrong."

"Is he trying to hit on you again?"

She shrugged. "I guess. He's messed up. He wasn't exactly an angel in high school, either. Oh, I know everyone thinks he was, but it isn't true. We did a lot of drugs together, a lot of drugs."

"But you're clean now."

She nodded. "But he isn't."

I wasn't surprised. Binky cheated on his wife and beat women. Drug abuse would only elevate him to King of the Donkey Dicks in my opinion.

"He's still into it. That was the argument. He wanted me to do a couple of lines with him."

My mind raced.

Cocaine habit.

Big bucks.

Charlene's money.

Buffy's fortune.

"Why'd he hit you?"

"I told him he needed an intervention. That I was going to tell his wife."

"Jesus, Bobette." Where were her brains? If Binky was the one knocking off the Song Dogs, she'd probably just achieved priority status with her threat.

"I just really wanted him to leave me alone." She looked like a tired raccoon, with the kohl smeared around her watery eyes.

"You could get a restraining order," I offered.

She shook her head. "When I go back to Luna I'll never see him again. I just have to get through this weekend."

I felt terrible for her. With all of her problems, past and present, going to the reunion was probably a bad idea. Still, it was her choice.

"You know, I've thought a lot about it, and I think Binky sent me that reunion notice," she said sadly.

"How'd he know where to find you?"

She shrugged. "Charlene knew about my grandmother years ago. Maybe she remembered about Luna."

Could Charlene have sent her the notice? How much sense did that make? Maybe it did if Charlene knew that Bobette had slept with Binky in high school. But I had no evidence that she did and why would she even care after all of these years? Besides, she'd gone with him to visit Bobette in Luna. I kept the possibility to myself.

"Some people look back on high school as the high point of their lives," she said wistfully.

"I guess so," I answered, having no idea what she was talking about. High school had not been one of my favorite times. In fact, if not for this being my first murder case, I never would have even considered attending the stupid reunion.

"Have you checked in with the police?" I asked.

She assured me she had and we talked awhile longer about her grandmother, who was recuperating from her open-heart surgery, and then I left, but not before asking her to call me if she needed anything.

She walked me to the front of La Posada and waved as I backed out the drive. She looked like a painted china doll, fluttering her thin white arms, and I found myself wondering if she could have managed to kill anyone.

29

Before I left the house Tuesday morning, a call came in from Emily Rose.

"More bad news, Trade," she began. "Did you hear about the fire?"

I remembered the thick black smoke I had seen on my way home the day before.

"The tire disposal area started burning yesterday," she continued. "They've still got the water cannons on it, but a lot of the tires are gone."

Shit. Now maybe the Williamsons' tires would never be traced.

"Was it arson?" I asked.

"Who knows? They're checking it out."

I thanked her and hung up. Tire profiles, moulages, what difference did it make if the tires had burned? The Williamsons' Explorer would never be tied in with the murders after this. Although it was a crappy development, there wasn't a thing I could do about it, so I went back to retracing my steps.

I talked to Jerry Higgins and Mrs. O'Hara again and went over old ground with both of them. Unfortunately neither had anything new to add, although both told me the police had also been back to talk to them. Well, at least I wasn't alone.

I tried to get hold of Elaine Vargas's family in Albuquerque, but they were away on a camping trip. I left my name and phone number with their housesitter and asked for them to call me if they phoned in.

That evening I grabbed a quick dinner with Bea at a dive in the University area before heading back down to Fourth Avenue. In the evening this part of the city is reminiscent of Mexican towns. Everyone is outdoors—congregating in doorways, leaning against buildings, strolling the streets. One of the most popular areas for panhandling, that doesn't seem to bother the revelers. While it's relatively safe, I was taking no chances and had my holstered gun on my hip. With a long, bulky cotton sweater over it, no one could tell by looking that I was packing.

A huge moose of a man was guarding the door at Justin's, carding people. I slid by him unaccosted, dammit, and found myself in a meat market. The bar had obviously hit it big with the downtown crowd, as I waded past a lot of white collar types and women in work clothes and heels.

The charmer that had been tending bar the day I came in was nowhere in sight. I ordered a C.C. and water and asked the barmaid if she remembered Valerie Higgins. She gave me one of those you've-got-to-be-kidding looks and disappeared for another half hour.

Somehow in the pandemonium I was able to nail down the bartender and another barmaid. Neither remembered Valerie, or anything special about the night in question, and both had already been interrogated by the police.

I debated the merits of a second drink and decided against it. I had a headache, probably from the secondhand smoke and bustling humanity, and was eager to go home and get to bed.

Outside there were a couple of transients smoking and sitting against Justin's wall. The younger of the two held a fat black and white cat wearing a knitted sweater. I dropped a dollar bill in the tin cup next to the cat.

"Great cat," I said.

"He's a good one." The man grinned, showing me the gaps in his smile. Wisps of dirty red hair peeked out of a brown wool cap that covered his ears, and red tracks ran through what should have been the whites of his eyes.

His neighbor clutched a crumpled, grease-stained paper bag against his considerable belly. He was wearing a T-shirt that read, LEARN FROM YOUR PARENTS' MISTAKES—USE BIRTH CONTROL. The message was easy to read, since the shirt was many sizes too small, stretched tight across his chest, and ended several inches above the top of his pants. A broad band of black flesh poked out below the shirt, making a convenient shelf for the bag. It didn't take much imagination to figure out where my contribution was going.

"Are you here a lot?" I asked the Cat Man.

I took his burp as an affirmative and handed him Valerie's photo.

"Ever seen this woman?"

He looked the picture over and then rubbed the top of his cat's head with it. I couldn't tell if he was just scratching his pet or looking to her psychic abilities.

"Sure, lots of times."

My triumph was short-lived.

"All in the last couple of weeks." He laughed as though he had told a wildly successful joke.

Bag Man took the picture from Cat Man.

"Cops." His eyes looked like they'd been sanded and he sounded like he had a wad of tobacco in his mouth. I couldn't tell if he was really drunk or just talked that way.

"You didn't see her that night?" I asked.

Cat Man looked in his cup. I added two more dollars. He immediately pulled them out and jammed them in the pocket of his filthy jeans.

"Nope."

I'd been had again.

"I hope it was good for you," I said as I left.

I was almost to Priscilla when I heard a running shuffle behind me. I turned to see Bag Man shortening the distance between us. Shit! This was the last place Valerie had been seen. Could she have been murdered by one of these homeless guys? I reached under my sweater and unsnapped the holster so I could easily get at the .38.

"Wait!" he yelled, and I noticed that he was dragging one leg. That made me feel better. He was fat, probably out of shape, and limping. Hell, I could probably outrun him if I had to.

I waited for him with my right hand hidden under the sweater, resting on the butt of my gun.

He was gasping for air as I mentally diagnosed an advanced case of emphysema.

"I seen her," he squawked.

"You saw the woman in the photograph that night?"

He came up to the truck and stood close enough to me that I could smell the cheap whiskey he had consumed and could easily tell that a shower hadn't been in his immediate past.

He took a long swig on the bag.

"Yeah, I seen her." His words were garbled. "But not where you think."

"Yeah, where?"

"I was pissin' out back." He pointed in the direction of Justin's. "Get in trouble if we do it on the streets, so I seen her when I was bleedin' my lizard. Out back."

"Was she alone?"

He gave me a blank stare. I remembered and fumbled in my jeans, handing him a five. At least he was telling me a good story.

"Nah, she had some dude with her."

"You're sure it was a man?"

Bag Man spit a long stream of something brown and yucky on the pavement. "Probably, but I couldn't tell for sure. Was pissin' on the wall when they walked out the back door."

"Didn't you see the color of his hair?"

He scratched his scrotum in reply.

"How tall was he?"

He pulled on the bag again. "Bigger'n me."

I looked at him. He was only an inch or so taller than I am, so I put him around five-eight. Bigger than him could still be well under six feet.

"Where'd they go?"

"Doan know." His speech was getting more unintelligible.

"Did you tell the police?"

"Shit, lady, why'd I do that? Hassle, hassle."

Bag Man had given me what he could. And I'd given him the last of my money. Perhaps sensing that, he shuffled off. Briefly I considered telling Uncle C about the guy, but I doubted that even sober the transient would remember anything else. Besides, if I told my uncle about the panhandler, he'd know I was still working the case.

If Bag Man was telling the truth, Valerie had left Justin's with someone. Could that someone have mutilated her and killed her? But who? Some man? Maybe. But Bag Man hadn't been sure at all about that.

It was after ten by the time I got home. I collapsed in bed, exhausted, and struggled with sleep as I tried to push Bag Man's muddled memories out of my troubled head.

It was pitch-black when I was jolted awake by a loud crash. Mrs. Fierce and Blue tore down the hall, barking furiously. I grabbed my glasses and fumbled in the bedside table for my gun and a flashlight, my heart pounding wildly.

I fought the desperate urge to turn on the lights. By the sounds from the dogs, something terrible was happening and I couldn't afford to draw attention to myself. My mind raced—if it was the killer, then I needed every advantage. I had no idea where the intruder was, but I did know my house, and turning on the light would only broadcast my position.

Terrified, I clutched my gun, my right index finger resting against the trigger as I tiptoed carefully down the hall to the living room, where it sounded as though the dogs were making their stand. Even though I knew the house, in the dark I couldn't see just in front of me. I tried to flatten my body against the adobe as I crept toward the living room, afraid that my thundering heart would give me away.

I knew Mrs. Fierce very well, and the sound of her snapping jaws and snarling told me that something was very, very wrong.

I peeked around the edge of the adobe wall, and although

the drapes were drawn, I could see that the center of them was billowing, as if pushed by something from behind. Shit! Was someone there? Could he see me? Was he alone?

My head snapped backward, as I checked the hall behind me, but there was no one there.

Looking again into the living room, I could barely make out a bundle on the floor and it was there that the dogs directed their energy.

My heart felt like it wanted to escape through my throat, and my hands were cold and stiff with fright. The gun and flashlight felt like lead weights.

I waited and watched the bundle.

It wasn't moving, and the dogs were calming a bit, dropping their serious barking to low-pitched growls as they moved away from the lump and sniffed about the room. Shaking, I was content to have them do the investigative work as my ears strained for strange sounds from the other parts of the house. I knew I should check everything out, but for the moment I needed to be sure that I was at least alone in the living room.

The curtains were still blowing, even though there was no reason for them to be. Was someone standing behind them? Or was he already inside?

I inched my way over to the window, holding my gun in front of me, keeping as far from the lump on the floor as possible. Shit! Could it be a bomb? Some kind of grenade? But the movement behind the curtain had me more concerned. I dropped the flashlight on the couch, screwed up my courage and with both hands bracing my gun, I crouched in a firing stance and I kicked the curtain aside.

I was met with a gaping hole in the picture window. It didn't look big enough for anyone to crawl through, but I couldn't be sure. Right now it was only filled with a slight evening breeze.

I stepped back and a sharp piece of broken glass ripped into the ball of my bare foot. As I jumped and whimpered, I nearly tripped over the bundle on the floor. Spinning around, I quickly retrieved the flashlight and turned it on the lump, and almost threw up.

A heavy rock had been thrown through the window. Roped to it was one of my beautiful Mallard drakes from the pond. Blood stained the iridescent blue-green of his sleek neck, which gaped open. And there was something else.

Around the duck's slit throat was a perfectly fashioned hangman's noose.

30

ALL DAY WEDNESDAY THE THOUGHT OF THE DEAD DUCK TOR-
tured my mind. It wasn't just the brutal act of killing it that
gnawed at me. Someone had come to the ranch, *my home,*
had caught one of the sleeping ducks, slit its throat and
stood outside my living room window without my ever
even being aware of the danger. I'd been violated. My sense
of peace and well-being at the ranch had been shattered by
my vulnerability. What was it that Binky had said? *And how
does that make you feel, Trade, to know that I can come onto your
ranch anytime I want, that I can take what I want?* Had he taken
the duck as a lesson to me? Had he actually followed
through on his threat? And if not Binky, who? I didn't think
it was a coincidence that the same knot that I'd found on the
hanging rag doll—a hangman's noose—was also used on
the Mallard. Fingerprints can't be lifted from ducks either . . .

Friday night came sooner than I would have liked. I still
had crummy feelings about Daggett and found myself
wishing I'd at least canceled the night for The Cork. Instead, pleading a tight schedule, I met him there.

The Cork is one of those venerable places that started out
years ago as a University hangout. Only back then it was
known as The Cork 'n' Cleaver. Those of us who stayed in
Tucson to go to college used to tip a few beers here, so it's

grown into a nostalgic watering hole. Anytime there's a reunion, or homecoming for old farts who were once college kids together, they go to The Cork. So it made sense to have our high school reunion here, too. Located on the east side of town, the place is rich in worn memories and cold draft beer.

The reunion committee had taken over a couple of back dining rooms and by the time I got there, the place was packed, taken over by the piggies from Javelina High. My cut foot was still hurting from the broken glass, and I hobbled through the throng. Fortunately, in spite of the crowd, there was very little cigarette smoke to contend with. Daggett immediately appeared at my side.

"Trade, I've been watching for you," he said, putting his arm around my waist possessively. I didn't like the slimy feeling it gave me. "We're back here."

The back dining room only held a few tables, but somehow Daggett had managed to find one. Buffy and the Williamsons were there, along with some stranger who appeared to be Buffy's date.

"What do you want?" Daggett was yelling close to my ear.

"Corona with lime will be fine."

I sat down next to Buffy.

"God, isn't this great?" Charlene said.

I looked at her to see if she was serious. Her fat face was flushed, and she looked like she'd already had too much to drink. I also suspected that her life had never been as exciting as it was in high school.

"I mean, when will we ever see all of these people again?" she gushed.

"Evening Mr. Muscle," I said, turning to Binky. The very sight of him made me sick as I remembered my trashed office, the dead duck and the red mark on Bobette's face. I glanced at Charlene. Her black eye had probably faded, but in any case it was hidden under thick pancake makeup. Buffy was unmarked.

Binky glared at me.

"Mr. Muscle? That's great!" Charlene laughed loudly

and punched Binky lightly on his arm. "Why didn't I think of that?" She hiccuped.

Buffy was ignoring us, involved in a whispered conversation with her date. She caught me staring at them and then made the proper introductions. "Trade, I'm sorry, this is Josh."

I offered my hand and he gave me a firm grip. It used to be that only men shook hands, but I like doing it. It not only sets you up on a par with them and says I'm here to be taken seriously, but you can also get a good feel, literally, for the person you're meeting.

"Joshua David—he was in school with us," Buffy explained.

"Happy to see you again," I lied, having no memory of ever having met him. I suspected the entire weekend would be like that—a troubling montage of strange faces with strange names, all professing to have shared a piece of history with me. Charlene could revel in it, but it was definitely not my idea of a fun time.

"Josh's living up near Battle Mountain," Buffy said. "He's working for a gold mining company."

"Well, I always liked gold," I replied lamely. I had no clue where Battle Mountain was.

Daggett returned with my beer, interrupting our scintillating exchange.

Having most of my suspects gathered in one room made my surveillance fairly easy. I eavesdropped as a constant stream of people hovered over our table and greeted some or all of us, and carefully watched the interactions. I paid particular attention to those alum who approached either Buffy or Charlene, since they were my clients. So far, it seemed like your typical reunion. As for me, the faces weaved in and out like a drunken tapestry. It was superficial at best. Like meeting an ex-husband years later. After a few minutes of "Remember when's" and "So whatever happened to so and so?" there was not much substance or common ground to explore with any of them.

Joshua David was all over Buffy Patania like a dirty shirt.

Binky's scowl grew blacker and blacker, but Charlene was so out of it, I don't think she would have noticed if he'd been banging Buffy right on the table.

"Here's Bobette!" Buffy jumped up and hugged the former cheerleader.

I stared at Binky. Trapped in the midst of his wife, his mistress and the woman he was pursuing, he did the only sensible thing.

"Gotta get more beer," he said as he jumped up from the table with a half-empty pitcher in his hand.

Charlene called to Bobette and motioned her to Binky's vacant chair.

"Oh, I don't think so," Bobette excused herself gracefully. "Thanks anyway, but I've got to be going. My grandmother's ill. I'll see you all tomorrow."

With excellent timing she left just before Binky returned with the beer. I followed her out to the parking lot.

"Are you okay?" I asked.

She looked exhausted, but nodded her head. "It's always hard having someone in the hospital."

"Nothing more on Binky?"

"No, thank God. I moved to the Plaza Hotel."

Her surroundings wouldn't be as cozy as at the bed and breakfast, but as long as she didn't tell Binky where she was staying, at least she'd be safe from him.

We said goodnight and I rejoined my table. Halfway through another Corona I looked at my watch. Eight-thirty, but I would have guessed midnight. Daggett had been up and down all night, but he never strayed out of sight. As near as I could tell, there was nothing peculiar about any of the conversations he or any of the others were having. I was just relieved that we didn't have to make small talk or discuss Indian ears.

Ron, one of the twins from the planning committee, came and sat in Daggett's empty chair and quizzed me about my work. I don't really like to talk about it, but I tried to humor him, making it sound a lot more exciting than it really is. I didn't mention anything about the Song Dogs. The way I figured it, the fewer people that knew I was interested in the cheerleader murders, the better my chances of hearing something important. So far I wasn't doing very well in that department.

Ron was asking me yet another inane question when I caught Buffy saying, "Well, I don't know, we'll have to ask Daggett."

As if on cue, Daggett reappeared beside her. "Ask Daggett what?"

"Josh has been talking about the gold mining that's going on up in Nevada. He wants me to invest in Echo Bay stock."

Ron, the annoying twin, repeated his question to me.

"We'll talk later," I said sweetly. "I'm an investor and I'd like to hear what Josh has to say."

Ron, clearly pissed, jumped up from the table, knocking over what was left of my beer.

"Great company," Josh began, and then held the floor for a solid five minutes while he extolled the virtues of Echo Bay. Finally done, he fanned out his business cards like he was dealing a game of five-card stud.

Buffy got up a few minutes later and headed for the ladies' room. I rose to follow her, and Charlene leaned over drunkenly and grabbed my arm.

"You know, he really does love her," she slurred.

"Who?" I asked.

"Binky. He really does love her." She pointed a big, puffy hand at Buffy's retreating back. "Just like a sister."

Right, I thought as I followed Buffy into the ladies' room.

It was crowded. After the requisite hugging and squealing from more reunion ladies, things settled down and we waited our turn. Buffy was two people ahead of me, and I waited patiently. When she came out, I stepped out of line.

"I've got to ask you something," I said quietly.

She was busy applying deep red lipstick to her full lips. That, coupled with her perfectly coifed blond hair, made her look like one of those perfect Texas society women. She glanced at me in the mirror and said, "Sure."

I nodded toward the door and waited until we were outside, our conversation protected now by the din of the bar.

"What was all that gold mine stuff?"

"With Josh? Oh, not much. He's involved in this company that he wants me to invest in."

"What's Daggett have to do with it?"

"I told Josh to talk to him about it, that's all."

"He's an investor, too?" I still wasn't getting it.

"He handles my money, Trade, I thought I told you that."

"Daggett Early's your investment counselor?"

"Yeah," she said, turning her cheek to receive yet another kiss from her adoring public. "Hi, Tommy, it's been a long time," she said in her throaty vamp voice as she greeted a fat, bald guy.

Jesus, it was a little late in the game for her to be telling me that. Why hadn't she put it on her bio? I'd never really considered Buffy a strong suspect, but what else had she withheld? This new information certainly elevated Daggett on my list.

We walked back to the table. I said goodbye to Daggett and got the hell out of there. The Cork wasn't giving me the answers I needed, but I knew where to get them.

It was ten after ten. Too late to call Charley Bell; his phone lines would be tied up with all of his computer stuff. But it wasn't too late to drop in on him.

I did mental gymnastics as I drove to Charley's. Shit. Why hadn't I known that Daggett Early was Buffy Patania's investment counselor? Could he have represented any of the other Song Dogs? Especially any of the dead ones? I scribbled names furiously on a Cork napkin while trying to keep the truck on the road.

The dogs started yapping before I even turned in the yard. I honked my horn and waited. Charley came out looking wide awake, and the dogs retreated under his trailer.

"Hope it's not too late," I said as I got out of Priscilla.

"Nope. I'm a night owl. Don't sleep all that well anymore, if ya want the truth. Let's get a cup of java." He turned to go inside.

"Wait. I can't stay." It felt weird to be at Charley Bell's

at night, like I was really imposing on him. "But I've got another mission if you're up to it."

He tucked his thumbs in his belt and grinned. *"Mission Impossible."*

"I hope not." I laughed and handed him the bar napkin. "But I need this stuff as soon as possible."

Charley looked at my notes. "Okey-dokey."

"Whatever you can get will be great."

I turned to get back into Priscilla, and I'd almost made it when Charley yelled, "Say Ellis, do you know why men name their things?"

"Because they don't want ninety percent of their decisions made by a total stranger," I yelled back, cocking a finger at him. "Gotcha."

I'd heard that one months ago. Sometimes it was fun to defuse Charley. Kept him on his toes.

On the way back to the ranch, I prayed that I'd struck gold with the Echo Bay deal.

31

EARLY THE NEXT MORNING I SADDLED GRAY AND HEADED OUT. My first stop was up on the mesa overlooking the Vaca Grande. I rode carefully, checking the ground for fresh tire tracks, but there were none. While I suppose I should have been relieved at that, I still felt vulnerable. I'd never had a case before that threatened my home and my animals. But then, I'd never had a murder case before, either.

As I dropped off the mesa I found a few Brahmas, off by themselves, with brand-new calves by their sides. After a day or two, they'd return to their social circles.

In the canyon, the horse flicked an ear to the south. I knew him well enough to know that meant he'd seen something. I looked over and found two coyotes, not fifty yards away in the brush, stopped in their tracks.

We sat very still as they studied me and finally decided I was no threat. They went back to their hunting; I watched them for a few more minutes before riding down to the Sutherland tanks. There was plenty of snowmelt, so there were only a few tracks around the water—a couple of birds, a coyote print and the ever-present cattle tracks.

As I loped up the Hackberry Grove road, I thought of the coyotes hunting in pairs. What if my killer was a pair? Could that be a possibility? The combinations that made sense were Charlene and Binky or Buffy and Binky, but I couldn't discount Bobette and Binky, either. What if they'd been arguing not about cocaine, but murder? Any way I looked at the pairs, there was a common denominator.

Binky.

I circled back to the ranch and trotted Gray up the lane. He was in good shape, and he barely broke a sweat. I unsaddled him, brushed him and gave him a couple of horse cookies before turning him loose in the pasture. Stopping at the chicken coop, I gathered the eggs, which I took into the house, where I threw two of them into a frying pan.

Fresh eggs are nothing at all like those anemic-looking things the grocery stores try to pawn off as eggs. These stand up proud and tall with thick, almost orange yolks, and when you've eaten one, you know you've had an Egg. Lots of country people can't eat the store-boughts, claim they're tasteless.

Anyway, I broke the yolks and flipped the eggs over hard. Topped with fresh salsa and lots of cilantro, then wrapped in a flour tortilla, they made the perfect breakfast. After eating, I showered, threw on some clean Levi's and then pulled out the Tucson telephone book. I made a few phone calls, and on my third try, I hit paydirt.

I jumped in the truck and headed for town.

Two blocks from my destination, I pulled over and got out of Priscilla. The toolbox in the bed of the truck usually saves me in any kind of crisis. Besides the hydraulic jack, flares, air compressor, halogen light, Fix-A-Flat and the myriad other automobile accessories, I keep files back there, and a few reference books. I pulled out what I needed and jumped back in the truck.

Ten minutes later my lies landed me in the living room of Evangeline Early, Daggett's mother.

A baby grand piano, covered with framed photographs, took up most of the living room. We walked by it and were almost to her kitchen when she stopped and saluted an old photograph resting on a bookcase.

I stopped.

"Aren't you going to salute it?" she asked.

"What?"

She pointed to the picture. "My husband's ship."

So, of course, I did.

The kitchen table was taken over with a paint-by-numbers set of a picnic scene. Mrs. Early had apparently been painting when I called, because some of the pigment was not yet dry. She was doing a pretty good job of staying in the lines, but I noticed that she had painted the people red and blue.

At the other end of the table was a long line of pill bottles standing at attention like toy soldiers. When I put my reading glasses on and looked closely, I could see that some of them had expired, like, five years ago.

"What magazine did you say you were with, Dorothy?" Mrs. Early interrupted my snooping.

"Tucson Lifestyle," I gushed, and handed her the December issue of the magazine, which I had fished out of the toolbox. Stapled on top was a card identifying me as Dorothy Gordon from the same periodical.

"And you're doing a story on my baby?"

"Yes, he may even make the cover." I felt like a rat, but I needed her to talk to me.

She beamed and I could see in her eyes that she was mine. She would tell me anything I wanted to know about her baby boy. Motherhood can be so dangerous to the progeny.

I pulled out a pad and pen. "Your son appears to be a very successful businessman," I began.

"Oh yes. Daggy's done quite well. He never finished college, you know, too smart for that."

"What did he do after high school?"

"Oh, he went to Rice for a year and then came home. It was difficult for him, you know, because he was very popular in high school. He'd been a big fish in a small pond, as they say, and I think the adjustment was too much for him."

I stared at her. Whatever Daggett had become was one thing, but he'd been a complete dork in high school. I'd been there to see it firsthand, but of course his mother didn't know that.

"Very popular?" I wrote on the pad.

"Then finally he got a job with A. G. Edwards. Took to it like a duck to water. Loved playing the stock market, and from there he just went up and up."

"Getting back to high school, did your son date anyone in particular?"

She gave me a funny look.

"A girl that may have influenced his life in some way," I added.

"Oh, Daggy was very private about his life back then. Still is. Of course he dated, and girls were always calling here for him. But no, he never was one to go steady. Too smart for that."

"And later?" I asked.

"He works all the time. In fact I hardly see him at all."

"It must have been very hard on him when he lost his son," I said.

"Son?" She looked at me like I was the crazy one.

"His little boy, Scottie. Didn't he die of leukemia?"

"Oh, you got your notes mixed up there, dear. Daggy doesn't have a son."

"But he was married?" I pressed.

"No, wrong again. He's always been just too busy to get involved with anyone. He always tells me he's married to his work."

My head was spinning. The lying son-of-a-bitch had really played on my sympathies that night at Anthony's. But why would he lie about being married and losing a child? Was he trying to distract me from suspecting him as the Song Dog killer? When he lies, he lies *big*. What else had he lied about? I couldn't wait to find out what Charley Bell dug up, for Daggett Early had risen on my suspect list again—more red checks.

We talked some more, and Mrs. Early verified that Daggett's grandfather had worked for Foster-Wheeler, and we both agreed that the shrunken head was a dreadful thing to have in one's house.

I thanked her for her time, and as I was walking out I stopped at the baby grand.

"What a lovely piano." I ran my hand over the sleek black wood.

"It was my mother's."

It wasn't the piano I was after. My eyes drifted over the silver-framed photographs that were clustered on top of it. I found the one I wanted and picked it up.

"Such a handsome pair," I said.

"Oh, aren't they? That's Daggy's sister Shannon and her boy Andrew. Of course that was taken a few years ago."

I put the photograph back on the piano. It was a copy of the one that Daggett had dragged out of his wallet that night at Anthony's. The people he'd passed off as his wife and child were actually his sister and nephew. Now I knew why Andy had seemed familiar to me that night at Daggett's. I'd seen him in the picture as a little boy. And now that I knew the connection, I could see the resemblance between Shannon as a mature woman and the young Shannon Early who had haunted me from the Javelina yearbook.

As I left Mrs. Early's I knew one thing.

Daggett and I would have plenty to talk about tonight. While I didn't have enough information to really nail him, there had to be some way to trap him.

I thought about it all the way home.

32

NORMALLY I DON'T WORRY TOO MUCH ABOUT WHAT I WEAR. I figure if my clothes are reasonably clean, my Levi's aren't so worn that I hang out in the rear and there aren't any real noticeable stains on the front of my shirt that I'm doing all right.

Tonight, however, was a different story.

You've got to plan your wardrobe when you're going out with a possible serial killer. Of course, I wasn't really dressing for Daggett. But since it was my high school reunion, I wanted to look as good as I could. Even to myself, I was almost ashamed to admit this vanity, but there it was.

So rummage I did. Discarding one outfit after another. I tried one on and even got as far as the front door before I dashed back and rechecked it in the mirror and decided it just wouldn't do.

I finally settled on a hand-painted turquoise silk dress with a dropped waistline that made me look thinner than I am. It was tea-length, so I knew I was safe. If most of the women were in long gowns, I'd pass, and if they showed up in short cocktail dresses, I wouldn't look too foolish. Those above-the-ankle lengths are real lifesavers.

I didn't have an evening purse large enough for the .3̶ and there was no way I was leaving my gun home ton̶ My black leather shoulder bag would have to do.

My shoes were the real problem. My foot was still bandaged from the encounter with the broken window, and most of my footwear didn't fit. I finally settled on some ancient black flats that I modified a bit by cutting the leather at the instep to give my bad foot the space it needed. They didn't do much for the dress, but at least they matched the purse.

I practiced trying to walk like a regular person for a few minutes but had to give it up, content to hobble slightly.

I was meeting Daggett at his house. He had really pressed me to let him pick me up, but I had held firm. I don't do killers at home.

It was after seven by the time I rang his bell. He opened the door immediately and looked absolutely stunning. He was not wearing a wrinkle and his black suit really set off his tan.

"Want a drink?" He was relaxed, which if he hadn't been a liar and my number-one suspect would have counted as a plus. Nothing is worse than those men who are always in a hurry. My ex-husband was like that. His idea of a driving vacation was to get from Point A to Point B as quickly as possible. But here I was on Daggett's doorstep, twenty minutes late, and he was asking me if I wanted to have a drink. There was no way I was ever going back into that house, so of course I declined.

His car, which I hadn't seen before, was a sleek black Lexus sedan. I'm lousy at cars, but I think it was probably the latest model. The interior had that wonderful new-car smell.

I knew I was going to confront Daggett with his phony wife story, but after thinking about it, I decided I'd wait and do it on the return trip home. If I kept quiet about what I knew, maybe I could get some more information out of him. Thinking about the ship I'd saluted and the painted people I'd seen at Mrs. Early's, maybe she was . Time would tell.

to the reunion, I decided to clear out some

"Didn't you tell me your bird was a male?" I asked.

"My bird?" He laughed. "Oh, that bird. Yes, yes, he's a male. Why?"

"Well, it turns out I have a cousin who's into falconry."

He kept his eyes on the road. "Really? What's his name?"

I gave it to him, but he didn't know Top Dog. "He likes hunting with females—he says they're better hunters, more aggressive."

"Well, you're a case for that." He reached over and squeezed my shoulder lightly. "But I like the bird I've got."

I flinched, feeling the heat of his hand through the thin silk dress. I didn't want the lying son-of-a-bitch anywhere near me. Quickly I changed the subject.

The parking lot at the Tanque Verde Guest Ranch was nearly full when we arrived. There were a lot of station wagons and older cars mixed in with some of the midlife male crisis machines: the Corvettes, RX-7s and even a Humvee, with a few Cadillacs, Porsches, BMWs and Mercedes sprinkled in. Most of the cars, like their owners, were the nondescript models that litter shopping malls daily.

My dress decision was validated as I saw women in pants, long gowns, and short cocktail dresses drift across the parking lot.

We made it to the registration desk quickly. After checking in, we squeezed into a room that had been set up for the bar.

It was a replay of the night before at The Cork. Dozens of people coming up and chatting about inconsequential things. Conversations springing up between adorers and adorees depending upon the status the alumni carried. I got my share of attention as the word spread that I was a private eye.

I ran into my good friend, Alva Caballero. We'd met in freshman English years ago and have been fast friends ever since. I was surprised to see her with Calvin MacKenzie, the past editor of the *Javelina Journal*. Since she and I had had lunch a month ago and she hadn't mentioned any hot romance, I figured he was just a convenient date for the evening. It made some sense, since she's the lifestyle editor for the *Arizona Daily Star*.

"Great outfit, Trade," Alva whispered with a dimpled grin, "but what's with the shoes and purse?"

"High style." I tilted my bad foot so she could admire the ripped leather.

"*Comadre,* what'd you do now?"

MacKenzie was pulling on her, wanting her to meet someone, so thankfully I didn't have to get into the story of the dead mallard duck, although I knew she'd be calling in the morning to find out what had happened.

As the cocktail hour wore on, several men began hitting on me, and I found that I didn't mind it in the least. Billy Harris was hauled away by his irate wife, and Joel Pressman was trying to convince me to ditch Daggett and have dinner with him. That part, at least, was fun.

The bar was getting crowded, and my claustrophobia kicked in. Crowded rooms will do it every time. If I get a dress caught over my head, I go into a real panic. Once I had to cut a gold bracelet off my arm with wire cutters, because the clasp was caught and I felt trapped. As for watching movies about people being buried alive, forget it.

Daggett was busy talking to someone, so I went out for some fresh air. This also gave me a chance to see what was happening outside. It certainly smelled a lot better than the bar. The grass had just been cut, and the smell of orange blossoms permeated the crisp desert air. There were a few other people outside. Some, I suspected, were renewing old liaisons.

I walked onto the grassy area toward the main dining hall, figuring I could kill a few minutes reading the notices posted on the wall. A huge eucalyptus tree shaded the north end of the porch.

I was halfway across the grass when I heard my name being called. I stopped, but no one was around. I hadn't recognized the voice, and as I searched the darkness, my heart started to gallop.

"Over here." The whisper was coming from the darkened north end of the porch, from my vantage point a black hole. While the reunion had been billed as a full moon affair, the evening was still dark.

I hesitated and then cut across the grass.

As I neared the end of the porch I could make out an old familiar shape. I sighed with relief.

"Uncle C!"

"Sssh." He patted the bench he was sitting on, signaling me to join him.

I wasn't surprised that the police were at the reunion. It was the perfect setting for the murderer to gain access to the remaining Song Dogs.

"How many are here?" I asked, sitting beside him. My eyes were adjusting to the dim light and I could now tell we were sitting on a wagon-wheel bench. Strings of dried chiles hung from the gnarled mesquite trunks that had been used as porch supports.

"Half a dozen or so. Mickey Jordan's inside. Did you see him?"

I shook my head. I'd met Mickey before. He was about my age and used to date Bea.

"Anything happening in there?" He asked.

"Yeah, a lot of people are getting drunk."

"We're watching a few of them. That Jarcik woman show up yet?"

"I haven't seen her."

"She'll show." Something in the way he said it told me that Uncle C didn't have much use for Bobette Jarcik.

I looked at my watch. It was so dark on the porch that the numbers were glowing. "I better get back."

"Be careful, baby." He sounded worried as I got up and walked back across the grass.

Daggett was waiting for me at the bar, which was nearly empty as we joined people filing along the cement path to a separate building for dinner. We funneled down the twin mesquite staircases into the Saguaro Room.

I was relieved to find none of the people from the previous night at our table. This was a new cast of characters, and I was grateful for the change. It also gave me an opportunity to check out Charlene and Buffy from afar and to check out who was also checking them out. They were three tables away from ours, toward the middle of the room, and I was watching them like a hawk.

Daggett introduced me to Troy Chavez, who was sitting with his wife across the table. Daggett and Troy had been on the track team together; now he was a veterinarian. I didn't need an introduction to Margie Chavez, a weaver, since we'd known each other since grade school.

"Hi, foxy lady." Stu Hansen leaned over and tried to kiss me on the lips, a wet gesture I barely deflected to my cheek. "My, but you're looking fine." While Stu had asked me out a lot in high school, I'd never capitulated. He'd been a wild man at Javelina; in fact, it was rumored he'd bitten off a canary's head once when he'd been drunk. He'd survived the prank, but of course the canary had not been so lucky.

Stu's squeeze was a hard-looking blonde about twenty years younger than the rest of us, with those real pointed boobs that look like they come out of a catalogue. One of her false eyelashes was crooked and it kept brushing up against her eyebrow, which was distracting if you were trying to have a conversation with her, which I wasn't.

Our table was rounded out by two empty chairs.

Daggett and I got settled and he ordered each of us another drink.

"Trade, may we join you?"

I looked up to see Bobette. She was with a tall thin man I didn't recognize.

"Sure."

She slipped into the chair next to me, disrupting the man/woman pattern. "Gordon Leach."

I shook Gordon's fishy little hand and introduced him to the rest of the table. Gordon had a strong New York accent and was pasty white, as though he'd just gotten out of prison. With Bobette's past, I guess that could have been possible.

I let everyone else carry the conversation as much as I could. Without being obvious, I tried to scan the room frequently, looking for something wrong with the picture. So far, everything seemed fine.

Halfway through my salad, Buffy and Josh sat down with Binky and Charlene. Charlene was decked out in a shiny gold caftan and loaded with jewelry. Her huge gold earrings were brushing where her collarbones should have been. The Williamsons were sitting with a couple of ex-football players and their respective dates. Then I saw Mickey Jordan walking along the outskirts of the tables, looking as though he was trying to find someone and trying not to look like a cop. Our eyes met briefly, but neither of us acknowledged the connection.

Dinner was standard fare for such events—Caesar salad, prime rib, duchess potatoes and broccoli with cheese sauce. I'd have no trouble keeping my cholesterol count up tonight.

"Daggett tells me you're a private investigator," Troy remarked, trying to pull me into their conversation. "How interesting."

"Well, it keeps me off the streets."

"Isn't it terrible about those cheerleaders being murdered? And Valerie Higgins! We were in Special Studies together," Margie Chavez chimed in. "You were a cheerleader, weren't you, Bobette?"

Bobette chased a piece of prime rib around her plate with her fork. "Yes."

"Are you afraid?" Margie never strayed too far from her loom. She'd been a ditz in grade school, and still was.

Bobette looked at me. "I'm always afraid," she answered ominously.

"Well, I'm glad they didn't do anything here for them. I guess that sounds selfish, but it would have been so grim," Margie bubbled.

"Honey, if they'd honored them, they'd have had to do something for all the guys killed in Vietnam," Troy said.

"And the ones killed in car accidents, and the suicides, not to mention those shot by jealous lovers," Stu said, winking at me as if to make a point.

"I'm going to the ladies' room," Bobette whispered,

giving me a pained look before leaving the table. She was still a strong suspect, and I debated following her. Was she really going to the rest room? I watched her walk out as Stu prattled on, without a clue as to what he had said.

"Yo Binkers." Stu stood and stopped Binky Williamson in his tracks. "What have you been up to?"

"Not much, Stuie," Binky looked nervously at the door and Bobette's retreating back. "Gotta go, know what I mean?"

"We'll catch you later." Stu slapped him on the shoulder and sat down.

With two of my three top contenders leaving the room together, there was no way I was going to stay out of it. I waited until Binky passed the threshold before I stood up and murmured some excuse. Mickey Jordan was disappearing through the exit behind Bobette and Binky.

I grabbed my purse and was right behind him.

33

OUTSIDE THE BANQUET ROOM THE CORRIDOR WAS FAIRLY EMPTY, with only a few partygoers and some serving people juggling bus trays filled with chocolate mousse. Neither Bobette Jarcik nor Binky Williamson was in sight.

I watched Mickey Jordan go into the men's room. The ladies' room was around the corner, and I headed there. Although the after-dinner coffee hadn't been served yet, the stalls were filled and two women were ahead of me in line. I didn't know the one, but the other was my cousin Bea. I fell into line behind her.

"He's cute," she said.

"Who?"

"Your date. What a hunk."

"I'll give you his number," I offered, having no intention of doing so. I knew Bobette could hear my voice, but she wasn't responding from behind any of the doors.

"You're a crazy woman. I sure don't remember him from high school, but he looks familiar."

"Well, he is in business here."

Sounds of retching were coming from one of the stalls. I made an effort not to think about what was happening in there. Instead, I stared at the shoes in the second booth. They were shiny gold high-heeled sandals. While I hadn't noticed Bobette's shoes earlier, I doubted she was the

Cinderella scooped into these slippers. They looked like boats, and Bobette wasn't that large. If her feet were that big, I would have noticed.

The mystery was solved as soon as Miss Gold Shoes walked out. It was Ingrid Johannsen, a foreign exchange student who had gone to Javelina our senior year.

Doreen Nichols came out of a stall on the opposite side and walked right to the upchuck stall. "Jennifer, are you okay?"

"No, I'm sick as a dog. It must have been the crab," came a miserable voice behind the door.

"Or the Manhattans," Doreen said. "Can I get you anything?"

"A new body," Jennifer gasped as she entered another round of you know what.

A woman I didn't know exited the handicapped area at the same time Celeste Jacobson came out of another stall. There was only one possibility left.

I was on the verge of calling out when Cookie Adams came out of the first cubicle. No Bobette. I quickly left the rest room and practically bumped into Mickey Jordan.

"Is she in there?" He asked urgently.

"No."

"She's not in the dining room, either. Neither is he." Mickey pulled out a small transmitter from his jacket pocket and spoke rapidly into it.

"They don't have her either," he said, replacing the radio in his coat as we raced up the mesquite staircase. When we reached the top, Mickey glanced across at the mezzanine, which was empty. We ran out of the building and Mickey stopped to check out the Board Room next door. As he flicked the light on we found Stacy Bohannon and Chuck Capelli going at it.

"Is anyone else in here?" Mickey said.

"What?" Chuck was trying to disengage himself.

"Nice dress," I said to Stacy, although there was really no way to tell because it was bunched up around her waist as she perched on the huge conference table. She was wrinkling the hell out of it, and I wondered if she'd brought her spray bottle. "And I just love your shoes." They were dumped on the floor and her legs were wrapped around his waist. She'd never been nice to me.

Mickey was just closing the door when I turned back. "Oh, Chuck, your wife's looking for you."

Celibacy can make you such a bitch.

Mickey sprinted up on the patio and I was on his heels. It was black and void of people as we hurried back down to the path in front of the building. Dashing around the corner, we found Uncle C standing there with a man I didn't know.

"No sign of them. Pork and Debby are checking the parking lot. Mickey, you take the stable area. Dave, there are some outbuildings down there." He pointed to an area south of the main building. "I'll check the pool. And you"— he turned to me—"get your ass back inside."

I didn't argue, since I had no intention of doing what he'd asked. The cops were spread out around the ranch, and they were the ones communicating with the radios, so it made sense to follow my uncle, since I had no clue where Binky and Bobette were.

I ducked inside the door for a minute before trotting after him. My foot was killing me as I tracked him along the concrete path. Uncle C trotted around a rock wall and I spotted a wrought-iron gate. I heard splashing water, so I knew the pool couldn't be too far away. I opened a tall gate and walked into the wading pool area. The shadows gave me a good vantage point from which to watch Uncle C.

Nothing floated in the pool.

Across from it stood a pair of large rock arches with water cascading over them and into the swimming pool. Uncle C crossed under the arches and then disappeared down a path. I jogged after him, praying he wouldn't turn around while I was beside the pool, because there was no place to hide.

He ran up to a rock building that I suspected hid the filter. I crouched, using the rock wall as a shield. The door, marked POOL CHEMICAL ROOM—KEEP OUT, was unlocked, and he disappeared inside and came back out immediately.

I hovered to see which way he'd go. Thank God he moved off around the far side of the building. If he'd come back toward me, I'd have been discovered for sure.

As he disappeared around the corner, I made my way down the sloping path and used the opposite side of the rock wall as my cover. Uncle C headed toward the parking lot. I gave him a twenty-second head start and then resumed my pursuit. The black flats, which would not have been my running shoes of choice, were slowing me down. Still, it was better than going barefoot.

He moved quickly through the parking lot and circled it to the north. This was easy, since there were plenty of cars to use as cover. He zigzagged through the lot and then ran down the road.

This was trickier for me because it was well lit and I again stuck to the shadows, which meant that I didn't see the rusted farm equipment that shredded my dress. I thought the rip of the silk sounded loud, but Uncle C kept going. Catclaw and mesquite continued to assault me as I chased after him.

He was almost to the main road leading into the ranch when the sound of a shot shattered the quiet.

My heart was pounding as I stopped long enough to fumble in my handbag and pull out my .38. Once it was securely in my hand, I threw my purse to the ground.

Uncle C made a 180-degree turn that would have put a barrel-racing horse to shame. He pulled his 9mm out of his shoulder holster and took off. I cringed behind the ranch's gas pumps until I saw his shadow clear the *estacada* corral fence. Then I followed him. Although I think of him as overweight and in fairly poor shape, he was a good match for a woman with a bum foot.

The stacked mesquite that made up the corral fencing continued the alterations on my dress and I heard more tearing as I climbed. As I jumped off the top of the fence, the shoe with the slit leather got stuck on the rough wood and was jerked off my bad foot. After I landed, I retrieved it, vaguely aware of pieces of turquoise silk hanging like flags from the top of the wooden fence. With no time to put the shoe back on, I quickly kicked off its partner.

Racing through the corral, I felt the sharp stones piercing my bare feet as I ground into the unforgiving earth.

Lights were beginning to come on in the tack room area. Suddenly one flooded the corral and I could see Binky draped against the hitching post. Detective Debby, one of the toughest women in the department, was patting him down. Not one of his better sexual experiences, I'm sure.

Uncle C turned and spotted me. We were both gasping for air.

"They got the son-of-a-bitch! By God, they've got him." He crowed. Victory apparently overshadowed my disobedience, and he ignored me.

Knowing the police would not be thrilled to see my gun, I stepped back into the shadows, lifted my skirt and tucked the .38 into the thick waistband of my panty hose.

"Look, there's been a mistake here." Binky was trying to negotiate.

Bobette was crying on a wooden bench in the corner of the porch. She held her left shoulder with her right hand, and I could see blood seeping out between her fingers. Mickey Jordan was gently trying to pry her fingers away to get a good look at her wound. He held a handkerchief between his teeth.

"I didn't kill anybody," Binky said.

"You have the right . . ." Debby began the program, reading Williamson his Mirandas. She finally instructed him to stand up straight as Uncle C cuffed him. Binky turned and caught my eye.

"This is a mistake, Trade," he said in a voice that approached humility. "A big mistake. I never killed anyone. I swear it."

I walked up on the boardwalk porch, keenly aware of the splintered wood tearing into my bare feet.

"Are you okay?" I asked Bobette.

"I think so," she whispered.

"It doesn't look serious," Mickey said. "But we've put in a call for an ambulance."

A cop wearing latex gloves came up holding a Buck knife, the collapsible kind sportsmen carry on their belts.

"What happened?" Uncle C asked.

"We found them back there." Mickey pointed to a three-sided open building between the tack room and the hay shed. I could see an anvil attached to a huge stump. "He had her up against the wall. They were struggling when I came around the corner. I saw the knife and fired a warning shot."

"It's not my goddamn knife," Binky growled. "It's hers." He tried to point his manacled hands in Bobette's direction. "She was attacking me."

Bobette began sobbing anew.

"Anyway," Mickey continued, "looks like I was a little late getting here. He caught her on the shoulder."

The word must have spread that something big was happening at the stable, and a crowd was starting to gather.

"We'll take statements downtown," Uncle C said. "Get the cars."

"I'd like to go," I said.

He turned to me, as though it was the first time he was aware of my presence since I'd seen him on the path. "Can't do, Trade. This is official police business."

Anger welled up in my stomach. I was pissed. I knew the rules, but I also suspected that this was his way of getting back at me for not giving up the case.

"Trade, are you all right?" Daggett appeared out of the crowd and wrapped a strong arm around my waist. "What happened?"

I stared at my feet. My right big toe was sticking out of the nylon and long runs and ugly snags dappled my calves. Hanes would never ask me to do a commercial for them. The bottom half of my dress was shredded by the catclaw, old ranch equipment and *estacada* fence. I was a wreck. I took several deep breaths to calm myself.

"I'll tell you on the way home," I said between clenched teeth.

34

WE WERE ALMOST HOME WHEN I FINALLY FINISHED MY STORY. I included almost everything, and we both laughed over his being a possible suspect.

"I'm glad they caught the bastard," Daggett volunteered after I had given him the rundown on my merry chase. "I never liked Binky anyway."

"Amen."

My cut foot was throbbing with pain. We were almost to Daggett's, and I had yet to broach the subject of his marriage. I was just too tired to deal with it, or a fight, and I decided that it really didn't matter anyway. He wasn't my type, and I wasn't going to see him again, although I was happy that he was just a liar and a creep, not a killer.

Daggett pulled into the driveway next to Priscilla, a concession, I suppose, to my foot.

He came around and opened my door. I like that. While I like to think of myself as an independent woman, I also like a man to extend some of the older, more formal courtesies toward me. My brand of feminism can be mystifying.

I hobbled out of the car with my black flats in hand.

"Why don't you come in for a drink?"

"Thanks, Daggett, but I'll take a rain check. I'm really

tired." Actually I was sick of talking. My adrenaline was still flowing, and I wanted to be alone to sort things out.

He walked me to Priscilla. As I opened the door, he pulled me back and tried to kiss me. I turned my cheek, and his lips slid across the side of my face. I could tell he was pissed, but I didn't owe him anything.

"Goodnight, Daggett."

He turned and walked into his house before I even cranked up Priscilla.

It was eleven-thirty by the time I was finally curled up in the La-Z-Boy, ready for bed in my ratty football jersey. I sipped on a cup of hot cocoa and thought through the events of the evening.

I knew that Binky Williamson was a jerk. And he had a bad temper—bad enough, I suppose, to kill people. But a rage killing didn't make sense considering the planned, thought-out, surgical removal of Valerie Higgins's arms or the interception of Connie O'Hara at the Tucson airport.

And I kept hearing Binky say, *It was her knife.* I couldn't forget that Bobette *had* stabbed her lover to death.

I knew eventually it would all be sorted out by the Pima County Sheriff's Department, but I had played with the puzzle for so long that I wanted to solve it myself.

I retrieved Buffy's Javelina yearbook from the coffee table and started searching for my cast of characters. I didn't really know what I was looking for, maybe some sort of divine inspiration that would come to me as I looked at their pictures.

I looked up Binky and Charlene, Buffy, Daggett, and Bobette. I checked out Daggett's sister, Shannon, and noticed the strong resemblance between Andy now and his mother twenty-five years ago. Just looking at her picture made me furious with Daggett all over again.

Then I looked up the other people I had seen that night—Calvin MacKenzie, Troy and Margie Chavez and Stu Hansen. Remembering Buffy Patania's date, Joshua David, I looked him up.

And hit paydirt.

Joshua David's senior class picture was right next to Daggett Early's. And on the other side?

Janet Eberlein.

The solution to one of my puzzles had been right in front of me all along. On page 210 of the Javelina High yearbook.

The pictures in the middle row, reading down the list of last names, gave me David Early Eberlein.

The genesis of David Eberlein.

Now I knew who he was.

And where to find him.

My blood ran cold and a deep-seated chill told me I was right. I knew Daggett was a liar, but this was his biggest one yet. Daggett Early was David Eberlein. Connie O'Hara's missing friend. Her boyfriend in high school who had continued her friendship through their adult years. Up until the time of her death. And who better to meet her at the airport than her boyfriend? Who better to take her out in the desert and kill her? Suddenly I was sure Uncle C had the wrong guy in custody.

The ringing telephone jolted me out of my reverie.

"Ellis? It's Charley. Sorry it's so late, but I've had some computer glitches here."

"No, Charley, it's fine. I'm still up."

"This Early guy you wanted me to check out? I hope you're not thinking of hitching up with him."

"Fat chance."

"A bad news bear, Ellis. Big into the Vegas boys."

"A gambler?" My head started spinning, recalling all the bits and pieces of Daggett's life that could have pointed me in that direction earlier. The quick business trips on a moment's notice, a private airplane, and access to a lot of money through his clients' accounts.

"I checked him through the usual channels and found a second mortgage he just took out on his house. That started me digging deeper to look for the debt and then I had this hunch, so I started in on the Vegas computers. Checked his player rating info."

"Player rating?"

"Yeah, the casinos keep records on all their high rollers. They track their gaming activity, stuff like their wins and losses. Anyway, our boy just got demoted from an ALL to an RFB."

"Charley, what in the hell does that mean?"

"He's gone from getting comped for everything—tips, phone, limos, you name it—back to just room, food and drinks."

"Why would they do that?"

"He's into them big, real big. Like about four hundred grand worth. Maybe they're worried about recovering it."

"Shit."

"I'm having trouble stirring up Early's accounts, haven't been able to get into some of them yet. He has one, though, Morning Star Traders, where he's been trading heavily, mostly selling."

"Morning Star Traders," I repeated. The name meant nothing to me as I listened to the clacking of the keys on one of Charley's computers.

"Uh, here it is. A Virginia Morgensen Patania."

Buffy was Morning Star Traders?

Daggett was bilking Buffy's account to cover his debts. It made sense now. He was living the high life. Airplanes, antiques, original Taber-Borcherdts—he'd even bought drinks for everyone at the reunion. The problem was, he couldn't afford it.

Shit. If Daggett really was using Buffy's account to cover his gambling debts, that would sure give him a motive for murdering her. But Buffy was still alive and well. Could he have killed the other Song Dogs, including his girlfriend Connie O'Hara, in order to cover Buffy's impending murder?

"Charley, call me as soon as you get anything else."

"You got it, Ellis."

After I hung up it occurred to me that Charley was as excited about this case as I was. He had forgotten to tell me a dirty joke.

I called Buffy, not expecting to find her home. When

her answering machine picked up, I left an urgent message for her to call me.

Dressing quickly, I grabbed my .38. As I rummaged through a kitchen drawer I found a couple of pieces of blank paper and a black crayon.

There was one other puzzle piece I needed to have before I could be sure about Daggett. And I was going to get it tonight.

I headed for the front door, and then my survival instinct clicked in. I returned to the kitchen and picked up the phone to call the Pima County Sheriff's Department. Uncle C wasn't at his desk. While they didn't tell me where he was, I knew that booking Binky and getting the truth out of him and Bobette would take hours. When I identified myself as his niece and said I needed to talk to him urgently, they said they'd page him. Before hanging up, I also left a voice mail telling him where I was headed.

I waited for ten minutes for Uncle C's call back, but it never came. Finally, I left.

I wasn't too concerned. I just wanted to check Daggett's garage, that was all. I'm not stupid. If I found what I was looking for, then I'd let the big boys move in on him. I'm not a cop. I don't even like to shoot my gun. It's noisy and it hurts my ears.

Besides, I'm a pretty crappy shot. I do okay with a rifle, but with a short-barreled handgun, I'm not that swift. No, when the time came for arrests and fanfare, the cavalry was welcome to it. I was just going to make their job a teeny-weeny bit easier, that's all.

I headed back out and was stopped by the telephone.

"Trade? It's Bea, were you asleep?"

"Just on the way out, actually." There was a lot of noise in the background and I figured she was calling me from the reunion.

Beatrice was too thrilled with her discovery to ask me where I was going.

"You know when I said that your date looked familiar?"

"Yeah?" I knew what was coming.

"He's the guy I saw that time with Connie."

"Thanks, Bea, I've got to go. Do me a favor, though, will you? I left a message for Uncle C. Will you try him in twenty minutes and tell him I'm at Daggett's?"

"Gee, and I thought you were going to give me his number." She gave me a phony whine, and then said, "be careful, cuz."

35

BY THE TIME I TURNED DOWN DAGGETT'S STREET, IT WAS CLOSE to one in the morning. The neighborhood, while in the heart of the city, featured homes with a lot of common space between them. There were only a few scattered streetlights at the corners. I slowed Priscilla and found an empty desert area just east of his house.

After turning off the engine, I opened the glove box and retrieved my gun. I took it out of its holster, grabbed the photo of the tire print left with Connie's body and a small pencil flashlight. I turned out the interior lights of the truck and opened the driver's door slowly.

In my rush out of the house, I'd forgotten to wear a belt, so I pulled up my shirt and stuck the gun in my rear waistband. I hate to do that, because I'm always afraid it's going to go off and take half my rear end with it, but I needed my hands to be free and had no other place to stash the .38.

I waited beside the truck for a long time, trying to figure out if anyone was looking out a bedroom window and would call the police with a prowler report. Although I really wasn't doing anything wrong, I felt guilty being up and about, snooping around a community when its residents were fast asleep.

In the distance a dog barked, but it just sounded like a chronic barker, not the Paul Revere of the neighborhood.

Daggett's house was half a block away. I crossed the street and walked toward it. The full moon was now up, but I still went slowly. I've never thought of myself as being very good at sneaking around, partly because I'm so noisy. Usually it's my heavy breathing and pounding heart, and I just assume that the rest of the world can hear it, too. Tonight was no exception.

Daggett's house was dark, except for his front porch light, which was probably left on every night. The Lexus was not in the driveway, so I assumed it was in the garage. A service road ran to the east of the house and I followed it.

I ended up in the alley behind Daggett's home with a wall of overgrown oleanders that seemed to delineate his property line. I found an opening and walked through them.

His backyard was protected by a tall concrete wall that I couldn't see over. The garage was at the back, a three-car affair with no windows and closed doors. From this angle, I was facing an impenetrable fortress.

A heavy wooden gate was at the end of the wall next to the garage.

I debated only momentarily before trying the gate. Could that alarm I'd seen inside also guard the perimeter of the property? The gate wasn't locked and I held my breath as I released the latch, half expecting to hear sirens.

Nothing happened.

I stepped over the threshold and into the yard. Training the light beam along the garage wall, I found the door.

It was also unlocked and I let myself in. As I stepped inside, my antennae were definitely up. Why was everything unlocked? Was Daggett's neighborhood *that* safe? Was this a trap? How could he be expecting me? I was being paranoid although there was no question I was at great risk here. Although I've never been delicate about putting my license in jeopardy, with the garage open I'd just removed the "breaking" from a possible breaking and entering charge. Like most private investigators, I've developed some pretty good rationalizations for surreptitious entry, so I try not to dwell on the consequences.

While the garage was built for three vehicles, there were only two inside. My flashlight roamed over both of them, the Lexus and what Daggett and Andy had referred to as his truck.

Only it wasn't a truck. It was a Ford Bronco.

I knelt down and let the light scope the sidewalls of the Bronco's tires. Yokohama Super Diggers.

Bingo.

They were the same kind of tires the Williamsons had on their Explorer. And the same kind of tires that had left tracks at Connie O'Hara's death scene.

I stripped the black crayon of its paper and placed a sheet of blank paper over the tire. I needed both hands for my task, so I held the flashlight between my teeth, directing it at the tire as best I could. I ran the crayon back and forth across the paper, getting a rubbing of the tires.

Still holding the flashlight in my mouth, I reached in my pocket and withdrew the picture that Emily Rose had given me.

Maybe it wouldn't hold up in court because Andy had driven the Bronco to the lake, and that had to be a couple hundred miles, but it looked close to me.

Alone in the garage, my heart was racing. My quest was nearly finished. I stashed the tire rubbing in my back pocket.

I had been so concentrated on the tires that I nearly lost another opportunity. As the tiny flashlight beam scoured the rest of the garage, my eyes were drawn to a wall of shelving units holding neatly stacked cardboard boxes. The lower half of the unit held drawers.

I walked closer and realized that they were old financial records, with the contents of each box neatly recorded on the outside.

As I passed the light over the records, I spotted the box I was looking for. It read CLIENTS M–O and was on the top shelf of the ceiling-high storage system.

I looked around for a ladder. How in the hell did he get up there to retrieve the boxes? He was so anal about keeping everything in its place, there wasn't even a garbage can I could overturn and stand on. The Lexus was just far enough away that I couldn't use it.

I opened one of the top drawers of the units and found it full of old *Forbes* magazines. It was risky, at best, but I wanted to get into that box and it was the only thing that could even remotely pass for a step up. Holding the flashlight between my teeth, I pulled out the second drawer in the section next to it, stepped up on that, and then put my full weight on the half-opened drawer full of magazines. As the drawer groaned, my fingers scrambled for the M–O box, knowing that I didn't have long.

I caught the edge of the box and pulled it toward me. It was a heavy sucker, but I was able to drag it across the shelf and into my hands. I felt the pull of the box through my back and shoulders as I held it over my head.

The extra weight was too much, as my ladder drawer gave a last sigh and collapsed, taking me to the garage floor with it. The flashlight flew out of my mouth and the garage was suddenly plunged into darkness. My back grazed the side of the Lexus on the way down, and I ended up sprawled across the cement floor on a bed of outdated magazines, with the cardboard record box crushing my chest.

"Shit." In spite of my resolve to keep quiet, it just popped out.

Amazingly, I had not hit my head on anything.

Pushing the box to one side, I sat up slowly, taking account of my battered body. Thank God I had only fallen a few feet. I was hurting, but nothing was broken.

Groping around in the darkness for my flashlight, I finally found it and twisted the cap several times, praying it would come back on. It didn't. As I played Helen Keller with the light, I realized the lens cap was missing. Probing further, my fingers found the jagged edge of the tiny broken bulb.

Shit! What good was getting into the records box if I couldn't see anything?

Not really expecting it to be unlocked, I tried the passenger door of the Lexus. Miraculously, it opened, its interior light casting an arc of illumination on the damning records. I opened the box and quickly thumbed through the file folders. There were three thick ones, all labeled MORNING STAR TRADERS. Knowing I didn't have the luxury of reading them there, I did the only sensible thing and stole them.

After placing the lid back on the cardboard box, I debated only momentarily about trying to return it to the top shelf. There was no way I could to it without risking another fall.

What difference would it make? Daggett must be guilty. I knew the combination of the tires and what I'd find in the Morning Star records would be enough to take him out of circulation for a while. By tomorrow, he'd be in custody.

Clutching the folders to my chest, I found myself tiptoeing out of the garage, a ridiculous act, since I was alone. Turning the doorknob as quietly as I could, I stepped out of the building.

And into the arms of Daggett Early.

36

I STIFFENED AND SHRIEKED, AND DAGGETT CRUSHED ME HARD TO his chest.

"Sssh, you're all right," he said.

I knew I wasn't, but I willed myself to relax. He continued to hold me tightly as my mind raced to form a lie.

"I didn't mean to disturb you, but I think I left my purse in your car. I hope you don't mind, I looked in your garage." I pushed lightly against him in a subtle effort to determine if he was going to let me go. He relaxed his hold a bit and for some silly reason I looked down at his feet.

I expected to see New Balance tennis shoes, but instead he was wearing the same black leather loafers he'd worn to the reunion. Could I possibly be wrong?

"No, I don't mind." His breath was hot against my ear. "Did you find it?"

"No, I probably left it at the Tanque Verde Ranch in all the excitement."

"We can call out there."

Neither one of us mentioned the file folders that I was still clutching.

His hold lessened a bit as he pulled my Smith and Wesson from the back waistband of my Levi's.

"Oh, don't bother, I'll check it out tomorrow," I said. This time I pushed harder away from him and was pleasantly surprised that he let me go. Except for my right wrist. It was trapped firmly in his left hand. I pretended not to notice that I was captured or that his right hand now held my .38. "I tried to be quiet so I wouldn't disturb you."

"Perimeter security system, Trade. The minute you came through the oleanders you tipped it off."

I prayed it was a system that alerted the police.

"It's our little secret," he said, as though reading my mind. "Well, we can have our nightcap now."

As though I was not connected to my body, I watched him pull me toward the house.

"I'm sorry, Daggett, I have to go home." Thank you, Mother. Or Mrs. Wright. Here I am trapped with a serial killer, and I'm still being polite. Maybe they had overdone things, I thought in a fit of hysteria, like that obscene phone call I had once ended with, "No, thank you."

He ignored me and I pulled back, feeling a terrible stab in my right shoulder as my arm was nearly jerked out of its socket. My cut foot was beginning to throb, and my back hurt like hell from the fall in the garage.

"Daggett!"

We were almost to the back door when I gave up the charade. I let out a howling scream and had just gotten the second one out as he dragged me through the door and slammed it shut.

As he set my gun on the counter, he kept his body between it and me, and with his free hand he turned the key in the deadbolt lock. He retrieved the gun and then released me.

"Behave yourself, Trade. We've got to talk."

I rubbed my raw wrist. A strange emotion overcame me. Embarrassment. Some private eye I turned out to be. My gun was now in the hands of a probable serial killer, and I was locked in his house. Lousy way to end an evening.

When I was done with that, the fear struck.

I was sure I would never leave Daggett's alive. Not if he was the killer. My breath quickened and I felt weak in the knees. My eyes darted around his kitchen.

"May I have my gun back?" It was a stupid request and we both knew it.

"Not just yet."

My mouth went dry.

"Into the living room," he ordered, waving the gun at me. I didn't argue.

"Whatever you say, David."

He chuckled. "You've got it all, don't you? I knew it was you when Mother called and said she'd been interviewed. But so what?"

"That really wasn't very clever. Any do-do with half a brain could figure it out. Why the alias back then?" I figured if I could keep him talking, it would delay his shooting or filleting me. We were passing through the dining room.

"It was Connie's idea. She was popular, a cheerleader and all that, so we came up with the idea of a mystery man for her. And David Eberlein was born. Saved her from explaining why she was dating a geek like me, or like I used to be."

I saw his reflection in the dining room mirror. A mask had dropped from his face. It was hard and stiff, and in spite of having spent time with him, I now knew that I knew nothing about Daggett Early. That scared me more than the fact that he was holding my own gun on me.

"And you continued to see her for all of those years?" I was mentally grappling with the psyche of a man who would use a fake name to date a popular girl because she was worried about what her friends would think.

"Sure, why not? We were friends. Good friends. She even did a lot of my business travel arrangements."

"What would have happened to her if you'd been enemies?"

He shrugged and looked puzzled momentarily, then nudged me with the barrel of the gun. "Move on in there."

I went into the living room, surprised to see that it was well lit. With the curtains drawn, I hadn't been able to see the light from outside.

For some reason I thought of Deborah Chamberlain. Anyone who had memorized the Periodic Table of Elements as quickly as he had in chemistry class could probably figure out a way to give someone salmonella. Another red check for him.

"You can put those on the table." He nodded at the folders. "I guess you've pretty much figured things out."

I couldn't help but look in the direction of the atrium. It could be a good choice for a slaughterhouse, I thought. The clean white tile, the center drain—he probably wouldn't even have to call his cleaning lady.

My palms were cold with sweat and my eyeballs felt sucked dry of moisture. My stomach shut down as instinct pushed my blood to my legs for flight. Thank God it had been a while since dinner.

I stepped around the coffee table, trying to keep my distance from him. My eyes darted to the alarm box near the front door. If I could get over there, maybe I could push the panic button and bring the cavalry.

"You were really going to do all of them?" I stalled.

"What?" He sounded confused. "Buffy's really my only problem. And now you."

I was still inching around the coffee table, getting ready to make a break for the alarm.

"Stop right there," he said brusquely. He was getting fairly casual with my gun, waving it around with the barrel pointing at the ground.

I was standing next to his lit cabinet.

"Covering up for a few misplaced funds, huh, Daggett?"

"Close to a million dollars, Trade. I don't think she'll understand, do you?"

Buffy's Morning Star Traders were going to keep Charley Bell busy on Monday, I thought.

As I glanced around for help, my eyes went to the cabinet. Some of the display had changed again.

"I have to fund my treasures," he said. I didn't like the way he was always picking up on what I was thinking. Was I that transparent?

"You've changed them again." My dry cracked voice was an octave higher than usual. Feeling like a kid who has sucked on helium from a balloon, the voice was not my own.

The pearls were still there next to the cameo brooch. And the antique derringer and the shriveled ear continued to occupy the bottom two shelves of the case.

"Is that really your mother's jewelry?"

"Not all of it." He laughed. "Why'd you have to go snooping around in my business? I don't know what in the hell to do with you."

I was dead meat unless I could get to that alarm panel near his front door. A red light was on. Was it armed?

I was surprised that the terror I had felt since he caught me in his garage was ebbing. The discovery that terror is not an emotion that the body can sustain encouraged me. Now rage and instinct were taking over.

"I guess you want this." I fumbled with the clasp on my watch while he hovered close to me.

"What the hell are you doing?" he asked.

I slipped the watch over my wrist and handed it to him. He seemed confused, as if he didn't know what to do with it.

"Take it." I shook the watch at him, thinking that he seemed pretty disorganized for the methodical serial killer that had been knocking off the Song Dogs.

As his eyes and hand dropped to receive it, I stepped back and my right hand grabbed the crystal obelisk from the coffee table. It was heavy, but I swung it underhand, catching him hard under the jaw.

Daggett let out a howl of pain and dropped to the floor. I should have hit him again with the crystal, but I was desperate to get away from him. I vaulted over the table and ran up and over the leather couch in a straight dash to the front door and the alarm.

I heard him scrambling behind me, and my adrenaline drove me on. I crashed into the wall, the flat of my palm smashing into the control buttons of the alarm system. It began shrieking.

I ran to the door and tried to open it. Like its kitchen counterpart, it had been secured with a deadbolt and key, and the key was not in sight. I was thinking about running through a window, and my mind assessed what broken shards of glass would do to my body, when I heard Daggett lumbering behind me.

I spun in time to see him jump the couch. I guess I wasn't surprised, remembering his track pictures in the yearbook. Hurdles, couches, what was the difference?

I backed away, with the obelisk, my only weapon, still in my hand.

"My God, what have you done? Drop it, Trade." He was yelling over the sound of the alarm and now pointing the gun at me. My blow had cut him and blood was dripping off his chin.

"It'll break." I was definitely feeling better, I thought, my smart mouth back in gear.

The telephone was ringing and Daggett looked anxiously toward the kitchen. It was probably the alarm company calling to see if we were really having a crisis.

I needed to keep him occupied so he couldn't answer it and give them his password or whatever. Holding the obelisk out in front of me like a knife, I backed away from him.

"Drop that goddamned thing," he demanded. He was only five feet away from me.

The phone was still ringing, the alarm howling.

"Okay. Catch." I threw the obelisk at him and ran.

I don't know what I was expecting, but it wasn't like in the movies where they drop the gun to catch the sculpture. He ducked it and came after me instead.

I flew around the couch and crashed into the treasure cabinet, sending it and me to the floor. I was flat on my back with my right arm embedded in the cabinet debris.

"God damn you, look what you've done." Daggett paused on the far side of where the cabinet had been, avoiding the mess.

I groped through the broken glass and splintered wood, pushing pearls and jewelry aside. A wet sticky feeling was engulfing my right arm, which was stinging. I grasped a dry wrinkled thing and with a wave of revulsion cast the shriveled ear aside.

My fingers finally found the antique derringer. As I

grasped it in both hands, I remembered the bullets were old, as old as the gun. Taking the chance, I rolled over and fired in Daggett's direction, and the derringer responded with a sick click.

I quickly pulled myself up into a crouch. He looked startled that I would try to shoot at him. My gun dangled at his side.

"Drop it, Daggett," I said, expecting him to either do so or raise the gun and fire at me.

He did neither.

I stood up. "I don't want to, but I swear if you don't drop my damn gun, I'll shoot you again."

"You don't know what you're doing. We need to talk. That's a single-shot derringer. You're done."

Shit. I thought it had two. Hadn't he shown it to me?

I left the gun aimed at him and checked it out. It looked to me like it had another barrel. But then what did I know about antique Remingtons?

He slowly raised his right hand, the one holding my .38, and pointed it at me.

What the hell, I thought, and pulled the trigger of the derringer one more time.

Again, nothing happened.

"You would have shot me," he whispered, as an incredulous look spread over his face. My gun was shaking in his hand.

"Police! Drop the gun!"

A black-clad figure stood in the doorway to the dining room behind Daggett.

He started to turn.

"Drop the fucking gun now!" Mickey Jordan had come to my rescue.

My .38 fell to the Berber carpet.

37

AN HOUR AND A HALF LATER I SAT ON DAGGETT'S LEATHER couch, my arm bandaged. He'd already been hauled downtown and I'd given a statement. While it could have taken a lot longer, Uncle C had intervened. A few detectives milled around, waiting for a signed search warrant to arrive.

"You better get over to the emergency room," Uncle C said.

"Right." I hadn't yet received the lecture that was surely coming from my uncle. He'd pick a more private time to deliver it. "What about my gun?"

"They'll have to keep it for a while, get his prints, run ballistics."

That figured. Even though it belonged to me, it had been in Daggett's hands when the police broke in.

I wandered into the kitchen and picked up the phone to call home. After punching in the code to my answering machine, I retrieved a message from Buffy.

"Trade, I'm returning your call." She was using her sensible voice, not the vampy one. "Also, Charlene just called me and she's a basket case over this thing with Binky. I'm going over there now. She really sounds like she's in bad shape." The call had come in at 2:45 A.M. I wondered what she would think when I told her how close she had come to dying. There'd be time for that later.

There was nothing on the machine from Charlene.

Relieved that Buffy hadn't insisted on my meeting her at the Williamsons', I headed for home. The clock in Priscilla read 3:23.

Driving up Campbell Avenue past River Road, I thought, what the hell, the night's shot anyway, and found myself taking the turn to Charlene's house. Fully expecting to have the gate man call her, I found him sleeping so soundly that I drove right by. Most people have to be deaf to ignore Priscilla's diesel engine.

The Williamsons' house was lit up like Christmas and I pulled in behind Buffy's Jaguar.

The spitting lion fountain in the front courtyard was quiet, which made it much easier to hear the yelling that was coming from inside. Clearly, Buffy and Charlene were having an argument. Shit! Had Charlene found out about Binky and Buffy?

The front door was unlocked, so I let myself in. Maybe I could get to them before they got into a real cat fight.

"You rotten bitch!" Charlene's voice rang out through the house as I scurried through the office/breakfast nook and into the kitchen.

"What's going . . ."

I stopped in midsentence.

Buffy was pinned against the refrigerator, arms raised, with her palms facing Charlene.

Who was holding a gun.

"What are you doing here?" Charlene asked, sweeping the gun in my direction. If I had thought she'd been dressed up at the reunion, I'd been mistaken. Now she was wearing a floor-length white lacy caftan studded with tiny seed pearls. Long pearl earrings dangled beside her face, and she sported several bracelets on her right arm, a huge blue opal ring surrounded by diamonds on her pinky finger, and an antique-looking locket on an old gold chain around her neck.

"I thought you were afraid of guns," I said stupidly, noticing that the floor was littered with something that looked like airplane tickets.

She laughed. "Get over there, next to her."

Buffy looked scared to death.

"He isn't worth it, Charlene." I still wasn't getting it. "He hit on Bobette, too."

"Shut up, Trade." Spittle dribbled down her chin.

"She's the one," Buffy said quietly.

"One what?" In spite of Charlene's holding the gun on us and drooling, I wasn't all that concerned. Surely I could talk her out of shooting Buffy for sleeping with the worthless Rodeo King.

"She killed them," Buffy said.

Charlene was smirking, obviously proud of herself.

Baffled, I let my eyes drop to her feet, which were clad in white tennis shoes. Why hadn't I noticed before how big they were? They were at least size 10. I could see an NB, The New Balance tennis shoe logo, outlined in gray and suddenly I knew I was in deep shit. Charlene had been the one up on the mesa watching the ranch. "You killed all of them because they were screwing Binky?"

"Of course not. He may have slept with them, but he always came home. This time he wasn't going to." She waved the gun at Buffy.

"I don't want him," Buffy said flatly.

"I've known about it since it started, you know," Charlene said. "And I know about the trip."

"What trip?" Buffy asked, looking baffled.

I heard a thud and looked to the window. Duke's nose was stuck to the glass, the Happy Face Frisbee in his mouth.

"Nice try. I ran into Connie O'Hara at Christmas when she was home visiting her mother. She slipped and mentioned that my hubby—that's really what she called him— was planning a little surprise." Charlene turned toward me, ignoring Buffy. "I started snooping around and found the tickets. Binky was going on an around-the-world fling with his whore."

I was right. Those were airplane tickets scattered across the floor.

"You really don't get it, do you?" Charlene said smugly. "Stupid."

"Why don't you put that gun down and we'll talk?" I

feigned trying to reason with her, hoping to buy some time. Boy, had I been wrong about Daggett; no wonder he'd seemed confused. He was just an ordinary embezzler, not a killer.

"I'm not a serial killer, Trade."

"Of course you aren't, Charlene." I lied.

"I just wanted her." She waved the gun at Buffy. "But it had to look like more than that so when she died and the police found out about her affair with my husband, it wouldn't be too significant."

I thought adultery was a pretty good motive, but said nothing. Funny though, that Buffy had been targeted by *both* Daggett and Charlene.

"You didn't kill all of them to get to her?"

"I had to make it look like something more so I shot Elaine. That was easy. Besides, she deserved it, that slut."

I wondered how shooting anyone could be easy. Most people wouldn't think so. Much less carving them up. I wasn't buying into Charlene's claim that Elaine Vargas had been a casual target. I remembered that in high school Elaine had been lectured for "public display of affection" in the halls with Binky. That was probably enough motive for Charlene's clearly deranged mind.

"But then I had to do something more spectacular, something they wouldn't tie to me."

"Valerie," I said, looking at the butcher block full of knives.

She had a strange smile on her face. It reminded me of the sexual flush she'd had when she'd been chopping the vegetables. "I didn't like all that mess, but I figured I'd be off the hook. Women don't kill that way, you know."

Who was she kidding? I'd seen the pictures of Valerie Higgins. She'd been butchered. This wasn't about making the police think they had a serial killer—she'd *enjoyed* it. She was going further with every confrontation, and now she'd gone over the edge. Holy shit.

"You mean Elaine and Valerie had nothing to do with this?" I asked.

"Nothing." I doubted she even realized that she was still smiling.

"Nice touch hiring me," I offered.

"That was her idea," she nodded to Buffy. "But I had to stay in it so I'd know what you were up to. Not that you were up to much." She laughed.

She'd been damned cagey, too. Charlene had led that first interview, so I'd always assumed she was the driving force behind hiring me. She'd been the one who had called me, all upset that the killer had found Bobette. Charlene had kept her nose in it the whole time, and I was none the wiser.

"Then I had to kill Connie, since she made their travel arrangements."

"So no one would know about the trip?" I asked, playing along. Who cared how she wanted to rationalize it? She'd killed those women for Binky, just like she was about to kill Buffy—and me.

"Exactly." She was smirking again.

"Or was it because she was working against you?"

"What are you talking about?" The smile was gone as she scowled at me.

I knew I'd hit home. "Connie was helping to take him away from you, wasn't she, Charlene?"

"I don't know anything about a trip," Buffy said weakly in her defense.

"Shut up, you filthy slut! You talked him into it!"

In one fluid movement, Charlene shifted the gun to her left hand, grabbed a boning knife from the butcher block and swung it toward Buffy's face.

"Charlene, don't!" I yelled.

Buffy's scream filled the air as her hands flew up to her face. Blood gushed through her fingers and I could tell that Charlene had scored a nasty cut across her left cheek.

Buffy, sobbing hysterically, was trying to hold her face closed.

Charlene was deteriorating fast. Butchering Valerie and Connie had been done without witnesses. But she'd just slashed Buffy in front of me. Not good. Not at all.

Charlene calmly laid the knife on the butcher block and returned the gun to her right hand.

"It isn't worth it. Binky's in jail," I said, trying for a rational approach.

"Thanks to that whore Bobette. But they won't keep him." Her tiny eyes looked wet. "Not for long. They don't have anything on him."

"If you're pissed, it seems to me that he's a likely target." Charlene looked at me as though I were the crazy one.

"I love him. Without money, he'll leave me."

Christ, could the white caftan have been her wedding dress?

"Jesus, Charlene. The guy's a coke addict who beats you and cheats on you."

Was she so insecure, twisted and afraid of abandonment that she'd do anything to keep the creep?

"He isn't worth it," I said, knowing it was a futile argument. She'd already killed for him and there was no turning back. I just wanted to keep her attention away from Buffy and stall for time until I could figure out what to do.

"Don't you say that!" she screamed.

I heard the rubber thump of the doggy door. Duke came running in with his toy and laid it at his mistress's feet. She ignored him and he nudged her.

I barely glanced at Buffy, whose blood was dripping onto the white tiled kitchen floor.

"The jewelry . . ." I started again, hoping to keep Charlene focused.

Charlene held up her left hand. As the caftan sleeves fell down, I counted four watches on her arm. I wondered inanely how she'd gotten them to fit.

"I guess you'll never be late," I said.

"Connie's was from Tiffany's." Charlene smiled. "She had nice things."

"That ring was given to her by her mother on her thirtieth birthday," I said.

"These things make me feel pretty." She sounded like a petulant child.

"You could have bought your own jewelry." How long

could I hold her attention? Sooner or later she was going to turn back to Buffy. This wasn't like Daggett's. No one knew I'd come here and no one would come after me. I looked around desperately for a weapon, But Charlene had the gun and she was also doing a good job of guarding the butcher block full of knives.

"It was just a bonus, for me. The money was running out." She pouted, staring at the rings.

"Rebecca DeVille," I said.

She nodded. "My sister, the writer. Only she didn't write her last two books. I did."

Pride and anger were evident in her voice.

"The complicated literary estate?" I asked Charlene while sneaking a glance at Buffy. Her eyes were beginning to glaze over, and I suspected she was going into shock. I had to act quickly or she'd be no help at all.

"Rebecca got blocked, couldn't write. But you can't explain that to her millions of readers, so I tried writing one. She did a little editing on it. We sent it in, and they bought it!" She was giddy with hysteria.

Suddenly the breakfast nook converted to an office was beginning to make sense.

"And the phone call the day I was here?" I asked, not really caring what she said—I was angling for time. There was a knife almost within reach and I edged toward it as she spoke.

"That bitch editor. After Rebecca died, I had to tell her what we'd done so she'd keep buying the books. But she didn't believe me. She wanted the money back."

"And you had to pay for all of this." I looked around the kitchen, hoping her eyes would follow mine and I could move closer to the knife. It didn't work.

"Worse. They'd paid a hundred thousand dollars on the proposal for the last book, the one I lied about and said Rebecca had just finished when she died. They wanted the advance back and I had to tell them. They didn't believe me, so I said, 'Let me prove it by sending the book in.' "

"And you did."

"The editors laughed at me. They said there was only

one great Rebecca DeVille and she was dead. They demanded the advance back." Charlene's voice dropped to a whisper, as though she were in a trance. "Without money, he would have left me, Trade."

Not only had Charlene had to share her husband with the other women, but when she finally did something right, no one believed her. Could the rejection have plunged her over the edge?

"What happened to the money, Charlene?" I was trying to keep her talking. She started out killing the other cheerleaders supposedly to cover up Buffy's murder. But then everything changed. Her money was drying up and she was going to lose her husband anyway.

Duke had the Frisbee in his mouth and was beating it against Charlene's fleshy leg in an effort to get her to play with him. She continued to ignore him.

"Binky spent the money. Some of it went to pay for that." The gun pointed to the airplane tickets scattered across the floor as her voice got louder. "If he left, what would matter?"

Jesus.

"I mean, why would I care about living? The money was all gone and he was leaving me anyway for his rich bitch." Her eyes were wet but furious as she turned back toward Buffy, raising the gun. "I never expected to walk away."

"Charlene, all of this is news to me, I swear . . ."

"Shut up or I'll cut you again, whore!" Charlene was sweating and her hands were shaking as she trained the gun on Buffy.

Suddenly there was a black flash.

Duke jumped up and in one magnificent leap ripped the gun from his mistress's hand. As I lunged for Charlene, I heard the thump of the doggy door as the Labrador made good his escape.

I tackled her behind the knees and we both fell hard on the tiled floor at Buffy's feet.

"Watch it! She's got the knife!" Buffy sobbed.

That was now obvious as Charlene rolled over and

lunged at me. She must have grabbed it on the way down. Now on my hands and knees, I scrambled backward in an effort to get out of her reach. She was only a couple of feet from me. The floor was slick with Buffy's blood and getting traction was impossible. Charlene stabbed the air furiously.

She was coming for me, there was no doubt about that. We were like two crabs sliding across the bloodied tile.

"Find the gun!" I yelled at Buffy, who seemed rooted in place.

"My God, she was going to kill me."

Buffy's whimpering told me that she wasn't out in the backyard searching for the gun, or on the phone with 911.

Charlene grabbed my wrist and, with an amazing show of strength, pulled me flat onto the tile. I jerked my head up, narrowly escaping a nasty blow. Her right hand came down with the knife as I rolled on my back. She straddled me, but as she attempted another strike, I snatched her wrist with my left hand. The knife hovered less than a foot from my face and I could smell the garlic from her banquet Caesar salad as I struggled to keep her hand from following through on its demolition expedition. I was severely handicapped as my left hand pushed against her right. Even without the weight difference, she held the advantage. I could barely move.

She was incredibly heavy on my belly. And she was strong. How could she have such strength? She may have looked like the Pillsbury Dough Girl but she fought like a wildcat. Her left knee was inching up as she tried to pin my right arm so she could use both hands to finish me off. My only chance was to feign weakness. It was a huge risk, but I slackened my hold on her knife hand just enough to let the blade drop a couple of inches closer to my face, as if I were losing strength.

She took the bait.

Confident of her imminent victory, Charlene released my right hand as she thrust in for the kill.

And in that split second my right arm shot out, my hand in a tight fist as I smashed it into her nose.

She howled in pain and rocked back as my right knee

hit her hard in her kidney and I rolled away from her. Lunging for me, she slipped on Buffy's blood. I heard the crack of her elbow as it hit the hard tiled floor and the clatter of the knife as she dropped it.

Scrambling, I pounced on her like a hungry cat on a spring ground squirrel. We had now changed positions and I held the knife at her fat throat as I explained things to her.

"Charlene, if you so much as twitch, I'll cut your friggin' throat out."

EPILOGUE

OVERALL, THE REUNION WAS A HOWLING SUCCESS. IT CULMI-
nated in four divorces, two marriages and one surprise late-
in-life pregnancy.

Stacy Bohannon didn't ruin her dress. I know this for a
fact, since I ran into her at the Metropolitan Grill a month after the reunion and she was wearing it. I was there with Uncle C, Josie and Bea, celebrating the conclusion of my first
murder case.

As much as I would have loved to have pinned something horrible on Binky Williamson, I finally had to admit
that he was innocent of any heinous crime. He was just one
of those terribly unpleasant people who come into our
lives, and unfortunately being a prick isn't illegal.

Turns out he was right about the knife, too.

It belonged to Bobette. Since she was the one who got
cut and she declined to press charges, it should have been
over. And it would have been except for the fact that she
was still on probation for the murder of Maude Evans, and
not carrying a knife was a condition of her parole. She got
lucky, though, and was ordered to undergo further counseling while under house arrest in Luna over the next six
months. She's wearing an electronic monitor around her
ankle, and last I heard, doing all right.

I was right about Daggett Early being an embezzler,

not a killer. Turns out that he'd been churning Buffy's account for years and she had so much money that she'd never suspected a thing. But then I'd come sniffing around and that made him nervous. When I talked to him later, he admitted that after he found me snooping around in his garage that night, he hadn't known what to do with me. He'd grabbed my gun because he was afraid I was going to shoot him with it. On that, he hadn't been too far wrong. As for his eccentric collections and egregious lies, I suspect that in a few years he'll be painting people red and blue just like his mother.

Thank God that little derringer didn't fire that night at Daggett's or my career would have been over. My gun nut friends tell me that while old black powder cartridges can last forever if properly stored, the primer's not as dependable and two dead rounds aren't that unusual for old ammunition.

One of the nice things about having a ton of money is you can afford the best plastic surgeons in the world and Buffy will probably only end up having a faint scar on her face. Her case against Daggett should keep her occupied for the next few years anyway.

Charlene's awaiting sentencing, and while Arizona has had women on death row before, the talk is she may be the first to hit that particular neighborhood in a long time. The chances of her actually being killed are slim, since only one woman has been executed in Arizona's history. That one hanging was rather spectacular, though. In 1930, when Eva Dugan dropped through the gallows' trapdoor, her head separated from her body and rolled into a corner. This unfortunate incident led to the outlawing of execution by hanging in Arizona.

Already I have a call from a friend of Rebecca DeVille's to return.

Something about murders she witnessed as a child.

ABOUT THE AUTHOR

Sinclair Browning is a "dirty shirt cowgirl" whose family ranched for years. Having lived in, and ridden, the Sonoran desert for most of her life, she still breaks her own horses, rounds up cattle and team pens. The license plate on her pickup reads "Wrider," a term she coined that describes her two loves—writing and riding.